WE
ARE
THE
MATCH

ALSO BY MARY E. ROACH

Young Adult

Better Left Buried

Seven for a Secret

WE ARE THE MATCH

MARY E. ROACH

This is a work of fiction. Names, characters, organizations, places, events, and incidents are either products of the author's imagination or are used fictitiously. Otherwise, any resemblance to actual persons, living or dead, is purely coincidental.

Text copyright © 2025 by Mary Roach
All rights reserved.

No part of this book may be reproduced, or stored in a retrieval system, or transmitted in any form or by any means, electronic, mechanical, photocopying, recording, or otherwise, without express written permission of the publisher.

Published by Montlake, Seattle

www.apub.com

Amazon, the Amazon logo, and Montlake are trademarks of Amazon.com, Inc., or its affiliates.

EU product safety contact:
Amazon Media EU S. à r.l.
38, avenue John F. Kennedy, L-1855 Luxembourg
amazonpublishing-gpsr@amazon.com

ISBN-13: 9781662529429 (paperback)
ISBN-13: 9781662529436 (digital)

Cover design by Hang Le
Cover image: © Eva HM, © Holiday.Photo.Top / Shutterstock

Printed in the United States of America

For Emma Warner, who believed,
and for Arynn, heart of my heart

ACT ONE: DEATHLESS GODDESS

CHAPTER 1

PARIS

On this side of the island, where the cliffs are stark white and brutal and the people are crammed together in small apartments like dolls in a dollhouse, your neighbors can hear every scream.

Or, in Thea's case, moan.

She and Perce are in my bed, as usual on a Saturday night, and the three of us have spent it as we always have—fucking, arguing about business, and then fucking again.

It's the buzz of my phone on the bedside table that finally interrupts us for good, and I clamber over Perce—who looks exhausted, poor man—and flip it over, silencing the alarm.

"So are you actually going to show up, Paris?" Thea flops back onto the bed beside Perce and arches a perfectly groomed eyebrow at me. "For the party?"

"I don't understand why you *want* me there," I say sharply, and there it is again. The argument that is always so close to the surface with us, the part where I ask her why she left me—left all of us at the group home—behind to play god with the crime families of the Grecian islands.

Perce groans. "Paris," he says. "I don't know what it will take to convince you. I really don't. You're our friend, and we haven't had a proper engagement party. So we want you there. *I* want you there, even if it's . . . well, even if it's Zarek's party, really."

Thea sits up and grins at me, the look on her face sharp. "Come on, Paris," she says. "This is how Zarek is. It doesn't mean we can't have fun at our party."

Thea works for Zarek in the same sense that we all do—he owns the mansion on the hill in name, but he owns all the rest of the island, city and all, in practice. Even on mainland Greece, far from the island, Zarek has reach that extends far beyond what it should.

"What's fun about a party with a bunch of high-up people from the Family?" I say.

Despite the number of times Thea's asked me to be one of her fixers, I've kept the Families and the work they do at a distance. Thea drills me with a look. "You always seem so sure you'll have nothing in common with any of them," she says thoughtfully, "when you've done similar work yourself over the years."

It's not that the work bothered me as much as *who* I'd be working for, though: after all, I've smashed a few fingers in my time. Convinced the occasional guard not to see something. Helped a whistleblower decide not to whistle.

Teach the bird not to sing. That's what the heads of the crime families say when they want someone silenced. It sounds innocuous enough to wiretaps and listening ears. Almost pretty, if you're the right audience.

"Will *she* be there?" I ignore Thea and direct my question at Perce this time.

He sighs, threads his fingers through Thea's, his bronze skin contrasting with her much-darker brown skin. "Are you asking about Helen?"

Helen. Daughter of the most powerful man on the island.

The reason I am going to this party in the first place.

Not that Perce and Thea know this.

"Of course she's asking about Helen." Thea's eyes narrow. "What's your obsession with her?"

"No obsession."

It isn't Helen I'm obsessed with; it's what her death will do to Zarek. He took my family, and I'm taking his. Pretty fucking simple by my standards.

"You know she doesn't often make public appearances," Thea tells me. "But I'm told she'll be there tonight to celebrate her close friend's engagement."

I snort. "Close friend? I don't see *her* here."

"Not for lack of trying." Thea releases Perce's hand and swings her legs over the bed. "If you want introductions, and if you want to play the game, I got you. If you want to make a scene, do me a favor and just tell me now."

"No scenes." It's a bald-faced lie, and if Thea still knew me like she did when we were growing up in the group home on Troy together, she would know that.

"What, are you finally ready for your leg up in the Families?" Thea asks me.

Thea's been on this shit for years, saying she has a place for me if I want it, and good money, too. The kind that could buy me a new life, if I wanted it.

If I deserved it.

"I just want to celebrate my friends," I tell Thea. "And maybe flirt with a pretty little crime princess while I'm at it."

"Excellent," Thea says, nudging me with her knee as she moves past me. "Now let's get a move on, Troy. I've got gowns to try on and guns to sell to some pesky off-island motherfuckers before I have to be at Zarek's tonight."

Troy, she calls me, as if we are not both shit from the same place. "Wear a gown," she tells me, and I laugh at her.

The mansion on the north end of the island will be everything I am not: glamorous, stunning, shrouded in wealth and privilege and unimaginable power. I intend to show up the way I always do—with a scowl on my face and a knife in my boot.

"I'm serious," Thea says, but the humor is still there beneath. "And you're sure you don't want introductions tonight, Troy?" She pauses after she pulls her tank top down over her head, the look on her face shifting into something I cannot quite read.

"You know there is no force on this planet that could make me want to be part of them." I look past her on purpose, because if there's anyone left alive who knows me at all, it's Thea, even if she sees less than she used to. She'll see this, though, written in my face, the fury that hasn't ever quite stilled.

Thea tilts her head at me, leaning closer. "Why do you stay?" she asks. "Why do you stay on this island at all, if you don't want any part of the Families who control it?"

My heart thuds harder in my chest. Why do I *stay*?

How can I *leave*, after what they did to my family?

"Do *you*?" I ask her. "Really want to be part of this?"

"*Want* is only a small part of the choices I make, Troy," she says after a beat of silence.

Thea has been in the game longer than I have. She's a few years older than me and left the group home before it was destroyed. Since then, Thea has leveraged her innate ability to sell guns to assholes all over the world, bringing in money from corners of the market Zarek had never played in before. If I was ambitious like Thea, I would ask for introductions to some of the players. They'll all be there tonight, not just Zarek and Helen. The queens—Hana and Altea and Frona, three powerful women who were once allied with the Family on Troy and now run different pieces of Zarek's Family—would not be left out of an event like this one.

"What about you?" Thea prods again.

"Just here for the sex," I say.

Thea barks out a laugh, her expression sharpening. "Well, if that's the case, I'd recommend Hana. For all Frona's reputation, Hana's got more spice. Unless you're angling for the big man himself?"

Oh, I am, I *am*, I always have been, if not in the way Thea means, because Zarek's pursuit of power cost me every person I cared about. But I, too, can play long games.

"I'll settle for Helen," I tell Thea. It's true in more ways than one, of course.

The three queens don't matter, not compared to Helen. *Zarek* doesn't matter, not compared to Helen.

"That's a stupid idea, Troy."

Thea is always warning me, and I am rarely listening.

"Yeah, but it'll be fun while it lasts."

Thea's gaze shifts to fury, but only briefly, and then she is still and placid, smooth waters covering the storm I know is beneath, the storm I have seen unleashed back in the group home on Troy. She put her fist through the drywall, broke noses, threw the first punch, always, *always*. The control she has now is new, and learned, and hard-won.

If I were honest with her, I would tell her I miss the brutality.

"All right, Paris," she says. "I'll get you an introduction, if that's what you want. But be careful. Helen plays a game more dangerous than you."

"She never leaves the castle," I say. "How dangerous can she be?"

Perce, who is pulling his boots on, pauses. "Paris," he says.

There is warning in his tone.

Thea is standing utterly still again, poised to slide her engagement ring back onto her finger. "You think *Helen* isn't dangerous?"

I reach past Thea for my shoes, but her hand closes over mine, her dark-brown skin stark in contrast to my white skin.

"Be careful." She leans close to me, her breath hot against my neck. "She can take everything from you without lifting a finger."

There are stories about Helen. She does not date often, but every girlfriend and boyfriend she has had—dead. She does not travel often, but everywhere she does—death trails in her wake. It has made people only more ferocious in their pursuit of Helen, the most beautiful of all these untouchable gods. As if they could be the one who survives her.

I have no interest in any of that.

I turn, my mouth inches from Thea's. "No one takes anything from me," I hiss back. "Not even this Family."

No.

Not ever again. No, I will be the one that takes something from *them*. I will take and take the way they once took from me. I am no god, but I have their viciousness, and if I had let Thea listen when she gave me opportunities to talk, I would have told her what it was like to be kept alive by a tenacity I did not want. To be the one who lived, even if I had not deserved it.

Thea draws back and laughs, the sound sharp as a slap. "Do you think you can do it?" She leans even closer, her lips almost brushing my jaw. "Do you think *you* can kill him?"

"I don't know what you're talking about," I say. We pretend we do not hate him, even here, in a room that belongs just to us, because in this world, people listen. Words can be recorded and twisted. Words can kill. "I don't want Zarek dead."

And it's true. I don't want him dead. Not yet.

He has to suffer first. Has to lose what he loves, what he keeps locked in the tower like a precious jewel, before I take his life, too.

I have a plan, and once I have enacted it, I am going to kill Helen of the gods.

Unless Thea is right.

Unless Helen is the end of me first.

CHAPTER 2

HELEN

My father does not make mistakes. He makes acts of strategy, and he makes acts of war.

It is strategic, then, that tonight's party comes ten years to the day since the bomb that ignited my father's last great act of brutality.

As my attendants style my hair, as I sit perfectly, perfectly still, I wonder which one tonight will be, the strategy or the outright violence. Both have a place here—in our home, on this island.

"Helen?"

Erin's hand is gentle on my shoulder. My personal attendant is sometimes my *only* companion, a carefully curated isolation to protect me from rival crime families, or to protect my father's alliances from me. From the bombs I once built, from the reckless way I once used them, and from the knowledge I still have—because everyone would try to use it.

Bomb-maker, they call me.

Death follows her.

Most beautiful, most deadly.

But most of all: alone.

Erin's hands are always gentle when she helps me.

Sometimes I wish they were not.

Perhaps then I could feel them.

I have to fight to feel her touch or anything else. I can see her hand on my bare shoulder, the silky lavender evening gown swishing to my feet, the thin strap of my heeled sandal, gold, ornate. And yet Erin could just as well be dressing a mannequin for as much as I can feel it.

I run my finger along the ridge of my phone, a new, sleek thing, because I am never allowed to keep the same phone for too long. Someone could find the number. Someone could use it to find *me*. God knows how many have tried, over the years.

There is a veil separating the world, and I am on the wrong side of it.

And tonight, if all goes as planned, that veil becomes permanent. My father and fiancé-to-be left grieving. A hole left in the Greek crime families once more.

And I—I will be away from here, free, while they fruitlessly search the waters below for my body.

"Helen?" Erin's voice is more insistent now, but still pleasant, mellow, compliant.

Perhaps it is this—the easy compliance, the deference—that made my father select her all those years ago. Every woman around my father had to fit the mold that this woman seems to have been born for. Every woman, except perhaps my mother.

I shake loose, move Erin's hand away. "I'm ready."

"Is there anything I can get you?"

I stare at her numbly.

Erin is a few years older than me, tall, dark-haired, attractive. In another world, we would be friends, or, at the very least, tangled up in bed together.

In this one, she does not meet my eyes.

In this one, very few people do.

But no matter. If I am successful in my plan to fake my death and escape tonight, I will never see her again.

"Nothing," I manage. My voice sounds hoarse. My tongue must be dry, my throat parched. "Perhaps some water?"

She pours a glass as shame worms through the edge of my consciousness. If I could feel my body right now, I know how it would feel, a squirming, cruel thing riling my stomach. This is a task I could—should—do myself.

Erin places the glass of water into my hands.

I suck in a breath.

Cold.

The cold of the glass against my palms, *that* I can feel. My palms are suddenly sweaty, slippery with nerves, and I bite down the panic, force it away before it bursts out of me in ways I have never been able to control. Before the glass in my hand shatters from the strength of my own fear, manifested in tightly clenched fingers.

Dangerous as we all are on this island, from the heads of crime families all the way down to the newest fixer, I am among the most dangerous. Few can turn the tide of power with just an appearance. Fewer still have the knowledge and skill to build bombs by hand that can lay waste to whole buildings. I am something unheard of, even here.

A heavy knock on the door nearly sends the glass I am holding to the ground. I cling to it, hands shaking.

"Are you ready, ma'am?"

Just Tommy.

My Tommy.

He has been my guard since before I can remember—by my mother's account, has been my guard since I was minutes old and she placed me in his arms.

My shoulders relax of their own accord.

Tommy is here, so all will be well. He promised me that.

"Ready," I call.

I glance back again at Erin. My father chose my dress for tonight, the accessories, all of it. Another strategic move, another move in a game that has lasted longer than I have been alive. But it is Erin who made the dress bearable, who added padding in the strapless bra, who chose the flowers she knew I loved. Erin who did not question when I set aside the bracelet laid out for me and chose, instead, the bracelet my mother gave to me before—*before*.

If I am to be a set piece, I will at least carry her with me. And when I jump from the cliffs tonight to fake my own death, this will be the only piece of the past to remain with me.

Erin folds her hands and drops her eyes to the ground respectfully.

"Erin," I say. "Are you happy here?"

Her head snaps up. "Happy?" she repeats.

"Yes." I am shivering in the gown, goose bumps crawling up my skin. But Erin cannot answer me. I should already know that; I *do* already know that.

I hold the power in the room. I *am* the power, wrapped in silk and glittering. Smooth skin, soft hair, clothes no one else on this island could ever afford. Even now, when I am no longer a bomber, no longer laying charges beside my mother or recklessly sneaking out at night to blow something up just for fun—even now I am too dangerous to be honest with.

"Of course I am happy, Helen," she tells me, in that same changeless, smooth tone, and then it is time.

Erin opens the door, and I step through, take Tommy's waiting arm to keep from falling.

I am no longer here nor there. I am in my body, just muted, feeling the solid weight of his arm, even smelling the subtle scent of cologne, but the pressure, the smell, it is as if neither sensation belongs to me.

And Helen—I, me, Helen, gone—I drift.

Perhaps I am just a collection of the spirits who died here.

My mother, the rest of the guards I had grown up with, the maids, the cooking staff, the doorman. They died here, and my father rebuilt when he should have left the ashes to rest.

My mother would have called this notion a foolish dream, but— but my mother is dead.

Tommy releases me before we reach the double doors to the staircase, releases me because the guests assembled below cannot see me leaning heavily on the arm of a guard. My father runs guns and topples elected leaders and still deals in the explosives my mother and I were so viciously good at. Their daughter cannot look as if she is about to collapse. Not in any version of this world.

"You gonna be okay on those stairs, k—ma'am?"

Tommy had almost said *kid*, as he always used to call me, but there is another, newer guard flanking us, and the guards here would report each other—or kill each other—just for the chance at rising in my father's ranks.

And Father has never liked the familiarity or the gentleness of Tommy's words, never liked that Tommy could calm my fear as a child, that I would seek out Tommy and not him. That it was Tommy who had seen me as I was—small, seething, cruel—and tried to teach me gentleness when no one else could.

"Of course I'm all right," I tell Tommy. My gaze skims past the other guard, who stares straight ahead, face impassive.

When I walk through the double doors onto the balcony above the ballroom, every head below turns.

It is to be expected, of course.

I am half god, half woman to them. Enough woman, always, to expect the gazes that rake down me, the hungry hands that graze me without permission on the rare occasions I pass through a crowd. Always, always enough woman.

Enough god, though, for men and women to worship whenever they see me.

Enough god. Enough woman.

And in all of it, I am always utterly alone.

My heels tap the pattern on marble floors.

Father looks up at me from the dais below, where he is elevated above the other guests—only two steps, a subtle but significant sign of the power he exerts here. I inherited his fair skin, but not his narrow green eyes, not his broad, tailored build. He is an impossible man to read, but he nods imperceptibly at me.

I have passed the test. I tilt my chin just high enough to be regal, but not high enough to be defiant. I have performed my part.

At least so far.

I am a shade of a daughter to him, just a piece on the chessboard.

So well trained now that I move without being commanded.

I take a step toward the staircase, and another. In the sea of color, of gowns and gold, one person stands out from all the others. A lean slip of a woman, dressed in black jeans, her shoulders square, her brown eyes fierce. She meets my eyes, and my heart catches. I descend.

There is silence, and beside the glittering, living souls who are here to celebrate stand the dead.

There is glass shattered across the floor, strewn in bloody fragments. My mother is there at the center, empty-eyed and bleeding. The soft clink of champagne glasses is the gentlest kind of violence.

I descend.

I am a sharp shard, the glass of the front windows blown in, blood spilled across the ornate marble beneath my father's feet. I am the glittering fragment they forgot to sweep up.

I descend.

The room is a mausoleum for me, and still they dance, they whisper, they laugh.

I descend.

I am Helen. I am half god, half girl, half fury, half grief.

And though they do not know it yet, my death is what they have all come to see.

CHAPTER 3

Paris

I know the games that power plays, and I am furious with myself when Helen descends and I allow myself to be carried forward in the crowd, craning my neck like every other fool in this decadent ballroom.

Helen is tall, or perhaps just wearing heels that make it appear that way, her dark hair brushing past her shoulders in long, loose curls. Her gown, soft lavender silk, whispers against the smooth curve of her legs. She fills the dress, generous curves in all the places where I am sharp edges.

Everything about her is simple, understated, elegant, and not one person in this damn room can look away. There is a bright-red flower—a poppy, maybe?—pinned to her dress.

Her brown eyes are distant, sweeping the room as if she sees past us all toward something we cannot.

I let out my breath in a *whoosh*, loud in the sudden stillness, and for a second—just a second—I could swear her eyes meet mine.

She is distant again a breath later, as if she were never here.

When she reaches the bottom of the stairs, she stretches out her hand, and a broad-shouldered man in a crisp suit takes it.

I suck in a breath, sharp and cold. The air tastes faintly of ash, though I know I am the only one—always—who can sense it.

Because this is him.

Zarek.

He is close enough that I can see him, can feel the heat of the flames of Troy around me, searing my skin but not destroying me. So close I could smash my glass on the bar counter and drive the shards into his chest.

They would kill me, of course. Probably before I reached him.

But the *maybe*—the *maybe I could make it*—haunts me, long game be damned.

Helen offers a small wave to Thea, who acknowledges it with a tight nod, and then the party lets out its breath.

Helen has arrived, and the music crescendos ever so slightly, a subtle change but a purposeful one. As the dancing begins again, the waitstaff floods the room with trays of brimming champagne glasses and hors d'oeuvres that probably cost more than I make in a month.

Zarek's people begin mingling. The voices here sound refined, polished, haughty—some tinged with practiced French accents from expensive study abroad, others brushed with Swiss or Russian or Korean or wherever else gods send their children to study before they return to grow their family businesses.

Does anyone else see it? Do they notice who the music plays for?

And I am just shit from Troy, a glass of mostly empty cognac in front of me, a trail of brutality behind me, and another marked out for me on the path ahead.

I kick one combat boot against the bar, my glass clinking in response.

The bartender sighs and looks at me. "More cognac?"

"Whiskey," a soft voice stops me. "On the rocks, please."

An electric current jolts my body at the sound of her.

Helen.

Helen, here beside me at the bar.

She moved so quickly, so quietly, that I did not hear her approach.

And I always, *always* listen for threats.

"Helen." The word escapes me before I realize I mean to say her name.

Up close, I catch the scent of her—whiskey and the softer note of vanilla.

She turns her head just slightly, her eyes slipping past me. "Yes?"

It is a trained expression, amicable but not personal. Friendly but distant. She gives me her attention while telling me I do not matter, not the way she does, not really, and I never will.

I see the game. I see the tilt of power, the force pulling me closer, and even though I recognize it, I am enthralled by her all the same. Behind her, a hulking man—probably her guard—moves closer.

He scans me from head to toe, searching for weapons, or perhaps he is the kind of guard who looks beyond that, who watches for suppressed anger in the position of my shoulders, the curl of my hands. He raises an eyebrow at me. "Who are you?" His voice is a dangerous sort of soft.

"Paris," I tell him, with a shrug of one shoulder and a grin that is too bold for my own good. With one finger, I twist one of the bands on my fingers, the cold steel, the raised indent of the flames engraved there, all of it a reminder. That my own damn tenacity may have kept me from dying, but it cannot save me.

I am not the kind of woman who can be saved.

"Thea's guest," Helen says, her expression curious. "But how do you know her?"

Helen may be curious, but this guard is looking at me like he can see the fury I have been tending all these years.

My hand strays to my pocket, to the lighter I smuggled in. There is a comfort to it, a security in flicking the lighter open, the small flame reminding me of—so much. Of what was stolen from me, of what I will do to those who robbed me. Helen included.

"Did you hear her?" the bartender snaps when I don't answer. He's staring at me, incredulity in his blue eyes. "She asked you a question. Answer the lady of the house."

Helen visibly recoils at the word *lady*, but her face smooths over a breath later. She leans slightly away from me, exposing her perfect white throat. The tip of my knife will sit nicely just there—above that thundering pulse point.

And for one mad moment, the truth is in my mouth. *I am here to destroy you*, I will tell her, watch her eyes widen, see her finally off-kilter. The flames engraved on my rings singe my fingers. *I am here so that you do not forget.*

"I'm an old friend," I answer Helen finally, pulling the lighter from my pocket.

Helen arches a single eyebrow. "Oh, of course," she says. She dismisses the bartender with a wave of her hand.

The bartender has not gotten my cognac yet, but he leaves because the princess tells him to.

I repress a curse.

"Some party." I slam my empty glass down on the counter.

Helen arches both perfect brows now. "Tommy," she murmurs.

The giant behind her steps a few paces away, and with a look from him, anyone in their vicinity moves back, including the guests who had pressed in toward Helen.

I flick the lighter open, flame in my hands as I watch them go.

"Why the lighter?" Helen asks me. Her voice is soft, a strange juxtaposition with me, all my sharp edges on display beside this woman with her soft dress and glowing makeup and full lips. Dangerous woman, she is, maybe more dangerous in the masking of it.

I meet her gaze as she reaches across the space between us, runs her finger down my hand and then down the lighter, her touch featherlight. I shiver, unsure whether to draw back or lean into the touch.

"A reminder," I tell her.

"Do you usually refuse to answer questions?" she asks me. "You are not one of us, but you answer questions just as vaguely as we do."

The question is so unexpectedly blunt that I laugh.

"Do you usually demand answers?" I return. Helen laughs, too, and then leans back, surveying me carefully. "It's my party," she says after a beat. "Did you know that?"

"Everyone knows that, Princess," I tell her.

Her eyes snap to mine, finally, a bolt of electricity straight to my spine.

Her eyes are dark brown, deep as the storm. There is something uncontained there, something almost feral. Perhaps this is the one thing she cannot disguise, cannot bury despite the years she must have spent learning to rule with poise and grace.

"Tonight, at the most opportune moment," Helen says. Her fingers stray farther down the bar, closer to mine. "When the guests are full but not quite sated, and happy but not quite ecstatic." She pauses, her eyes boring into mine. "We will give them an engagement they could never have anticipated."

"Yours." I stare at her soft lavender dress, at the curves of her filling it, at the smooth line of her legs beneath it. There will be pictures of her in this dress, looking perfect, smiling as she receives a ring that could buy whole islands or set a whole group home free from the poverty that dogged them.

"Don't you want to know who the lucky man is?" she asks. Her head tilts, but again her eyes have left me. "Before anyone else?"

It is maddening to look at her and not be seen by her. I saw that look in her eyes when she met my gaze earlier, a mesmerizing violence, and I crave another glimpse of it. And *that* is the danger of Helen, after all, not the charm and poise and power. But the raw, vicious look in her eyes that makes me want to look again and again and again.

"No," I tell her, just to see if I can bring the flash of her eyes down upon me again like vengeance. "He's not important, is he? Whatever alliance you make, you are doing it to shift more power into your own hands."

"You speak as if *I* was making the choices." Her laugh is soft, a careful, practiced thing.

I want to rip a real reaction from her throat. I want something *real* from her. She owes me that much, after so many of us died because of her family and the power she upholds. "The power in this room? It's your father's. And it's yours."

How can she not know this, swathed in silk and here to make someone else's party her own? How can she not, when both her parents are tangled up in the war that destroyed my sisters? I shove my glass away from me, letting it tip over the edge of the bar top and shatter on the marble floor.

Behind me, Tommy surges forward.

He can see my violence.

They will kill me for it, too. Too soon, if I'm not careful.

But Helen waves him away. "You must be new to the game," she tells me.

As if I have not been surviving her family's games my whole life.

"And you are a fool if you think you have no power," I tell her. "You *are* the power here. They bend to you. If you asked, this room would kneel for you."

"You would not kneel," Helen says. Her throat bobs, as if the breath is caught there.

My blade—her throat—I can hardly breathe. I am so, so close to her now.

I could do it here, instead of dragging her all the way to Troy. Set my knife just—*there*.

"Would you?" Helen's chest heaves just slightly, the shallow rise and fall the only sign that she is as caught in this moment as I am.

"I kneel for no one," I tell her.

Not since Troy.

Her cheeks are a soft pink, maybe from the whiskey, or maybe the opiate intoxicating her is something more—something strange and tenuous and unexpected.

I lean close to her. Take the drink from her hand, tip it back, and down it, grinning at her as I do. I can imagine, instead, Helen of the gods on her knees for *me*. Throat tipped up, eyes trained on me. *Begging.*

This time, Tommy ignores her hand wave and steps forward.

His hand is on his sidearm, the warning clear.

Helen is watching me, mesmerized, and the other partygoers must be, too, though she is the only one I can see. She is the only one here with me.

"Tommy, please," Helen says gently. "She won't hurt me."

Oh, but I would. I intend to. I *will*. Now it is not just ash I smell. No, the rest of it burning, the bodies, their flesh. That smell, *that* smell is the one that haunts and haunts and haunts.

I grin at Tommy, raise Helen's now-empty glass in a salute. "I was just thirsty," I say.

His eyes narrow. "I will kill you," he says softly. "Do you understand?" He is not an average guard. He is not doing this because Zarek pays him to.

He is doing this because he *cares*, because he cares about *her*. I can see it in his eyes, and that thought nearly makes me gag. Because this guard—he is one of us, one of the pawns. And pawns should never love the queens they die for. If you can't help the dying, you can at least help loving the thing that kills you.

I set down the glass slowly, raise my hands. "Of course," I say.

He takes a step back, but his hand remains on his sidearm.

"Anyway." My voice is louder, sharper now. The risk, the danger, has only made me bolder. "Who are they marrying you off to?"

Helen's gaze drifts to the dais where Zarek stands next to his new favorite business partners, a pair of brothers.

They were not part of Zarek's Family when he bombed Troy, so they could not matter less to me. Still, they matter if they end up in my way. After Zarek consolidated smaller crime families—like the ones belonging to Altea, Frona, and Hana—he reached further to find new allies.

"Really?" I ask. "You could have anyone in the world, and you're choosing the new blood?"

It is no secret that the Families traditionally have allied only with people they've known for generations. Men like Marcus and Milos, heirs to a shipping empire, have probably found that some doors remained closed to them despite their wealth, new money never reaching quite as far as the connections of old money could.

"You think I could have anyone in the world?" Helen asks a little dryly, her gaze flicking between the two brothers.

Milos is the elder brother, the calm one, the face of their family. Rumors abound that he doesn't like the Family's brutality, that he prefers a subtler angle.

Marcus, his younger brother, is handsy and volatile and has a violent reputation. They are new blood, new in a world that leans heavily on its traditions, but Marcus makes up for that with the amount of money—bloody goddamn money—he has brought to invest in the Family's work. Or pay for much-needed cover-ups.

"Marcus is the pretty one," I say, mostly because he's less likely of the two and the suggestion is more likely to get under her skin. And more than anything, I want something real out of Helen tonight.

Helen's perfect lip curls, ever so slightly, and I can see it again: her fury barely contained.

"So not Marcus, then." I grin at her.

"As if I would let a man like Marcus lay a hand on me."

"Milos, then," I say. "He'll shift the power into your father's court the way your mother did years ago. When Zarek owns all the ships, he'll own the whole Mediterranean." I slam my hand, palm open, on the bar. In my other hand, I flick the lighter open again. "And you are happy with that?"

She meets my eyes, her gaze level. "I was always going to be sacrificed for this Family," she says.

"If you don't want to do something," I say slowly. "You snap your fingers. You wave your hand. The world bends for you. The bartender leaves before pouring my fucking drink."

Something flashes in her eyes. "*He* doesn't bend," she says. She glances across the room. Her father is still on the dais, though his eyes are on us. "And waving my hands at my employees doesn't mean *I* am free."

We've reached the point of the evening Helen mentioned. The surrounding people are full but not quite sated, happy but not quite ecstatic.

They are restless, waiting for the moment they were promised. *The* moment. The moment that should be Thea and Perce's, but will instead belong to Helen and her waiting, watching father.

"You could change that," I tell her.

"Do you want to know something?" Her voice is quiet, so quiet I have to lean in closer.

"Do you want to tell me?" I shoot back.

"I am going to die tonight." She says it with a smile on her face, something desperate and dark but something *real*.

My own heart thunders against my rib cage, so hard it is almost painful.

"And who would dare kill the princess?" I ask.

Because she *can't* know.

Can she?

Helen is still smiling, but the look in her eyes is distant now. She is far away from me, far out over the stormy blue sea beyond the windows.

"What is it *you* want, Paris?" she asks.

You, I almost answer. *At my mercy.*

"An introduction," I tell her after a beat. "To your father."

Disappointment flashes in her face, sharp and clear before her expression smooths over, and then she steps back toward the great windows looking out over the sea, alone on the symbol carved into the marble floor, a Z and an L, tilted and interwoven. Zarek and Lena. Their family, their godship, their love for each other, immortalized in marble.

How fitting that Helen will die on the anniversary of the bomb that started it all.

They will crowd Helen soon, but now, just briefly, she stands alone, framed by windows that open to the yawning mouth of sea and storm. She looks almost wistful.

I am going to die tonight.

What is it you are planning, Helen of the gods, or what is it you have learned? What bloody nightmare will these families unleash tonight?

It is the right moment for something, though. The moment Zarek will call for everyone's attention, when Milos will descend the steps and kneel in front of Helen, ring in hand. When she will pretend to be surprised, ecstatic, perhaps a little teary but still somehow perfectly composed. She will smile for the first time tonight—other than the smile she sneaked me when I stole the whiskey from her soft, perfect hand—and the guests in the room will fall even more in love with her than they already are.

It is *Zarek's* moment.

Except it is also *Helen's.*

Except Helen is alone for a breath of time that lasts too long, and I smell something faint, something out of place, something devastatingly familiar.

I flick my lighter open out of habit, but the soft comfort of its click cannot calm me. Because this smell, it is an acrid smell, like flame, like—

bomb.

I am moving before I can call it out; I am moving on instinct and instinct alone; I am faster than guard and god alike. Because Helen is *mine.*

I am hurtling straight into Helen of the mansion, Helen of the island, Helen of the gods, my body colliding with hers, just as the windows behind us explode in a shower of glass.

CHAPTER 4

HELEN

The woman is on top of me, and the shards of glass are in her back and her neck and her head and in my bare arms and I am bleeding and I feel it. I *feel* it.

I feel, for the first time in years.

I feel *her*.

Paris on top of me, her body covering mine in a wall of lean, hard muscle. Her hands are braced on either side of my head, her knee digging into my thigh, pinning it to the marble floor beneath her.

There is screaming, incoherent and distant. The only thing in the world is Paris, is me, is glass on the floor and the storm outside now audible, now raging at us for believing we could keep it out.

Her eyes are blazing.

She is *furious*.

All the chaos around me, and that is the only thing real, the only thing I am sure of. That Paris is as furious as I am, and that she is furious with *me*.

And then hands drag Paris from me, Tommy's hands. Tommy tosses her aside carelessly, as if she is nothing, this woman who stole my drink and laughed at my Family and saved my life.

He kneels over me, hands gentle as he checks each place the glass has marked my skin. "Kid," he says. "You okay?"

I nod my head.

My neck is sore, a bit of glass has scraped my arm, but there is no head wound, no scorch marks, no jagged gash in my chest.

No blood spooling across the floor where Mama died. Where, tonight, I was meant to die—and not the false death I had planned, the escape to freedom.

I become conscious of the rest slowly:

The guards are holding the crowd back, weapons drawn. They are keeping the peace with the threat of violence, my father's usual solution. And then Father is rushing down from the dais, arms outstretched to me. My almost betrothed, Milos, is behind him, concern flashing in his blue eyes.

Paris is on her feet, staggering but still standing. I look at her there, wavering, bleeding, and I get the distinct feeling that she would still be standing even if her wounds were much deeper than the surface injuries she sustained. Blood runs down the sharp line of her jaw, but she barely grimaces.

"You okay?" she asks. Her voice is unrefined, a jagged thing that does not belong in a place like this.

I stand.

I am still the one they all came to see.

Every head turned to me, all eyes on me.

Your place, Father said to me.

If my mother was here—well.

If my mother was here, the air would not smell like ash and soot and destruction. As long as she was alive, it was only ever our enemies who suffered like this. It was only ever them who burned.

Now, I lean hard on Tommy's arm, and I do not tremble. "I'm fine," I tell Paris, because if I look at my father or if I look at the man he's marrying me off to, everything in my perfect facade will crack.

But Paris.

Paris, the woman who met my eyes and did not look away. Paris, who told me exactly what she thought of me, of all of us. Paris, who does not belong at this party and walks like royalty despite that.

Paris, with the lighter in her hands and the smirk on her lips.

I am going to die tonight, I had told her.

My gaze falls on the shattered glass, the windows wide open. I could pull away from Tommy and step through them now, waver at the cliff's edge and then fall.

Few could survive that kind of fall, but *I* could. It is a hard dive, but not an impossible one. Not if you know there is a gap between the rocks below, where the landing will just be the hard slap of water and not the breaking crush of the rocks.

And it is the only way I will ever be free.

"What the *hell* happened?" Milos asks my father, who looks to Tommy and then me and then Paris.

There is a hole in the wall, and the storm is still raging, rain and hail falling through the gap in the glass, the floor slick as blood. The metal bars that held the windows are bent outward, warped from the heat of the bomb.

My father has that look in his eyes, that barely caged thing in him that came out when the blast killed my mother ten years ago, a mixture of raw violence and determination.

"I intend to find out." He wheels on another guard, one holding an assault rifle. "No one leaves," he hisses. "Not until you have searched and questioned every single person."

I place a hand on my father's arm, firm and calming. I can feel that, too. I can feel every sensation in my body. I have been able to *feel* ever since Paris touched me, tackled me to the ground and covered my body with her own.

It was her touch that shocked me back into my body, and I am not sure yet if I missed feeling or if I would like, now, to return to its absence.

I sway a little on Tommy's arm, and he shifts to support me. "Come sit," he says quietly. "The physician will be here soon."

"Marcus," my father snaps at the man beside my almost fiancé.

I suck in a breath, trying to still the raging beat of my heart.

Marcus ducks his head toward my father.

"Gather my fixers."

Many in the room are already cowering.

My father will do what he does best—rule. And after he lets the party guests sink deeper into their fear, after he reestablishes his own power however he needs to, I will step in and I will pick up the pieces and I will make them feel as if all is well again.

Unless I—unless I jump.

I look out the ravaged windows to the storm raging outside, the sea below calling to me. I could do it. I could make it. I could make it to freedom. Or I could break on the rocks or be lost to the water, tangled in my gown in the perilous sea. It would be freedom regardless.

The fixers surround my father within seconds—half a dozen of his most trusted employees, brutal people who have served him for years.

"Should we evacuate, sir?" Tommy asks. "There might be another explosive."

My father's face hardens. "No. No one leaves. Sweep the room and remove my daughter if you deem there to be a security threat. But everyone else remains until I find the person who did this."

No. The shattered glass, the shattered daughter, all of that can be swept up later. My father must have his blood.

"Look." Marcus's voice cuts across the chaos of the room and splits the crowd in two as surely as if he were carrying a blade. He is holding two halves of a round golden object that fits in his cupped palms. "By the window. Someone blew out the windows with *this*." He holds it out to Father, who nods to one of his fixers to take it.

It is a grenade, not the kind of complex explosive I am used to laying. If it were, if I had been the one laying the explosive, this whole room would be in the Mediterranean.

There are too many people between me and the gap in the wall now. I could run for it. I could force them to move if I wanted, cut my path with the brutality befitting my father's daughter.

They expect it of me, even if I am no longer brutal enough for my father's liking.

The investigators gather around, but with a look from Tommy, they take a step back.

Except Paris. Still bloody. Still furious.

If I jump—

Paris moves into my path, solid and real.

Everyone else might move from my path if I made for the windows, but not Paris. She watches me with cold, immovable disinterest.

I shiver with the weight of her gaze but turn back toward Marcus and the grenade.

"Careful," Father snaps at his fixers now. "That could still—"

"It did its damage," I tell him. I step back toward him, toward this life, toward the fragments of the grenade. The sea behind me mourns my choice. "Let me."

When my mother was alive, she taught me what she knew, let me pore over the materials in her workshop. Let me set them off on the small, uninhabited islands around us. The shards of the grenade are hot to the touch, the twisted metal singeing the pads of my fingers. It is beautiful: even warped, I can see it was made in the shape of a golden apple, lettering engraved on one side that somehow survived the flames. I lean closer, awe and horror at war inside me. This is a grenade even my mother would have been proud of.

"*Careful.*" This time it is Milos, back with the doctor, lecturing me as if he has any right to tell me what to do. As if he is anything but a man my father is selling me off to. He hovers at my elbow. "Don't hold it so close to your face."

Anger uncurls beneath my ribs so quickly I nearly strike him with the remnants of the bomb. This man, this man from the world of finance and ships and *business*, knows nothing of explosives like this. This was my world, *mine*, long before it was ever his.

I bring the grenade closer, turn it over to see a message engraved on the other side.

FROM THE QUEEN.

"From the queen," I whisper, and Paris surges forward, a strange, knowing expression in her eyes.

She looks as curious as any fixer now, hungry for answers. "Is that what it says?" she asks. "From *the queen?*"

Father's gaze finds Paris. "Who are you?" he asks. I can see it on the tip of his tongue, the *thank you* he knows he owes her, but he hesitates. There is suspicion in his eyes, and for good reason. No one ever does the Families favors without expecting something in return. And sometimes—sometimes the circumstances around those favors are staged.

"Paris," she tells him, with no further explanation. Something strange and unsettling flickers in her eyes, but she does not move closer to him, does not speak further.

The corner of my lip quirks toward a smile. I have never heard someone speak to my father with such minimal deference.

Just briefly, she looks as if she belongs among the gods, despite the black jeans and scarred knuckles. The set of her shoulders, the tilt of her head, the thing in her eyes that tells me she, too, has stood too close to death too many times—

A scream cuts the air before either my father or Paris has the chance to escalate the tension rife in the air between them.

Near the bar, the guards sweeping the room have stopped a young woman in a server's uniform.

She is tall and lean, her hair dark red, her skin freckled. Her green eyes are snapping with a fury that reminds me of Mama. Fiery, and then gone.

Two of the guards are holding her while a third searches her, and my stomach tightens.

They will kill her. Or my father will.

She will die.

She will die, and she is so young, and she is furious, and someone so young and so furious should not die here.

"She has the pin," one guard says. "She has the pin to the grenade."

And then everything—

Everything happens too fast.

My father, raising a hand and shouting *wait*, and Tommy moving in front of me, wrapping his body around me to protect me, and then: a gunshot.

Nothing about it feels real—not the screaming, not the surge of the crowd like a frantic wave, not the shots that follow, not silence settling over the crowd again. The fear, though. That pulses in the air.

That is as real as my own heartbeat.

Beside me, my father is trembling with rage.

Beside the bar, the girl's body is splayed across the floor, blood still leaking from her temple.

Paris's face is a hard mask, my father's face a twist of fury, his stare deadly as he looks at the guard who shot the girl.

"Bring. Him."

His words are quiet, but they are a thunderclap.

I force back a flinch, drop my hands to the bracelet from Mama instead, rub the pad of my thumb along it, over and over. It is a thin black metal band with words engraved on the inside, an oath we took so many wars ago.

Méchri thanátou.

Unto death.

Unto death, Mama would say as we lit a charge together. *Unto death,* she would say as she taught me to fire a gun. *Unto death.*

They drag the guard who fired the shot before my father.

I should have chosen the jump, the sea below, the chance of escape, because I do not want to watch the rest, do not want to see, do not want to *see*—

"Helen." Paris is beside me, her voice soft, her eyes furious. She will not let me leave my body behind. "Looking away changes nothing."

"How," my father asks quietly. "*How* am I to question a corpse?"

The guard is trembling.

He is so young, and he is so terrified. And someone so young and so terrified should not die here.

But I cannot stop them from dying. I can never stop them from dying. I look out toward the storm. I beg it to drown out the noise, but even the storm's rage is dying, rain slackening at the blown-open gap in the window.

The boy does not answer my father.

There is a crack. Ringed fingers against bone. Cartilage and bone breaking.

There is more blood on the marble.

There is Mama's blood on the ground, and the girl's, and they have bold, furious green eyes, and they are afraid like the boy and they are all dying, they are all dying—

Paris's hand closes over my arm, so hard her fingers dig into my skin. "No," she says.

Tommy is watching her carefully, but he is not moving, not driving her backward or holding a weapon to her face. He appears, for half a minute, strangely hopeful as he looks back and forth between us.

Another crack, and a low moan, and beyond Tommy and Paris the guard is kneeling before my father.

The others in the room are kneeling, too. They are all kneeling.

Just not me or Tommy.

Or Paris.

"*How,*" my father repeats, his voice a snarl now. "*Am I. To question. A corpse?*"

"I—" the guard attempts, finally, too late, too late. "I am—sorry—"

"No one dies unless I *say* they do." And then my father crouches, and it is over, it is over, and I am a coward, so I do not watch.

If I were braver, I would choose this moment. I would walk to the edge of the wound in the wall and I would say *I do* and step off.

But instead, I am frozen, and Paris is holding me fast.

I look at her, look at the sharp angles of her face, and I tremble on Tommy's arm, and Tommy and Paris, who are not cowards, watch my father and the knife and the boy.

They watch the slash of his blade as it opens the boy from his diaphragm down to his abdomen, and they watch as the boy tries, just briefly, to hold his intestines inside his body, and then. Then they watch him die.

Paris releases my arm and steps back, and the instant she is no longer touching me, no longer holding me here with the ferocity of her grip, I—I leave.

The noise is muted. The colors are blurry. The red of the blood is not quite so violently bright. Not quite so harsh.

My father strides toward us, the body behind him inconsequential already.

"Why are you here?" he asks Paris, that dangerous edge still at the forefront.

If I were here, if I were in my body, I would feel the fear churning inside me.

The guards shift, ready for the command to take Paris, to put a bullet in her, or to hold her while my father guts her.

And I, I may be nothing, I may be unable to stop anything, but I—I make another choice. I chose not to jump. And now I choose—

Paris.

Impulsively, I take her arm. Perhaps this one woman, sharp edged as the grenade that blew up my party, I can save.

She looks at me with something akin to shock, but she shifts her balance so that she can hold me up.

"What do you think it means?" I ask her.

33

We stare at one another, Paris and I. She is furious and dangerous. She is the edge of a cliff. She is a mistake.

I want to draw closer.

"I can investigate this," Paris says, twisting one of her rings slowly. She is looking at me, and only me.

I turn my gaze to my father. "She's a fixer," I tell him, loud enough that the men nearby and anyone standing just beyond the ring of guards can hear. The dead boy and the serving girl and Mama, they can hear, too. They are all holding their guts in with bloodied hands, and they watch me defy my father. If it was not true before, it is now: she is a fixer because I said she is. "Father, we should let her help."

Father's eyes narrow. "We have our bomber," he said. "Helen—"

"The queens," I murmur. "Father, it says *from the queen.*"

"I saw." His eyes sweep the crowd.

The three queens are *here.*

They are all watching us with great interest, and all three of them are far from the source of the explosion.

"I can vouch for Paris." Thea has breached the ring of guards, slipped right past them. She is standing too close to the blood, so I cannot look at her, cannot look at her straight on. There is a smear of red on the edge of her pink tulle engagement dress. "She has solved more than a few problems for me." She stares straight at Paris, something almost like surprise on her face.

Paris holds Thea's gaze unflinchingly, a moment passing between them that is entirely their own.

They are saying something to one another, these strange blood-drenched women at my party, if only I could decipher it.

"We need someone far from the usual circles," I tell my father, soften my voice so that the tone—gentle, demure—is one he can hear without rage.

Because if Paris is working, Paris is alive. Because if Paris is alive—maybe she can be my way out.

"Paris is welcome to assist, then." My father's shoulders are perfectly relaxed, his hands open. He is the picture of ease, of calm in the chaos. Only in his eyes do I see the storm still rages. "Find us this queen."

Paris's eyes flick to the queens, one by one, but she knows as well as Father and I do that even in his house, we must use a subtler hand with the queens than outright accusations. Powerful as my father is, a war with them would be bad for business.

Where most people would look frightened, or at least intimidated at the idea of going toe-to-toe with those more powerful, Paris has a flicker of excitement in her eyes. As if she has gotten something she wanted.

Thea taps the heel of her boot against the floor. "Good luck, Troy," she calls. Paris's shoulders tighten imperceptibly at the word.

Tommy wedges his way between Paris and me, but the look he gives Paris is one of grudging respect.

She takes the grenade from me gingerly, as if expecting it to go off again in her hands.

It is nothing but a shell, though.

From the queen.

There was only one queen on this island. My mother, Lena. And their bombs incinerated her ten years ago today, Troy betraying their own because she favored my father over the Family she was born to.

The room is a tomb around us. There is blood on the floor, and I cannot tell if it is my own, or from the girl who carried the grenade, or the boy my father killed. Or after all this time, if it is still Mama, the little that is left of her bleeding at my feet. I cannot tell if I am a woman standing here for all to see, or a little girl who just found her mother's body.

But I stand tall, my bleeding shoulders rigid like the queen my father expects me to be. In this moment, *needs* me to be.

"Now," I tell Milos. "The people need their moment."

Understanding follows confusion across Milos's face, and then a hurt deeper than I imagined I'd see. "You want to make our announcement *now?*"

How could he have confused the state of this union? Has he thought, all along, that he and I were anything more than an alliance?

I squeeze his hand, offering what reassurance I can. "We have an announcement." My voice carries. Every head turns. "I know tonight's events must have shocked you. Terrified you, too. And for that, I grieve deeply." I hesitate, and they lean forward, eager, desperate.

The bodies are already being carried away, and the people in this room are already looking past them. They are looking beyond the smears of blood on the floor. They are looking to *me*.

I brush my thumb along the bracelet again.

Méchri thanátou.

I am their safety. I am everything they think they need. I almost went over the edge of this cliff tonight to buy my freedom. "I cannot imagine your terror. No, perhaps that isn't true."

I do not have to force my words to falter, my voice to tremble.

Mama holds her guts inside her body, hands weak and then slackening entirely. Blood spatters the edge of my soft silk slippers.

She has fury in her eyes. She is afraid.

And then Mama's body burns.

There are ashes all around me.

The crowd, the real, the now, all blur before me. I want Paris to take my arm so that my body does not forget to hold on to me. I want the force of her colliding with me, the pain of her knee jamming into my thigh, the fury of her eyes staring into mine. I want her fingers to dig into my arm, closing over my skin hard enough to bruise.

I waver on my feet.

Milos steadies me, and I do not feel his touch.

"I can imagine it," I breathe, but the room is so quiet that I know it carries to every person in this room.

Even the guards, the ones who must detach from it all, the ones who must pay attention to threats and not to me, have their heads tilted toward me, listening even as their eyes scan the crowds.

"I was here, in this room, the last time someone hated my family enough to attack us." I stand taller, but I allow Milos to continue to support my arm. "The last time this happened, it did not go unpunished."

I look to my father, whose face is a hard mask. He will spill more blood tonight, a thought that should give me pause.

It is *my* words, power cloaked in civility, that enable and embolden him in that brutality tonight, makes him almost sympathetic to those watching.

You are the power, Paris said so viciously. *You.*

I catch Thea's eyes, stone cold, boring into mine.

Well, sympathetic to *most* of them, that is.

"And I am here to tell you that hatred will not stop us." I lift my chin. "Milos and I have something to tell you."

That girl, with the bright eyes and the rage, holding the pin to the grenade. She may have been hired for a job or played like a pawn. But she hated us. That hatred was all her own.

I look back at Milos.

At least I will allow him to tell them. I can grant him that.

"Helen and I are engaged to be married."

The crowd sucks in its collective breath. I should smile up at Milos, the picture of love and devotion, but this was always for our audience, and not for him, so it is our audience I turn to. Most faces hold surprise, excitement, joy.

Among them, I find the three queens, their expressions pleasantly neutral, because even now, they mask. I imagine they are calculating what this means for their alliance with my father. Do they wonder, now, if those alliances are coming untethered, their place in Zarek's family made unimportant by the arrival of Milos and Marcus?

I should care more.

But I am watching Paris, watching her stone face. She is framed by the storm and shadow of the sea beyond as she cradles that grenade in her hand and stares back at me with unmistakable violence in her eyes.

37

Violence, and something else.

I have let her in, and premonition tells me everything will change because of it.

And then Milos tilts my chin toward him, and we kiss there in front of the watching world, the gathering sea.

The crowd lets out a breath.

We are beautiful, defiant but not enough to give anyone else ideas that they, too, could defy their circumstances.

I close my eyes, an illusion of pleasure for the crowd and an escape for me so I can imagine how it would feel to step off the edge of this mansion and choose freedom.

I close my eyes, and I feel nothing at all.

CHAPTER 5

Paris

It is Helen herself who gives me the idea for her own destruction. I watch her intently as she mends the party back together in front of me until her guard guides her away. I saved her. Somewhere in that split second when I knew it was a bomb, I decided to save her.

It was not any sense of goodness left in me, no: Helen of the gods is *my* kill.

The Families—whoever is playing a game at this party, Zarek included—are going to topple.

And Helen is going to help me do it.

I may have lost my window of opportunity tonight, but if I am Helen's fixer, working this case, finding this bomb-maker, I will have another. And when I have her, and an audience to boot, I will carry her home to Troy.

Helen's path takes her past me, her eyes on me as if she is riveted.

She stops her guards with a hand, and then pulls off the flower that was pinned to her gown. Despite the bomb, despite the hard landing on the marble beneath my body, it is perfectly unruffled.

A poppy, the flower of remembrance.

Kore had said she would grow them for the lost girls of Troy. It was the last thing she told me as I dragged her out of the rubble, the last thing she told me as the last breath left her body, soot still in her hair and ash dusting her skin. It was the closest thing to goodbye I ever had from Troy.

En morte libertas, Kore had whispered in my ear before the end. It was the words engraved above the door to the group home, a building that had once been a church. In death, liberty. We had joked about it, when we had all lived there together. When we had all *lived*.

Now, Helen leans close, presses the flower into my calloused palm, her thumb brushing my hand.

And then she is gone, and I am left with a poppy in my fist, glass embedded in my skin and hair, and Thea's warning thundering in the back of my head.

Helen is dangerous.

Oh, and she is. Whiskey and vanilla. Poppies and blood and rain.

But it is already too late for me.

"Fixer," Zarek calls me over to him now.

I step forward as the guards guide other party guests away for questioning.

Once we are out of the ballroom—up the stairs, down a long corridor—he pauses in front of his office. "What use are you to me?" he asks.

"You want me to find you a queen," I answer.

Zarek tilts his head, surveying me intently. Behind me, his guards step closer. "So find her."

"Hana, Altea, Frona." I pause, Thea's name next on my lips—she is the fourth queen, after all, rising through the ranks like a meteor, and just as destructive. Loyalty stops me, as much as I have tried to cull personal loyalty and feelings over the years.

"Those three," Zarek says. He is standing close to me, so close I can smell expensive cologne and the faint scent of woodsmoke. "And only those three."

"Yes," I say. Not because Thea is loyal to him—I am not even sure she is loyal to *me*, not even after all these years—but because she loves Perce.

"Tell me why those three." He moves again, his steps quickening as he enters his office. "And why not Thea."

Hana controls elected officials, swings local elections, and influences national ones. She has been gathering more connections, more power.

It was only a matter of time before she moved on Zarek.

Altea ran weapons for one of Zarek's rivals before he decimated them in the last round of brutality. She runs weapons for *him* now, but it has always been an uneasy alliance.

Frona is *the* fixer, the one with a whole team of people like me.

They were all complicit in the war that killed us, even if only tangentially—though none of them matter as much as Zarek and Lena and Helen.

"Because Thea loves who she loves," I tell Zarek. "Because she doesn't want to find his head in a bakery box."

"Then why those three? Are they not my loyal allies?" Sarcasm is thick in his voice.

"The three queens were never your first choice—not for connections, not for weapons, not for information and fixers," I answer bluntly. "And you were never theirs."

"Wasn't I?" Zarek stops, turning to me so sharply he nearly elbows me in the face.

"No," I say. "They saw you take Troy and knew they could be next or they could be yours. The question is—which of them has decided to move on you now?"

Red blooms in his face, but then he shakes his head. "I appreciate honesty," he says finally. "But you would do well to remember your *place*."

"Of course, sir," I say, dipping my head in his direction.

The guards part for someone. Zarek raises an eyebrow at the commotion.

Helen's new fiancé, Milos, stands behind me in the doorway, and behind him, his brother Marcus. Zarek nods to them but looks back at me.

"So, *fixer*, why would she sign the explosive, whoever she is?" Zarek asks me. "Why would she blow up my party and risk being caught or killed by her own bomb?"

I snort and then pretend to cough into my arm to cover it. It is unwise to let the gods know you are laughing at them, especially when you are in the belly of one's mansion. "Of course she wants you to know who she is," I say. "She wanted a spectacle, and she got one. Hel—your daughter salvaged it, so whoever sent the bomb will want a second chance. They want something you cannot walk away from."

A decade of hating him, a decade of imagining revenge, and I am an expert at how someone would go about it. I am well versed in ripping power out of the hands of a man too used to having all of it. And I know exactly what someone who hates Zarek would want when formulating a plan to destroy him.

It is a question, now, of who thinks they can throw a grenade into *my* plan for revenge, if they are working together, if we share the same hatred—and if I can use them to speed my own plan on its way.

Milos's gaze lands on me squarely now.

"I have never heard of you," Milos says coldly. "Until tonight. What are you to Helen?"

What am I to Helen? Is that *jealousy* I hear in his voice?

I push the poppy deeper into my jacket pocket. "I am nothing to Helen. Just a body that stopped her from dying."

They saw her rip the flower from her dress, press it into my palm, sweep away across the ballroom, away from all of us as if we were nothing. As if *they* were nothing, but not me. With me, she left the flower.

Marcus laughs. "We are all nothing to Helen," he says. "Even you, *fiancé*."

"Marcus." Zarek's voice is a whip.

To his credit, Marcus turns his head slightly to listen to Zarek, his only reaction to the harshness and fury bound up in Zarek's voice. A lesser man would have flinched.

"Find my daughter," Zarek commands. "See to her. I have no further need of either of you."

Milos's disappointment is evident in both the slump of his shoulders and the disappointment in his face as he and his brother turn to go.

"Do you trust them?" I ask Zarek as soon as they leave. "Because other than the three women downstairs, they are the only ones who might be foolish enough to challenge you."

Zarek turns to me, eyebrow raised.

"Sit."

I consider, just briefly, that I could comply by dropping into the spacious desk chair behind his mahogany desk and sitting in *his* seat.

Instead, I sit in the chair he motions to, a guard dropping heavy hands on my shoulders as soon as I do.

Zarek pulls his chair forward and sits opposite me, his knees almost touching mine.

I taste ash and soot and bomb.

I bite down hard on my tongue.

"Tell me," he says softly. "Tell me the truth."

I meet his stare. I will not fear. I will not allow my hands to tremble. *En morte libertas.*

"The truth?"

I lean forward, and the guard jerks me backward, my shoulder blades slamming into the wooden back of the chair.

Zarek's lips tip upward in a smile. "The explosive," he says. "You knew. You knew before it went off. Tell me how."

Because this is not the first time for me, because I am a survivor of his violence, because flame is as natural to me as breath. Because I crawled over girls who deserved to live, girls who burned in flames that did not manage to kill me.

I cannot lie, cannot hide that much. So instead I offer a manageable truth.

"Because I am shit from Troy," I tell him, baring my teeth as I do. "And I remember the stink of your bombs."

Surprise flashes in his face, and he leans back in his chair, satisfied.

"Your honesty is refreshing," he says. "So tell me, Paris of Troy. Do you blame me for those bombs?"

I shrug one shoulder. "They didn't kill *me*," I say.

This time, he smiles, and for the first time I can see his resemblance to his daughter. "You have the spirit required for the Family," he says finally. "Very well, fixer. Why would the brothers challenge me? They are about to *join* me. Helen solidifies that alliance."

He must have used her for just such a purpose many times over the years—because who has seen Helen of the gods and not tried to use her? There is war in the tilt of her jaw. There is power in the red of her lips. There is violence waiting in the hollow of her throat. "If they have Helen, is she really your asset anymore?" I ask him. "Or is she Milos's bargaining chip? Is she the face of *his* endeavors? And what of his brother?"

It must twist in his chest, that this was exactly the case with Lena all those decades ago. The marriage was meant to be an alliance, an end to the squabbles. Lena's Trojan family and Zarek's family united, and more powerful for it.

Except Troy didn't want Zarek, something he could never forgive.

Zarek stands, pushes his chair back to its proper place. I get a look around me for the first time as he does.

The office is as opulent and pristine as the rest of the house, with high vaulted ceilings and a hand-carved desk that probably cost over five years' living expenses for the entire group home back on Troy. Zarek waves a hand to his guards, who step out of his office, their obedience silent and immediate.

The door swings shut with a heavy *thunk*.

"Do you know why I brought you here?" he asks softly.

"Someone blew up your party and you're desperate to—"

I am propelled backward off my feet until I am pinned against the wall, my head slamming into an oil painting of Lena.

Zarek holds me there, one hand around my throat, my feet dangling above the ground.

His face is expressionless, almost calm, but the flicker in his eyes betrays him. "You will show me *respect*," he hisses. His breath is hot on my face. Perhaps it is only my imagination, the fear and fury tricking my own brain, but in this moment his breath smells of ash and burning flesh.

"You will follow orders," he continues. "And if you fail, I will send your head back to Troy and leave the rest of you for the crows."

He releases me.

My knees buckle when my feet hit the floor, and I stagger.

A smile flickers across Zarek's face but does not linger. "I have already had Marcus and Milos investigated," he says conversationally, as if he had not just pinned me against the wall by the throat. "They are under surveillance even now, but they are no threat to my power, and there is no chance my daughter will have loyalty to them over me. My daughter . . . my daughter is largely uninterested in the power we hold. But she is loyal to *me*. She has no one else."

The truth burns in my throat, the ache of withholding the truth: that it is not as true as Zarek believes. That there is someone else, and if Helen knew—well, she might not be so easy to use.

"But you sent them away anyway," I rasp. "To talk to me alone."

Surprise flashes in his eyes.

I do not show fear. I do not *feel* fear.

If I practice this enough, it will be true.

"You fascinate me, Troy." Zarek surveys me, head tilted. "I had you pinned to the wall, and you only looked *angry*. Is that why my daughter spoke to you tonight? Did you fascinate her, too?"

He makes me sound like someone's toy. Someone's object.

All of us on Troy were. It was the smallest of the islands, never much of a city even in its most prosperous days. But Troy was the home of a rival, so when he was furious, his violence consumed it. Even the group home. Even the girls inside.

"I think Helen was just bored," I tell him.

"Yes." Zarek's tone is frigid. "Well, you have already wasted enough of my time. Be on your way, and be discreet, little fixer. Find me this queen."

From the queen.

It is all pretentious bullshit—the party, the gold-plated modified grenade, the type of woman who labels *herself* a queen. But when it is time, this work I am doing will bring me their heads on a fucking platter.

I nod. "I'm sure you already know where to find me," I tell him. I shove one hand into my pocket and find the poppy there. My fingers linger.

Helen.

Oh, Helen.

"I do."

I am not afraid. My fingers clench around the poppy.

"Would you like the doctor to attend to you?" Zarek asks. "You look a bit . . . scraped."

It's an understatement: I look like shit. Absolute shit. There is glass in my arms, and my pride wants me to stalk out of this room and ignore his offer, but years of paying my own bills stills me.

"Yes," I say.

"As thanks for saving my daughter—"

"Didn't you already thank me?" I gesture to the fingerprints around my throat, already purple.

There is a small smile on his face.

The gods like when their playthings fight back. It amuses them.

"You have boldness, Troy," he says. "You remind me of a woman I once knew."

The doctor patches up my injuries, and then leaves me. I have memorized the floor plan, so now I walk the halls. I can feign confusion when a guard finds me. I can pretend I am lost.

I have enough favor, for saving Helen, to talk my way around a guard.

I am going to die tonight.
En morte libertas.

I still have her poppy in my pocket, the memory of us tangled up on marble, limbs crashing together, glass shattering. We were a damn cacophony. And what was it Helen knew, moments before a bomb went off? Does she know the queen? Is she making a move to become one in her own right?

She was famous, once, for the explosives she and Lena made together, though it was said Helen stopped making them altogether after the Trojan bomb destroyed her home.

The mansion, the party, the grenade, Helen—all of it runs through my mind on a loop. It would take a dozen of my tiny studios to fill one room in Helen's mansion. I imagine what *her* bedroom must look like for the briefest of minutes before I stop myself.

I find my way to the floor below her wing of the house, a long, mostly empty room with an easel and paints that are covered in dust, a lounge chair, a long mirror. Someone's studio, once.

I am not directly below; her balcony is several rooms over, partially visible from where I stand.

I push back the curtain so that I can see her balcony, the length of it extending out from the house, over the white cliffs and the raging blue waters below.

Helen stands there, curves barely concealed by a black silk dressing gown. She is barefoot, lips slightly parted, gazing out at the sky.

I can imagine her room, even if I cannot see more than the balcony and the window into the room.

Silk that smells of whiskey and vanilla. Glass skylights and rain. Poppies at the bedside.

Bare skin, tangled sheets.

Hot breath against my neck.

I crumple the poppy in my fist.

Damn all the gods.

Especially the beautiful ones. Especially the one that's *mine.*

CHAPTER 6

HELEN

The sea is a siren below me, calling for me as I stand on the balcony far above the raging water. The doctor has left, Erin has left, and I am finally, blissfully alone.

Could I jump from here? Make them think I had fallen, make them wonder why?

My father would tie up loose ends with Paris, of course, and that bothers me more than it should.

I can still go, after her investigation concludes. And she is not connected to the Families, has no loyalty to any one of them in particular, so maybe—with the right money, the right leverage—I can even convince her to help me disappear.

I close my eyes and I *feel* it. I feel the way the water thunders against the cliff, feel it thundering in my chest. I can feel the cold of the guardrail against my bare arms, the firm, smooth marble beneath my feet. What spell did Paris cast on me that sensation has rushed in like a wave and demands my presence here? It is disorienting, deeply, but so is everything about Paris.

I can feel the silk robe against my legs, smooth and recently shaved. I can feel the bruises, too, on my back, my arms, where Paris knocked me to the floor to shield me from the glass, the bomb. I can feel the raised welt that her knee left in my thigh, and I want *more.*

And more than anything, I can feel the warped, round metal in my hand that says *from the queen.*

My father's investigators collected most of the pieces and took them downstairs to start the work of tracing the materials, to follow the dark paths they must walk to find answers for him.

But this fragment, with its beautifully carved letters. This fragment I keep for myself.

I press my body harder against the railing. I feel. I *feel.*

I can just barely see the nearest island in the distance.

Twin islands, they called us.

My island, and Troy.

One for the gods and one for the monsters.

And it is where Paris—drink-stealer, investigator, savior—is from. It is my mother's home island, but I have never visited—not before the violence, and not after the skirmishes that obliterated most of the city.

I turn from the balcony. An idea pulls at me, sharp and ugly.

I retreat from the balcony momentarily. The guard outside my suite is young, sandy-haired and too nervous to look directly at me.

"Is Marcus still in the house?" I ask him.

"Marcus?" the guard asks blankly. "Not Milos?"

I bristle. *"Marcus,"* I repeat. "Send him here. I need to speak with him."

The guard nods as I shut the door, and I return to the balcony, watching the waves and wondering, wondering just what Marcus would do if he thought I was a threat to his brother.

Waves crash below me as I pace, hand on the guardrail until I stop again, leaning out to look on the night-dark water below.

"Careful."

I whirl around. Marcus. Marcus, the younger brother, the violent one, the brother of my fiancé. He is owed my civility, my smiles.

I must not bare my teeth.

I must not snarl.

I must not lose control, not now that I have laid a trap as surely as if I had set a tripwire at the door.

"Are you advising yourself?" I ask coolly, but I wear the smile that I must as I slip the piece of the grenade into my pocket. There is an idea burning there, something snagged on the sharp edges, the gold plate to the grenade. There is something to the smell of this that is familiar, that is—

"My brother is looking for you," Marcus says, but his smile is a sharp, waiting thing. He places a hand on the guardrail, too close to me. "Your father asked us to see to you. But when your guard found me, he said it was *me* you asked for."

I do not flinch or move away. I stand tall, meet him eye to eye. He must know I would throw him into the sea before I would allow him to touch me. It is not this kind of meeting between him and me, not tonight and not ever.

"Kind of you to help your brother." I gentle my tone. "I hope you are well after the disturbance this evening?"

It is a challenge, but he does not see it.

When Mama was alive, she taught me how to conceal a knife beneath my robe. When she was alive, she taught me how to use it.

My hand moves slowly down to the gap in my robe, the gentlest tilt toward violence. If I can no longer bear to use the explosives I once loved, then at the very least I can use this knife.

And now, if Marcus touches me, I will take his hand from him.

For a second, he leans closer.

I pull the knife free of its sheath, still tucked beneath the folds of my robe.

Just right to center of the chest, upward angle beneath the ribs. And then twist, my love. Always twist the knife.

And then Marcus steps back. "Of course," he says. "I wanted to congratulate you, Helen. My brother . . . my brother is a good man."

"He is." I wait, lengthening the pause, my eyebrows rising just a hairline. Not enough to be openly rude, just enough to make him feel like I am waiting for him to continue. Because I want more. I want to *know*, to know exactly what Marcus thinks of me. To know if he, perhaps, is making his own moves to clear the playing field, to ensure I have no living allies once I have married his brother. To set up Altea or Hana or Frona for something *he* has done.

"My brother," Marcus repeats. "Helen, my brother loves you. Do you know that?"

He should not. If Milos were from this world, he would not have hopes that an alliance could ever be more.

"Of course," I tell Marcus.

"Milos deserves—well, you know," he says. "I am . . . protective. Of my brother, of our family. Of our *interests*."

"As you should be," I murmur, leaning in a little as he spills more of himself in front of me. "We are all protective of our families, Marcus."

"Ah," he says. "Yes. This is the part where my brother would say to keep things civil, pretend we are talking about our kin when I am talking about threats. Your father's fixers will look outside of his family for a threat. But if I find you staged any part of this—that you are planning to overthrow your father's rule and use my brother as a plaything along the way—"

He steps closer, and my knife flashes in the dark between us.

I hold it the way Mama taught me, fingers wrapped around the hilt, tip of the blade just under his throat. "The only one looking for a plaything is your brother."

So it was not Marcus playing with my life and the lives of all the partygoers, then. Unless he is more skilled at this game than he lets on.

Marcus's intake of breath is sharp, his broad chest rising and falling, corded muscle beneath his tailored suit. He is smiling now, an expression as beautiful and dangerous as us both. "Well," he breathes. "There is more to you than the pretty plaything, then."

"Get out of my room, Marcus." I press the knife in just slightly, a bead of blood appearing at the end. "I have learned all I have wanted."

He does not flinch. Instead, he smiles back at me, looking at the blade as if death is a companion he is well used to.

Finally, he takes a step back. "Good night, Helen," he says, and then he is gone.

When he leaves, I call for the guard outside my door. It is on the tip of my tongue to send for Tommy, but he would not approve of me playing this game with Marcus, so I do not call for him, after all.

"Can you get me out of this house undetected?" I ask the young guard standing in my doorway.

He opens his mouth and then shuts it again, and then nods.

In the early days after my mother's death, bold recklessness drove me more than it does these days: I would sneak out at night, down through the passageway beneath my room, to the boat in the hidden cove that only Tommy, my father, and I know about.

But this is simpler: many cars are coming and going tonight. I will not be noticed.

"Yes?" the boy-guard answers faintly. "I think I can?"

"Go and get a car ready, and then come back for me," I tell him.

I call Tommy as soon as the boy is gone. He answers on the second ring.

"Kid," he says.

"I'm sorry to bother you—"

"Skip the apologies," Tommy says. "I figured you'd be shaken up tonight."

"Keep an eye on Marcus," I say.

"Already doing that," Tommy says. "Any particular reason why?"

I cannot lie to Tommy, so the news that Marcus was in my room will not be kept forever, but at least—for tonight—I will keep him at bay.

"I don't know what his angle is," I say. "And I need to. He's volatile, and he might pose a problem."

We Are the Match

My father used to say that to my mother—but about me. Volatile, he called me, because I was emotional where they were both controlled. Once, when a girl I had been dating had been killed in an attack by a small rival Family, I had laid charges at the Family's marina and blown it all to hell. There was more along the way, of course. More volatility. More death. More loss.

My parents were only annoyed that my recklessness cost them trade partnerships.

Tommy was the only one who seemed to care about the humanity of it—who cared to teach me any different.

"I'll do my best," Tommy tells me now. "But we should talk about your investigator." The warmth returns to his voice as he talks about Paris.

My cheeks are strangely hot. "What about her?"

"Are you going to have her chase after Marcus, too?" he asks. "Or are you just going to keep giving her flowers?"

I choke and then cough. "That was—Paris saved my—*Tommy*." I shake my head even though he cannot see it. "I'll tell her. I think."

"Don't trust her too fast," he says, his voice heavy again. "She is dangerous. You know I'm not wrong about that, Hel. So give her flowers all you like, but don't trust her until I find out more about her, you hear me? She's too young to really have connections to the old cartels, but let me make certain before you get in too deep."

If he had given orders to me like this in front of my father, my father would have made him bleed for the insubordination.

But Tommy is right.

And Paris *is* dangerous. She looked at me with violence in her eyes when she stole my whiskey, with fury when I pressed the poppy into her hand. Even when she saved my life, she stared down at me with fire in her gaze.

So no, I do not trust Paris. Even if she mesmerizes me.

"I trust no one," I tell Tommy. "Except for you."

"All right," he says finally. "Are you going to be okay tonight? Do you want me to come up?"

"No," I say, a little quickly. "No, no, get some sleep."

"Night, kid," he says. "You call me if you need anything."

Soon after I hang up, the young guard returns.

"There's a car downstairs, ma'am," he says, ducking his head. "Where to?"

Everything blurs, pain pounding at the edges of my temples like a drum. Mama died today. Paris tried to shield her from the blast with her body, and the glass got stuck in her dark hair. Father started a war. I am eighteen, cowering in fright as bombs go off throughout my home. I am twenty-eight and Paris is saving my life. I am then and I am now. I am Helen and the memory of her. I am Helen and the idea of her.

I am no one at all.

The glass shatters.

I give the poppy to—

"Paris," I tell him. "Find me Paris of Troy."

CHAPTER 7

PARIS

The storm is raging now, thick sheets of rain and rapid flashes of lightning across the sky. No one would be leaving the island in this fury, even if Zarek had not closed the harbor and airfield.

But me?

I have work to do.

Thea's house is not far from mine. The city is a cramped little thing, crawling up the south side of the island and clinging to the unforgiving rock. The wealthy members of the Families—like Zarek and his queens—have vast properties and mansions on the north side, but Thea has chosen to live closer to the rest of us, her house on the southwestern shore.

When she moved into her place, a three-story, she rented with roommates, other girls who had aged out of the group home on Troy. Then she bought the house. Then she no longer needed roommates. Then those girls she grew up with became her partners or employees or faded away when her life intertwined more and more with the Families.

She has always been willing to leave the rest of us behind.

I am here often enough to have a key—courtesy of Perce, not Thea—so I let myself in the unguarded side door, and then slip down the hallway.

I shake rain from my coat onto the rug in her entryway. It's pristine, new, like some of that handwoven shit you can buy from charities to support women's small businesses. It's a very Thea move. Beneath, the recently finished hardwood floor gleams.

She has money, and she wants everyone to know it as soon as they enter her house. But *new* money, too. She wants them to know that part. That she can be Family and not. That she can play at their level without belonging to them.

A click, and my breath catches at the sound of a safety sliding back.

Not a rifle, then. Just Thea and her handgun.

"Come out," I call. "You aren't happy to see me?"

She steps out from the doorway, gun leveled between my eyes. There is something akin to humor in her dark eyes, but the gun does not waver. "Why are you in my house, Troy?" she asks, as if we had not been tangled up in her king bed more evenings than not.

"Thought I still had an open invitation to spend the night." I shake more water off my jacket, this time above the newly finished wood floor. It pools at my feet. I do not break eye contact with Thea. "Why are you awake in the middle of the night, Thea?"

Perce appears in the entryway behind her as she opens her mouth to speak. There are dark circles under his eyes and his curls are tangled, as if he has just gotten out of bed. "My love," he says wearily. "Why are you threatening Paris?"

"She's not," I say.

"I'm not," Thea says at the same time.

"What is the gun for then, my dear?" Perce asks patiently. "Is this some new foreplay I'm not familiar with?"

"Thea," I say. "Let's take a walk."

"No," she says. "Give me a reason not to throw you out of this house right now."

Perce makes a noise in his throat. "Thea—"

"Enough," she snaps. The gun has not moved.

I am close enough to smell Thea's perfume, something like bergamot. That's Thea, bergamot and bullets.

Not the perfume that I smelled at the mansion tonight, the one mingling with TNT. But I had to know. I had to be sure.

I stare down the barrel of her gun.

"Why are you here?" she demands again. "You've refused to work with me for *years*. And one night at the big house, and you're a fixer now?"

I bite my tongue. How do I snap back at someone who has saved my life, not once but twice now? She vouched for me tonight.

And worse, she has cared for me since I crawled out of the rubble of Troy.

"The explosive was not from you tonight," I say.

Because if it had been—if she was vying for a new place within the Families, I am not sure what I would have done.

"A useless fact we all knew," Thea says. "Not one you needed to break into my house to tell me. It was your terms when we all started fucking, wasn't it, Troy? That we were nothing but what we are in bed? Not friends, not allies. So if you're not here to fuck, why the hell are you in my house?"

"Zarek asked if you were one of the queens I should investigate," I tell her.

The gun falters in her hands, just briefly. Just for a second. Just long enough.

She was not the bomb-maker, no.

But her loyalty to Zarek is as fragile as my temper.

"Why would you ask me before going to Zarek?" she asks. "If we are not even people who can be honest with one another?"

Why would I?

We all claw our way upward.

"We are friends from Troy," I say. "Even if you wanted to leave us all behind."

Thea snorts. *"What?"*

I open my mouth, but she holds up her free hand in one commanding motion. She holsters the gun and shoves dark-brown hair behind her ear. "Sit down, Troy," she says. "And spare me your self-righteous bullshit. I took my sisters with me when I left, the ones who wanted to come. You ran for yourself and yourself only, didn't you? What did you do for any of the girls left behind?"

I open my mouth and close it again.

I carried the ones I could, I want to tell her. *I went back for all of them.*

And I was too late.

It sits there in the air between us: I would not have survived at all if not for Thea.

"I gave them a home," Thea snaps when I don't answer. "I kept them safe. I gave them work when they wanted it."

"This isn't just about Troy," I say.

"It's always about Troy," Thea says softly. "You've been carrying Troy around with you for years. And we would have—Perce and I, we would have—"

I hold up my hand, stopping her words. They would have let me talk about it, if I had wanted to. They would have let me say the names of the girls who died, and rage about the Families who let them. They would have listened, even, to the story of my singed flesh and the goddamn stubbornness that would not let the fires consume me.

Something flashes in her eyes, and she nods, just once. "All right, Paris. Have it your way. I don't know the bomb-maker," she says. "I didn't see anyone. A shard of the grenade went through my arm." She holds up her left arm, which is bandaged along the forearm. "If it's a queen you're looking for, you'll have to look higher than me."

Perce shifts beside her, and then he looks at me. "Won't you come in, Paris?" he says gently. "You can sit down. I'll get some food. We—"

"*We* are not friends," I tell him, and hurt flashes across his face, because I am telling the truth.

We used to be friends, Perce and I. When he was just a baker and Thea and I were just girls in secondhand donated clothes hanging around his family's shop. Before Thea fought her way up through the Families.

Before a bomb in the mansion blew open a path for me to take my revenge.

Before *Helen*.

"Stop being an asshole to my husband for no reason," Thea says icily.

I don't have a way to respond to that, don't quite know how to back down or apologize. So instead, I smirk. "Did you say *husband*? Thought tonight was your engagement party."

Thea's face reddens.

Perce's slight smile confirms my guess.

"Was it private?" I ask them. "How did you keep it a secret?"

Perce's smile saddens, just a little, and he places a hand on my arm. "It was just us and a priest on the mainland," he says. "We would have had you there, Paris. We invited you for drinks—a few months back?"

I shake his hand off. "I'm not bothered," I tell him. Thea has chosen her path: a place among the Families, a piece of their power. A husband to protect.

And I have chosen mine.

I scuff my foot against her rug.

"Don't ruin my goddamn rug," she snaps.

Perce rolls his eyes. "Well, I'll leave you two to sort this out then," he says. "Good night, not-friend and not-wife."

Thea and I snort at the same time, both near-laughs that sound so similar I want to turn around and get the fuck out of there right now.

We were close, so long ago.

"You know something," I say when we're finally alone. "I know you do. I'm going to look into the other queens. You know that, too. But I came to you first, because if you're doing shit with any of them behind Zarek's back, I'm going to find it. You know I am."

I don't say the rest: I'll burn them all on my way to ending Zarek, because while this is personal—he took my fucking *family*—it is bigger than just him. Bigger than just me.

The girls of Troy have never rested quietly, and I intend to make sure that all my sisters—Kore and the others, Cass and Milena and Yara and all the rest—have their vengeance.

Thea's eyes blaze. "I don't know you anymore, not really," she says finally. "I will not insult you by pretending I do. But I know this isn't about an investigation or a bomb-maker. I know you don't give a fuck if they all kill each other."

I can hardly breathe, cannot look away from her.

She *knows* me, she does, and I cannot deny that it is almost a relief to be known, even like this, especially when I had thought her largely cold and indifferent.

"Paris," she says. "You can't win, especially if you pull Helen into your games. But you can still get the fuck away from them."

I hesitate, and then shake my head.

"Paris," she says my name again, softer this time. "I know. I *know*."

My stomach drops, fear heavier than it was when the bomb went off beside me tonight, thicker than when Zarek had me pinned to the wall. Because part of me thinks she *does* know, that she can see in my eyes that I am here to destroy them. She could tell them that—could tell them with one line in a text message, and I'd be dead by morning.

She has enough power in the Families to be believed, and I have nothing.

Finally, Thea sighs, jaw tightening into something unyielding. "Whatever it is you're actually planning—whatever *shit* you intend to dig yourself into. If it comes back on me or my husband—"

"Yeah," I tell her. "Got it. I promise not to come for any more nighttime heart-to-hearts."

"I didn't say *that*." A smile tugs at the corner of her mouth. "You can come any night you like, so long as you're here for the right reasons. Though I think your nights may be occupied for the foreseeable future."

We Are the Match

I scuff my boot against her rug again. "Thea, what I said about you leaving us—"

"No," she says. "Stop."

We stand there, staring at each other, the years hanging between us. The moment is as tense as if the gun was still between us. I could apologize, or I could—

I grab the front of her jacket and haul her toward me, press my mouth against hers. She gasps against me and then kisses me back, hard, her tongue pushing into my mouth.

"Ah," Perce says as he pokes his head through the door again, and I spring backward, but there is humor in his eyes. "So it *was* foreplay, then. Are you staying, Paris?"

"No," I say. Bergamot and bullets. Whiskey and poppies and gold-plated grenades. "No, I'm not staying."

"You're always welcome." His eyes sweep down Thea's body, hungry, but too soft, too emotional.

I cannot fall into bed with these two tonight, because they—they care too much, tonight has showed me that, and I cannot be a person others care for, not if I want to do what I have to. Not if I want to survive.

It solidifies, too, what I told Zarek: that Thea could not have planted the bomb, that she has made the mistake of falling in love with someone who can be ripped from her. That she knows better than to risk someone she loves this much.

"Good night, Perce," I say finally. "Goodbye, Thea."

He nods to me, slips back down the hallway, but Thea remains where she is, feet planted.

"Whatever you think Zarek deserves, whatever you plan to *do* to get yours," she says softly, so, so softly. There is a *click*, the safety sliding back on her handgun again. "You'll do it, and I won't stop you. But whatever else may come, you *keep my husband out of it.*"

When I leave Thea's, I keep my hood low as rain batters me.

It will be worth it when all this is done.

That is enough to propel me forward. That is enough to carry me through this dark, rain-soaked night. Helen will be mine, and the Family will fall.

My hand moves to my pocket instinctively, searching for the poppy.

Zarek's fixers will start researching the queens, some of them exploring the forensics, picking apart the remnants of the explosive and tracing its origin. The others will comb the islands. Still others will be on secure lines talking to connections on the mainland, in all the dark corners of the continent and beyond.

They have the might of the Family, of blood and money and power going back decades.

But I have something they do not.

I know the smell that surrounded me before the grenade went off—the TNT was mixed with something, something that was used on Troy. I recognize the smell—solidox and sugar—and I knew the girls who once used them for their bombs.

When I finally return to my apartment, I am bone-tired.

I tread lightly, kick my boots off at the door, and then—

Stop.

There is a scent here that does not belong.

A note of vanilla, a note of poppies, a note of—

Helen is standing in the bedroom doorway, hair loose around her shoulders. She has one of my blankets draped over her, and her lips are parted, chest heaving slightly as if she is winded, or nervous.

I drop my rain-soaked jacket with a wet *thump*. "Helen," I say. "What the *fuck* are you doing in my apartment?"

CHAPTER 8

HELEN

Paris has a knife in her hand, she smells of TNT, and she is dripping wet.

"Um," I say. "Hello, Paris."

She snorts. "That's not an answer."

"I came," I say finally. "Because I need to *know*. And because I think you can help me."

The other fixers, the ones who work for my father, have been around long enough to know that they are to keep me away from the work of this world. If I asked for updates, for answers, they would simply call my father. Everyone keeps me at arm's length. Everyone keeps me in the dark.

But Paris isn't one of us, and Paris doesn't know that. So Paris will let me work with her, and if she does—*when* she does—I can convince her to help me escape.

"What do you need to know?" Paris is shrugging off wet clothes and moving around the cramped studio, but her eyes track me as she goes, as if I am a threat she must not turn her back on—or prey she is determined to catch. "And what do you want from me?"

It isn't that I care, not entirely, about who bombed my party. I am a target wherever I go; I have been a target before in my own home.

"I—I just want to know," I repeat. "More about the attack. All of it. I want to be part of your investigation."

She runs a hand through her short hair, tousling it, her rings catching the light as she moves.

"You want to work together." Paris says the words like they are weapons. And then she crosses the room in long, confident strides, stops so close in front of me that I can see her throat bob slightly as she swallows. Can see the flecks of gold in her brown eyes. "But why would I need you, Helen of the gods?"

"I think—" I swallow hard, watching the rise and fall of her chest as I do. I almost feel drunk, unsteady just because of the proximity to Paris's magnetism. "I think we can be of use to one another," I finish finally.

Paris tilts her head to one side, amusement in her eyes as her gaze roves down my face, lingering at my lips. "All right," she says. "I'll bite. What is it you propose?"

I open my mouth and close it again. "You are leading this investigation," I say. "My father is keeping me out of it. And I want in."

She arches an eyebrow, leaning closer to me. "And why is that, Princess?"

"My father has his reasons." Reasons that have something to do with the volatile, violent girl that I was, or with the timid woman I became—or perhaps reasons that have more to do with his own fear, sowed deep in him after we lost Mama. "If my upcoming marriage is being targeted, I want to know. Besides, you need me. I have connections. I can get you inside their homes—Altea and Frona and Hana. If you work for me, I can—"

"I can get all of those things by working for your father." Paris's smile is mocking. "And I have no interest in working for someone who cannot be honest about what she wants."

I open my mouth and then shut it again with a click. It is not honesty I lack, but courage. And besides, who in this world is honest about what they want? Who among us does not have secrets that could kill?

"Now get the hell out of my house." The smile is still on Paris's face, fixed in place as if welded there, but that danger Tommy mentioned—that danger is sharp edged and obvious in her dark eyes. "Unless there was something else, Helen?"

"You will not speak to me this way," I tell her, summoning every piece of decorum and control I can. "I am—"

"We both know *exactly* who you are, Princess," Paris says. She shrugs off her button-up and slings it over the stool along the little countertop island next to her kitchenette. Beneath is—not much. Smooth, toned skin. Faint scars on one wrist. A tangle of tattoos circling her ribs. Her bra is lacy, black, and shows most of her beneath. "Anything else?"

It is difficult, suddenly, to focus on the conversation, with Paris so bare before me.

"If you had spoken to my father this way, you would already be dead," I tell her coldly. "Do not think for a second that I can be pushed around just because I did not show the same level of brutality tonight."

Paris leans back against the high-top, folding her arms and raising an eyebrow at me. "No," she says. "You just enabled it."

"You can choose not to work with me," I tell her. "But then you'll have to explain to my father how you knew the bomb was going to go off a second before it did."

Paris's expression does not slip. "You think he has not already asked me that?"

"But would that matter?" I ask softly. I can be dangerous, too, and wrap it in silk. "If I confide in him that I think you are dangerous? Would it matter to the bullet with your name on it?"

Something settles in Paris's expression, half a smile flickering across her face, and then she shrugs one shoulder. "So I update you as I have leads," she says easily. "What is the endgame here, Helen of the gods?"

"You destroyed my plans tonight, Paris. And I want your help finishing what I intended."

She surges forward, her knife flicking open, and then I am being propelled backward until I am pinned against the wall, rough wood digging into my shoulder blades.

The tip of her blade edges against my throat, and I feel every beat of my heart thundering within me.

"Was it your bomb?"

"No," I breathe.

I am so close to Paris, I can almost taste her. She smells of TNT and woodsmoke, and I am as intoxicated as I am afraid.

She eases back, but her knife remains where it is, the tip digging into my skin.

"Talk."

It is not the knife that loosens my words, but the fact that I really do need her. So I offer a piece of honesty, if not the whole of it.

"At the right moment," I tell her. "The perfect one, when the party was at its height. I was going to step off the cliffs and be free of this world."

Confusion flickers in her dark eyes. "You were going to kill yourself," she says. "Why?"

"No," I tell her. "I would have survived the fall. I would have been free. If I leave, I will be hunted. But if I am dead—there is no one to hunt."

Her knife eases away from my throat.

I inhale deeply, grateful for the gasping breaths I can take now that the pressure of the blade is not robbing me of the ability.

"So you want me to what? Help you fake your death at the end of this?" Paris is watching me carefully.

"No, I can do that on my own. But someone already wants to kill me. If you help me find out who, it will be easy enough to frame them for my death. And I can give you enough money and resources to get away from the Families and start over," I promise her. "Or enough power to get a better, higher rank and continue playing the Family's game. If you help me be free, I can—I can give you whatever you want."

A smile flickers across her face now. "Yes, Helen," Paris says. "I think you can."

She steps back, flicking the knife shut and stowing it in the pocket of her black jeans so fluidly I barely see the movement.

"Should we talk terms?" I ask, my voice shaking more than it has any right to.

Paris steps away, though she remains facing me. She hooks a chair with her foot and pulls it closer to her and straddles it, leaning her forearms on the back. "Sit down."

I glance at the stool at the bar and the ragged love seat on the other side of the room and then, flustered and uncertain, I sit down on the floor in front of her, folding my legs neatly beneath me. It puts me at an immediate and unexpected disadvantage, because Paris is above me, looking down.

"You don't—you don't give the orders here," I manage. "I need to ensure my father doesn't find out you're working for me, rather than him."

Paris raises an eyebrow and waits.

A blush creeps up my cheeks. "So what is it you want, Paris?"

"*I* saved *your* life. So this? This will be on my terms. Do you understand?"

A flash of movement, and her hand flicks out, tracing the place on my neck where she held her knife just moments ago. One of her rings just brushes my throat, the cool metal sending my pulse racing.

"My terms," she repeats. One ringed finger hooks my chin and tilts it forcibly upward. "Look me in the eye, Princess."

I swallow, meeting her eyes. My heart pulses against my ribs. I have never ached so much as I do when Paris is staring down at me, fire in her eyes.

But I can do this. With Paris's help, *I can do this.*

"Your terms," I say hoarsely, and she drops her hand from my face.

"Then we have a deal, Helen," Paris says as she stands, her rings clicking gently, and I notice she's retrieved her lighter from somewhere. "I'll see you tomorrow. Your place."

I nod, push myself to my feet. "Tomorrow," I say breathlessly.

I hesitate. There is no reason for me to stay, now that I have said my piece.

Paris gives me a searching gaze. "You want something else?"

"I want—"

Paris waits, and when I say nothing, her smile slips into that mocking look again.

She is still watching me when she opens her fridge and grabs a beer. She is still watching me when she sits down on her love seat, twisting the top idly off the bottle and then sips. Her lips part, and her throat moves as she swallows.

"Are you going to talk, or just stare?" she asks me.

"I—that's all? We don't need to talk about the bombing? What you already know? I want an update now."

"I think you're far too used to getting exactly what you want," Paris says, any trace of amusement evaporating from her face. She swirls the liquid in the bottle. "I have theories, but nothing substantial. I'll update you tomorrow when I know more."

"At least tell me the theories, then," I tell her. "If we are to work together—"

"If we are to work together," she cuts me off. "You'll learn to fucking listen."

The words sting. Sharply.

"We could be civil," I say breathlessly.

"No," she tells me. She is godless, storm weathered, so vividly *alive.* "*You* could be civil. But on me, it would look like compliance."

I touch my fingertips against my wrist and then my throat, ever so lightly. Having Paris as my fixer—and my eventual liberator—is like trying to hold a flame in the palm of my hand.

Every inch of me is singed by her fingerprints.

Every inch of me demands more. But instead—

"Now." Paris sets down her beer and leans forward, elbows on her knees as she looks at me. "Get the fuck out of my home, Princess."

CHAPTER 9

PARIS

The sight of Helen staring up at me from the floor of my apartment, lips parted, tugs at something relentless and wild in the pit of my chest. It leaves me breathless, long after she is gone from my room.

She will be mine.

Regardless of how much or how little Helen really told me, what I learned at the tip of my knife was enough.

After she leaves, I sit in the same spot on the floor of my apartment, staring after her, imagining the way the hollow of her throat felt against my palm. Her hair, wild around her shoulders, just brushing my arm. The curve of her body beneath clothes that are wet with rain, clinging to her and leaving nothing to the imagination.

I take the poppy and kneel near my bed, where I retrieve the box beneath it. This box represented an ending, once. Of Troy, of us.

And it is a beginning, now, of the plan that will end the people who hurt us.

Inside the box are keepsakes, of a sort. A shard of metal from the group home doors, part of it melted again to make the three rings I wear, part of it saved here in remembrance.

And then—

A handful of photographs—a woman with dark hair and a regal bearing leaving a bombed-out husk of a building on Troy. The same woman, over and over again throughout the years since the bombing, making a hideout out of my sisters' tomb.

Because there is one more player in this fucking game, one that—as far as I can tell—none of them but me know about.

Lena, like me, did not die when she was meant to.

And if it was her supposed death that started the war that killed us, then Lena, like Zarek, is to blame for what happened to us that day.

Beside the warped metal and the stack of photographs I place one more token:

The poppy, a gift from the woman I am going to kill.

ACT TWO: AND BURNT THE TOWERS

CHAPTER 10

HELEN

I wake early the next morning, head aching. Last night—grenade and storm and girl—feel like a hazy dream, but when I sit up, Erin is there, also looking the worse for wear.

"Are you all right?" I ask her.

She raises an eyebrow as if the question is unexpected. "I'm just fine," she answers. "And yourself?"

I push myself up on the silk sheets and lean against a few of the pillows scattered around the bed. I must have tossed and turned last night, kicked wildly by the look of the tangled sheets and pillows. I must have dreamed, violently, but I can remember none of it. "Did I—how long have you been here?"

"A few hours, ma'am," she says quietly. "I waited in the sitting room to avoid disturbing you. I called for fresh fruit when I heard you stirring."

I am overwhelmed by curiosity, as always, to know what I had dreamed. I wake like this often, sheets and blankets and pillows tossed as if I have been fighting all night. And I can never, ever remember what I dreamed of.

"Did you . . . ?" I let my voice trail off. I have asked her that question before, if I have said anything in my dreams. "Did you hear me?"

"I did," she says. Her gaze finds the smooth, cold mahogany floors.

"And?" I lean closer, my hand pausing midair as I reach for the glass of water.

"Forgive me, ma'am," she says. "It seems . . . inappropriate."

I raise an eyebrow. "Inappropriate?"

She hesitates. "You were moaning," she answers finally.

My face warms, and I draw the tangled covers farther up my body. "Moaning?"

"Yes," Erin says, twisting her fingers together. There is a trace of a smile hiding on her face.

"Oh."

I do not remember the dream, but a flash of it hits me—sheets of rain and the smell of a leather jacket and the cold steel of a knife and ringed fingers sliding across my throat, smooth as silk and—

My door slams open. Tommy is in my doorway, eyes flashing. "What the *hell* did you do?" he snaps.

Erin jumps, startled at his tone.

"Erin, out," he orders.

She looks at me, and I nod.

As soon as she is gone, he whirls on me. "You went *out*," he says. "Helen, what the fuck? Someone tried to set off a grenade next to you and you sneak out hours later? Do you have a death wish? Your guard certainly must have—"

"He . . . he wasn't supposed to tell you," I say weakly. "It's not his fault, Tommy. It isn't. He did what I commanded."

"Helen." Tommy isn't looking at me, and his voice is lower, careful.

"Tommy?" I don't want to hear this. I want to beg Tommy not to say what I've realized too late was always going to come next.

"I tried to send the guard away quietly," he says, and then he clears his throat. His eyes are haunted. "I did, kid."

I press my hands down hard on my thighs, fingernails digging in. No. *No.*

Did my father gut this guard like he gutted the other boy with the gun at the party last night? Did he make him suffer first?

"I'm sorry," Tommy says, his voice almost crumbling. "I am."

"Did you do it?" I ask him, but I am looking past him, because I cannot look *at* him, cannot bear to see him, to see our shared brutality.

But it isn't shared, is it?

It was *my* choices that killed the sandy-haired boy who guarded my suite last night. It was my choices, and I don't even know the boy's name.

Tommy nods once. "I made it quick," he says.

He swallows hard, Adam's apple bobbing. Despite the long years he has been in this work, protecting me, killing has never sat well with him—unless he is doing it to protect me.

"Tommy," I say finally. "It isn't an excuse. But I didn't think—"

"He was dead the minute you pulled him into your game with Marcus," Tommy says. "There is nothing you could have done after that."

"Fuck," I whisper, guilt settling heavy in my chest.

"Where did you go?" Tommy sits down on a chair near the bed, leaning his elbows on his knees and looking at me carefully. "Were you out walking the cliffs?"

It was my place, when I was a child. Wandering as close to the edge as I could without falling.

I shake my head. "I went to see Paris."

Tommy closes his eyes, pinching his fingers over the bridge of his nose as if staving off an oncoming headache. "Kid."

"I wanted—"

"Is it a fling?" Tommy asks when I can't manage to finish my sentence. "It's all right if it is. Everyone has them, and I can help you keep this one discreet."

I blush scarlet. "*Tommy.* I'm not having an affair!"

He shrugs, unbothered. "You know the way it goes in this house. You want to have an affair before you marry for an alliance, you're allowed. But that little fixer will die when this is done either way."

I want to deny the truth in his words, that just by being tangled up with me the woman who has saved me once and may save me again will die when this is done. But I know who my father is, and I know how the game is played.

My chest is suddenly tight at the thought that Tommy, who knows me better than anyone, who is maybe the only person who *really* knows me, cannot know what I am planning and cannot come with me.

"I just want to find the person responsible for trying to kill me," I tell him with a huff. "And you know my father will never allow me close to the investigation."

He nods slowly. "And you know I will protect you," he says. "No matter what. So I hope you tell me enough truth to make that possible."

I duck my head. "I—I am telling you the truth. Paris is tough. And Thea says she's good. She'll help me sort out this case. Will you send for her, Tommy?"

"Your father might have already sent for her." Tommy pushes back his chair and stands. "But there's no need to fuss. It will be all right, kid. It will."

"Promise?" It is childish, this need for reassurance, but I ask for it all the same.

"Promise," he tells me.

It has been our tradition since I can remember—any problem the rest of the world could not solve, Tommy could. The first promise he gave me was one awful, impulsive day when I had taken some of Mama's bomb-making supplies and laid charges out on the cliffs at the edge of our property. I had timed it poorly, leaving me stuck on the wrong side of my own trip wire with a timed explosive ticking down.

The guard that found me ran when he saw it, and I remember it in a strange, disembodied vividness: the first time I left my body. I was frozen, unable to feel the cold ground beneath my feet.

Tommy found me crouched there, so far back he couldn't reach me. He had crouched down low so we were eye to eye. I stared at him, pressing my back against the wall, wondering why I could not feel the bite of my fingernails digging into my palms.

"Put your hand on the ground," he told me. "Press down hard, and then breathe. That will help."

I did what he told me, and I could feel the ground just faintly. I could feel myself returning to my body.

"It'll be okay, kid," he said.

Promise? I had asked him.

He helped me slowly, carefully, across the poorly laid trip wires, away from the danger.

Promise, he told me, over and over again.

"You with me, kid?" Tommy asks now, and I am drawn inexorably back to the reality I am living in, the one where the girl and the guard died last night, where the boy and more will die today, and eventually Paris, or maybe even me, if I do not escape.

"I'm with you," I say.

"Then we should talk about your next move," Tommy says. "I can't say that I care for strategy and countermoves—except where it keeps you safe."

"I suppose I have to talk to Milos today," I groan, and flop back onto my bed. "Can you make him leave?"

Tommy chuckles. "No," he says firmly. "If you want this engagement to end, you have to be the one to end it. You know that."

"As if my father would allow me," I say.

"You know," Tommy says thoughtfully. "Outside of this island— and the mainland, I suppose—your father isn't all-powerful. You're twenty-eight. You could just leave."

But my father can shut down airports and harbors with a single command. He sells weapons all over this part of Europe, and he has expanded to buying political leaders where he can, too. The Mediterranean may be his primary playground, but there is nowhere in the world I could be free of him. Maybe not even in hell itself.

Still, the words light something in me. Something in me I cannot quite face.

You are the power, Paris told me, lip curling.

She sees me like she saw him, cruel and powerful and complicit.

And maybe I am.

I shake my head at him. "I wish it was that simple."

He folds his arms across his chest. "And what about this fixer?" he asks.

"When this is over," I say, the face of last night's guard appearing at the edge of my memory, his dark eyes wide with fear. "Will it be you he sends to kill her?"

Grief flickers in Tommy's eyes. "Pray that it would be me," he says heavily. "That would be the most merciful outcome."

"Bring her in quietly today, please," I tell him, as if that will be enough to save her.

The look Tommy gives me says he knows it as well as I do: it is already too late for Paris of Troy.

CHAPTER 11

PARIS

The summons comes in the form of heavy footsteps and then a sharp knock at my apartment door just before 9:00 a.m. "Paris?"

The voice is vaguely recognizable.

"Who are you?" I shrug on my tank top and scramble into jeans.

"My name's Tommy," he says. "Can I come in?"

Helen's guard.

I pull open the door, knife in my hand.

He raises a single eyebrow, amusement flickering in his eyes. "You're about as friendly as I expected," he says, holding up his keys. "You ready to go?"

I shove my knife back into my boot.

"I can't let you bring that into the same room as Helen," he says quietly. "I'm sorry."

I roll my eyes. "If you can't trust her in the same room as one little knife, you should have taught her self-defense," I tell him.

He barks out a laugh, though it doesn't quite reach his eyes. "I can see why she likes you. Doesn't change the rules, though."

I am not sure *like* is the word either Helen or I would use, but she at least finds me interesting—or useful. She will hate me soon enough, though.

I straighten. "Let's go," I tell him. "Gods don't like waiting."

"No one on that hill is a god," Tommy says. "No matter how much they like to believe they are. No matter how much money and weapons they possess. Though I have never heard someone say the word *god* with so much disdain before."

I stare at him.

The corner of his mouth tips up like he's fighting a grin. "Let's go," he says.

"Tommy," I say. "Do you promise not to drive somewhere remote on this island, kill me, and dump my body off a cliff?"

He grins, though there is a shadow on his face. "You'll be just fine, kid."

Kid.

"You promise?" I hold out a pinkie finger. His pinkie is about three times as wide as mine.

I say it sarcastically, but the shadows deepen on his face, some emotion there I cannot read.

I follow Tommy down to the car, shrugging my hoodie up over my face as I go.

It is not a large island—about a twenty-minute drive from the southern edge, where I live, to the northern tip, where the mansion is. The warehouse–turned–apartment buildings are well behind us now, and we are passing mansions like Thea's, three- and four-story homes set close together on the hills.

And then soon after, we pass mansions that belong to the higher-ups in the Families—sprawling, towering creations that attempt to rival one another but cannot come close to the mansion still ahead of us.

We pass a few layers of security—a lift bridge over the river that can be retracted to prevent any crossings, two gates, and a guard tower. Tommy shows ID at each one, until finally we're parked in an underground garage. There are over a dozen vehicles, some nondescript limousines like the one we're in, a few sports cars, a few black Suburbans.

I follow Tommy to an elevator, where he swipes his key to enter and then again when he chooses floor seven. A family of two, and it has seven fucking floors.

How many of us could the resources spent on this home have cared for? How many of us would have never gone hungry?

When the elevator stops, Tommy scans his key card again and we step out onto an open-air rooftop garden. Helen is dressed in some soft, flowing rose-gold thing that flows over curving hips, thighs. I see a flash of calf beneath the folds of the dress. She wears a soft white wrap, hung loosely over bare shoulders. Her dark hair is pinned at the nape of her neck, a few stray curls spilling over her shoulders.

The wind whispers, ruffling Helen's hair and exposing one bare shoulder.

The hairs on the back of my neck stand up.

She holds out a smooth, immaculate hand to me. "Paris," she says, as if she wasn't practically begging on the floor of my messy apartment, just last night, breathless and bright-eyed and desperate. "I hoped you would come."

Beyond her, there is nothing but sea and wind and sky, and I cannot breathe.

"I—" I stare at her and clear my throat. "Who can refuse a summons from a god? Especially one that can tattle to her daddy on you."

A shadow falls across her perfect face. A brief second where I pulled a thread of power back into my hands.

"Tommy, leave us," she says gently, and her voice is music, the gentle lilt, the notes hitting just right. The desperate woman in my apartment last night is gone, replaced with the tightly controlled, regal woman before me.

"Helen," he says firmly. "There must be no threat. No matter who it is from."

She rolls her eyes. "Then I won't invite Marcus again, or Milos. This woman won't hurt me. And I need to talk to her alone."

This woman.

Even girls from Troy can be something, I want to tell Helen. Even girls from group homes can bring gods to their knees.

And something that even guards like Tommy don't know is that women like me?

We always have another knife.

It is hidden lower in my boot, a small thing, barely the length of my little finger.

Tommy steps back into the elevator, and then it is just Helen and me, windswept. Breathless.

Alone.

"I am sorry about that," she says.

I don't acknowledge her apology, but I do nod my head. "He's loyal."

"He has known me my whole life," she says. "My mother placed me in his arms when I was hours old. He has kept me safe ever since."

"Plus," I say. "He didn't find my last knife."

Helen's eyebrows shoot up, and then, unexpectedly, she laughs.

"That's all right," she says. "He doesn't know about mine, either."

She reaches beneath the fold of her skirt, showing a soft expanse of skin as she does.

My face warms despite the chill of the wind.

Helen pulls out a small, sharp blade. She turns it over in her hand, her fingers moving with the dexterity of someone who has long been familiar with a blade.

"Who taught you?" I ask. "Your father doesn't seem as if he'd approve of his princess playing with blades."

"My mother," she answers.

I want to ask more about Lena, to look for some sign that Helen knows her mother is alive, that they have been working together—or confirmation that Helen is truly in the dark. But more than that I want to learn about the woman whom I am trying to destroy, to lean close to Helen and inhale the scent of her, to ask the things we are never allowed to know about her.

I want to know it all, before I bring her to her knees.

"Were you—close?" My words almost catch in my throat. "You and your mother?"

It feels wrong to toy with Helen in this particular way—to ask about Lena, when I may be one of the few who have actually seen her since she faked her death.

"We were." Helen's eyes are anywhere but on mine.

For the first time, I wonder what kind of mother would leave her child to grieve the way Helen is now; for all her usual control, Helen cannot hide the sorrow on her face.

"She was from Troy, too." The words rip from my lips before I can call them back.

That was where I saw her. I visited them every year—the ruins, the memory of my sisters. Because who else would come to visit the burned-out shell of this place, except for the only girl left alive? I had felt like I was the only one who would haunt a place like that—except on the first anniversary of their death, I saw her—Lena in the flesh, strolling into the group home as she once did when we all lived there.

Helen's hands are clenched around one another, her knuckles white. "She spoke often of home," Helen says finally.

Revenge had felt like a far-off dream before I saw Lena. Hatred for Zarek burned bright, but he was a god, untouchable. It was seeing Lena—seeing her there, rebuilding her empire little by little, that set me on a new course: revenge that would encompass them all.

Helen turns away from me toward the white couches and chairs, the table at their center laden with food, a clear end to this topic.

"I had Erin—my attendant—bring up a little breakfast." She takes a seat on the couch opposite me, legs crossed, one arm extended gracefully along the back of the couch.

For one wild moment, I consider sitting down beside her instead of across from her, our bodies just touching.

Instead, I drop onto the couch across from her and reach for a croissant. I shove it into my mouth and then raise an eyebrow at her.

83

"Don't you eat?" I ask through the croissant, before pausing to think about how rude and abrasive I sound in the presence of royalty.

"Of course." She lifts a scone more daintily than I ever could and takes a single bite. "I have been thinking about our conversation last night. And I've—" She clears her throat, her hands dropping to my hand, to the rings there. "I've, well, I've decided—" She squares her shoulders. "You will bring me along when you go in . . . in the *field*. I want to attend at your side."

"No," I tell her.

Helen chokes on the dainty bite of scone, her eyes widening. She laughs a second later. *"No?"*

I set down my scone and lean forward, elbows on my knees. "My terms, Helen," I say. "Remember?"

She blushes. "It's just—I want to be part of this. It's going to be messy, and my father . . . well, you know what he's willing to do. But I would like to minimize the loss of innocent life if I can."

The light, flowing rose-gold dress she wears has slipped below her collarbones, and I could hold my knife to her again—just there.

"Where do we begin, Paris of Troy?" Helen says quietly, the wind almost stealing her words from me.

I have to lean close to catch them, so close I can see one tiny, perfect freckle on her flawless skin.

"Three queens to choose from," I tell her. "One of them is testing your father, maybe even telling him a war is coming. It's a threat, or a promise. It's either a bold queen showing her hand too early, or a calculating one trying to unsettle him at just the right time."

Whichever queen is moving now, will it draw Lena out of the shadows sooner than she had planned? The one thing I remember of Lena during her rule was that like Zarek, she was infamous for her brutal response to any threat to Helen.

My plan had felt perfect: revealing Lena before she was ready for the world to see her, breaking Zarek with the depth of the betrayal. So while I do not need Helen to survive this in the end, I do need her to survive long enough for me to destroy this Family.

"Last time," Helen tells me quietly. "My father ignored the warnings until it was too late. This time we can't let that happen."

"And then your father obliterated an entire Family," I say. "Yes, we all know what happened."

I was there.

I was there when he dropped his bombs on my island. I was there when the doors melted shut, sealing my sisters inside. I was there, holding Kore's hand while she choked on ash and soot.

Helen swallows and looks away from me. "I know my father was involved in the violence against Troy," she says. "I remember—well, I remember his face when he found my mother. She was so unrecognizable they had to identify her with her *teeth*."

Again, we skirt toward Helen's grief, this loss that sits at the center of her, and if I gave myself time to think about that look in her too long, I might almost feel for her.

But still: plenty of the girls from the Troy group home were never identified at all, because no one cared enough.

I clench my jaw shut.

"Anyway," Helen continues. "My father will take this threat seriously, but he also knows better than to move on the wrong queen. If you imply they are suspects, you will offend them. And you will destroy trade relationships that have taken years to solidify."

"He'll get less money," I translate for her. "And if he gets less money, people die."

Helen's face is pale. "I have heard no one speak of my father as you do," she says.

"Then you have been lied to all your life," I tell her.

They could kill me for this.

And they will, when they learn I am not here to stop a war. I am here to push them over the edge of it.

"How will you do it?" she asks. "You know that discretion is paramount to the success of this investigation. How do you plan to find out more about each of the queens?"

"We start with Hana," I tell her.

"Hana the horrible," Helen says, and then claps a hand over her mouth in horror. She glances around, as if making sure she was not overheard.

The wind sweeps over us in a gust, tossing her curls off her shoulders. Her fingers ghost over the bracelet on her wrist, a thin band of metal devoid of decoration.

"You were wearing that last night." I gesture to the bracelet.

She jumps, her hand covering the bracelet involuntarily. "Yes," she says. "It was a gift. A message from my mother."

"What does it say?" I set down my croissant, twisting one of my own rings around my middle finger. What kind of messages do gods leave their daughters? And will it be one more thing forcing me to confront the ways in which Helen and I are the same?

Helen hesitates. Then she tilts the bracelet so I can see the writing engraved on the inside.

Méchri thanátou.

Unto death.

"That's not your Family's slogan," I say. "Not any of the Families that I've heard of."

"Not my father's," she says. "Not Troy's. Just my mother's words, her very own. And what about you? Your rings?"

My hands still, thumb and index finger still touching the rings on my left hand. Three steel bands, each with a flame engraved. One for all those I lost on Troy. One for the unwanted gift of life still beating in my chest. One for the Family I will punish for it all.

"Also a gift," I tell her finally.

"Paris," Helen says, and for just a second she actually meets my eyes. "Why do you want to be here?"

To get close to you. To get close to your father. Because he has taken everything from me, and I wanted some of it back before the end.

But I cannot say that.

So I say: "I had a few options. This one looked like it would make me the most money and leave me the least dead."

"There are jobs that make more money," Helen says thoughtfully, but now she cannot meet my eyes, a muscle in her jaw tightening as if there is something to my response that caused her pain. "I—Tommy said . . . he said he thought you were dangerous. Violent. That you looked at my father like—" She shakes her head. "You're from the group home. I heard there was an accident during the war, that part of the house was destroyed."

I lunge forward, leaning across the table, my hand inches from her throat. "An *accident*?" I snarl. "A fucking *accident*? Don't bullshit me, Helen, not here."

She shifts just slightly, the soft skin of her shoulder exposed. There is terror in her eyes, and it rushes through my body. "What are you talking about?" she asks.

"You can't be serious."

Helen shivers in the wind.

"He killed them," I say finally. "Your father dropped bombs and killed them to make a point, Helen. And they all died, except for me."

Helen gasps as if I have struck her, and I am frozen there, watching emotion play out over her face.

I want to wrap my hands around her throat. I want to push her back against the chair and make her *pay* for what happened to the girls of Troy, make her pay for not bothering to *know* the way we all died.

Instead, I reach across and tuck her wrap over her shoulders again, my fingers brushing her exposed collarbone as I do.

She nearly jumps out of her skin, and I freeze, my fingers still touching her shoulder.

We stare at each other, our faces inches apart, and then Helen of the gods reaches for me in return.

CHAPTER 12

HELEN

Paris is sharp teeth and lean muscle. She is wind and rain. She is a lethal blade of a woman, and then she is kissing me as I have never been kissed in my life. She is kissing me as if she cannot get enough of me, as if she will never have me again, as if she wants to hurt me, and I want it all.

Does it matter if she is dangerous, if she feels like this? And she may have been the one who leaned in and kissed me, but I am the one who scrambles across the space between us, nearly knocking the trays of breakfast over as I do.

She pulls me to the sofa, nips at my lip, and then I am straddling firm, muscular thighs, her tongue in my mouth.

She is taller than me by at least a few inches, but I am curvier than her. Still, she is strong enough to flip me over a second later, and she straddles me, pinning me to the cushions beneath us. She draws back, her mouth hovering a breath away from mine, her hands pinning my wrists.

"Helen," she says, my name a growl in her throat.

I lean toward her, but she pushes me back down.

"No," she says. "No, Helen."

No one ever, ever tells me no.

Everyone wants more of me, always.

But this damn woman has said it to me so many times in the last twenty-four hours, and now she is staring down at me with her wild storm eyes and she is holding me here, unmovable.

"Tell me what you want," Paris says softly.

It is both command and question.

I am at her mercy.

"I want—" I am staring at her lips now, so very, very close to mine. So very, very unreachable. "I want to . . . stop a war. I want to leave the Family behind."

I want you.

I want to be free.

I want so many, many things.

Paris's fingers brush mine. "Will you do as I say?" she asks.

"Get *off*," I growl, and then I gasp.

I am smooth and soft-spoken. I am half goddess, half girl. I never get angry, and I certainly never growl.

But this woman, this *woman* with her lean muscle and short-cropped hair and wild flashing eyes. This woman drew that growl from me like it belonged to her.

Paris releases my wrists. I ache with missing as soon as the touch ends.

I can feel.

I can feel everything.

Every beat of my heart, every place where her legs touch mine. In all the long years where I walked on the other side of a veil, never quite in my body, I never knew I could want this much, and now it intoxicates me:

I want to be tangled up in her forever. I want to feel her heartbeat and mine. I want the weight of her body, holding me down, tethering me to my body, tethering me to hers. I want her. I want this.

I want it all.

What do you want? she had asked me.

And I had not had the strength to say *I want you, this, more.*

89

She swings a leg off me and stands with more grace than I can manage.

I just lie there on her couch, panting. "I—" I begin, and then I stop. There are no more words to say.

Mama would think it was disgraceful to throw myself at anyone this way, let alone a fixer whom no one on this island knew until yesterday.

"Paris," I whisper.

When she takes her seat on the couch opposite me again, she has the audacity to lick her lips. They are swollen, puffy—like mine, which I touch gingerly.

"Paris. Paris, I have a fiancé, such as he is." Though, in truth, it is not Milos's feelings on the matter that concern me—I will be gone before we are ever married. It is his brother, watchful and protective, who may act if he comes to see me as a threat to his brother's work.

"Do you, though?" she asks. "You have an upcoming alliance. Nothing more, and everyone knows it."

"His brother Marcus cannot," I say quickly. Shame follows a moment later. "He cannot know."

Marcus and his broad, heaving chest, and his furious, snapping eyes. Marcus, who already mistrusts me.

Paris raises an eyebrow. "He doesn't like you?" she asks, eyes growing darker, a storm there I had not anticipated. "I thought everyone was obsessed with you." I sit up at last. I wish I could take my eyes off this woman. I wish I could take back the kiss.

I wish I had told her to bend me over the back of this chair and fuck me.

I wish it was just me and Paris, and no one else on the whole godforsaken island.

I wish she belonged to me.

"Is it not enough?" I ask her. "That I have hired you? That I will give you whatever you want in exchange for helping me escape?"

Paris stares at me. "It will never be enough," she says, so softly I almost miss it.

"Paris," I whisper.

"Helen," she repeats. "What do you *want*?"

But how can I answer her, when I don't quite know myself? When I am not sure, at the end of this, what will be left of me? And how can I do this—kiss her and know she will be expendable, if she steps too far into my father's sights? That no matter what happens to her, I will put my own freedom first?

Paris stands, drawing back. "When you finally have the stones to say it," she tells me. "You tell me, Princess."

And then she leaves me there, windswept and breathless, and descends to face god.

CHAPTER 13

PARIS

Zarek is seated in his office when Tommy and I arrive, his hands steepled, his eyes distant as if he is deep in thought.

He raises an eyebrow when I enter. "You're late," he says.

I have to hold back the growl in my throat. Something woke in me on the roof as I kissed Helen, something rough and raw and ambitious. She will be mine, wrapped in silk and vengeance. I want to *win*. I want this whole goddamn house.

He slams a hand down onto the table when I say nothing.

I do not flinch. The crash of his palm against the solid wood is a practiced move, the power, the violence, the noise. I will not let the power slide back into his hands. I will not.

"Do you have a name for me?"

Behind me, Tommy stands squarely between Zarek's personal guards. None of them move.

"I have a theory," I answer. "Helen and—"

"You come into my office with no leads to share," Zarek cuts me off. "Speaking of my daughter by her first name? Who gave you the *right*?"

"Helen did," I answer.

We Are the Match

There is silence, stark, white, measureless silence, the kind before a storm strikes the rock, the kind of silence you find in the burned-out husk of what was once a home. A violent, living kind of silence.

"She has asked to work with you," Zarek says, his voice quiet, measured, endlessly cold.

More specifically, she asked me to answer to *her*, not to her father. But Zarek doesn't need to know that.

"She did." Zarek sits back in his chair, eyes never leaving mine. "Give me the information you have gathered, and you will be paid and sent on your way. I have no further use of you."

"If you have no further use of me, you will throw my body out with your guard from last night," I say. "And I have already agreed to see this investigation to its completion. I'll keep any location or lead I might have until I finish my investigation. You will have your results, Zarek. But I will not die for it."

Zarek's pupils expand until black nearly fills his eyes. "Everyone else out," he says softly. "Not you, Tommy. You stay. You, Kaleb—send for my daughter. I want her to see this."

Tommy makes a noise, low in his throat. "Sir," he says quietly.

Zarek's gaze locks on Tommy. "Is there something you want to say to me?"

Tommy clears his throat. "She may be . . . upset."

His voice is weighted with meaning, with something I cannot quite suss out. *Upset* seems to say more than either Zarek or Tommy is willing to articulate.

Thea hinted at it, too: that there is more danger to Helen than meets the eye, that there is a reason she remains locked away, rarely making appearances even at small gatherings of the Families. What unstable, violent tendencies mar that perfect facade? And why does this hint only heighten my desire to make Helen *mine*?

"Very well," Zarek says. "But I want Helen informed after." His gaze snaps back to me. "And you."

"I am doing the job you hired me for," I tell him firmly. Whether I answer to him first or his daughter should not be relevant.

I will not fear. I will not waver. I will not break, or fall, or die, not today, not after everything I clawed my way through to survive.

Because what else is there to take from me?

Zarek reaches forward and snatches my hand, pulling me forward, just off-balance enough to matter. He meets my eyes as he twists my fingers in his viselike grip. "This is what happens," he says. "To people who forget their *place*." In a flash, there is a blade in his free hand.

Behind me, I hear no noise from Tommy, no surprise.

"You do not speak to me as if you own me," he says. He leans forward, his face so close to mine I can smell high-end cologne and cigar smoke.

I am not afraid.

The thought beats in my chest.

"If you do not have a name for me within a week, you lose something that matters to you," Zarek says. His voice is still soft, but rage flickers all the same, barely controlled. "If you attempt to give *me* an order ever again, if you speak to me again the way you have today, you lose a hand. Are we clear?"

Fury thunders against my rib cage.

You will not make me afraid.

"Very," I breathe, and then he cuts my pinkie finger off at the knuckle.

A sound rips from my throat, half growl, half guttural scream.

There is a knife in my boot, and it takes everything I have, every ounce of bleeding strength, not to draw it and put it through his fucking throat.

There is a longer game to play, I know there is, but I can hardly see it through the haze of blood.

I stare down at the bloody stub remaining at the end of my left hand. At the knife in Zarek's hand, covered in my blood.

My finger is on the table between us.

Zarek smiles.

And then the pain arrives, wave upon wave, and my stomach heaves violently.

Blood is running down my arm, but there is something there, amid pain, amid adrenaline, amid fear.

Fury.

Raw and animal and overtaking every part of me.

"Will you question me again?" he asks softly.

Yes, I want to say to the knife, to the man, to the silent, watching guards. *Always, over and over again. I will always question those who think they rule.*

"No," I say through gritted teeth.

And beneath it all I make myself a silent promise: *I will not always be the one powerless in this room. One day, I will be the one to take your whole fucking hand.*

I eye the fingers on his left hand, covered in my blood. *Mine.* His fingers are well manicured. He wears his wedding ring and a ring with the Family symbol on it, covered in my blood.

Kill him. The thing inside me roars. *Kill him here.*

Not yet, the whisper that follows, the logic, the thing that has helped me survive. *Take her first.*

I straighten my shoulders.

I bleed.

I have felt pain worse than this before, pain unimaginable to a man like him. I have felt worse, and I have *survived.*

I press my free hand around the bloody stump of my finger to stanch the bleeding. Spine straight. Bloody, unbowed.

He leans back in his chair, his expression calmer. No, more than calm. Sated, as if he has just eaten a meal, as if I was the feast.

I bleed.

I lean forward, closing the gap between us again, closer. Closer.

I bleed.

How do you rip power from the hands of a god?

95

"You will have a name," I say, closing my hand over my severed finger. *You will bleed.*

You will lose all of this.

And then you will bleed.

And then I stand, bleeding, unwavering, and stalk out of the room without waiting for a dismissal.

I take my severed finger with me.

Tommy follows, catching my good arm without speaking. He helps me into the elevator and then down to the doctor, the same silent man who checked me over for injuries after the party.

I clench my free hand into a fist, and I do not scream when the doctor begins his work.

I let pain roll over me in waves, and I plan until the pain—or whatever pain meds the doctor gave me—takes me under, until blackness opens up and swallows me whole.

Zarek cut off my finger.

Before I end him, I will take his whole fucking hand.

CHAPTER 14

HELEN

Tommy takes me aside on the rooftop garden and tells me, in a few words, about Paris. About what my father did to her.

Her finger, just her finger, he tells me, but everything is suddenly muted—Tommy's voice, the wind, the crash of the surf below.

Paris. Brave, brutal Paris, who compels me even as I do not fully trust her.

"Come back to me, kid," Tommy is saying gently. "Come back."

I think, for a moment, of what I could do. If, instead of running, I took my father's place on the throne. I could do it. I could lay the charges. Hide the explosives, the way my mother taught me. That I could lay waste to anything, even something that is supposed to be a home. He puts his hand on my arm, and I jerk backward. *"Don't,"* I say. "Don't be gentle with me right now."

He tucks a strand of hair behind my ear. "I will always be gentle with you," he says.

I am trembling as he guides me to one of the chairs.

"Is she okay?" I ask.

"The doctor is reattaching her finger," Tommy tells me. "She tried to refuse medication, gritted her teeth until she passed out. He has her sedated now to finish the job, but your father wanted you to know. He wanted you to *be* there. Why, Helen? What is it your father thinks is so important about this woman?"

"Because she's close to me," I whisper finally. My father cannot know I plan to run. I have been careful, more careful than those who did not survive him. And yet—and yet he sees danger in this alliance I am forging with Paris. Tommy shakes his head, his face clouded. "I stood there," he says. *"I just stood there."*

"There was nothing you could do," I tell him, but he will not believe my empty words. We are all of us complicit here. "You know that."

"Kid," Tommy says sternly. "You know that's not true. There is always something we can do, and I didn't do it." He turns away from me, his face toward the wind and the sea.

My knees weaken as I clutch Tommy's arm for stability. "What can I do?" I ask. "Should I remove her from the investigation? Hire someone else?"

I could let her go now, tell her to leave this island and me behind. Do I owe her that, for saving me? A life for a life?

"She said you wanted to work on this with her," Tommy says wearily. "Stay away. From her, from this, from your father's business."

"Someday I will inherit this," I say, but even as I say the words I can taste ash. It coats my teeth, and the blood spills over my fingers and Mama is dying in front of me, dying because of the Family, because of the money, because of the blood we have spilled here.

"Stay far, far away," Tommy repeats. "Do you understand me, kid? You will not be involved in this."

Briefly, I fight the urge to be obstinate with Tommy just because I can, because he is the closest thing to a father I have had, at least when it comes to telling me no. But then I see the bloodstains along his arm, undoubtedly from Paris, and I swallow my words. "Tommy," I whisper. "Thank you. For helping her."

He grunts in reply, and then he looks at my thin wrap and scowls. "You should come in from the cold," he says.

I should.

My eyes wander to the overturned breakfast. Tommy's gaze follows mine. He looks back and forth between me and the table and the toppled cushions, and when I blush, the faintest smile touches his face.

It is tinged with sadness, though. "You really like her," he says, wonder threading his voice.

"She fascinates me," I admit. Can you like someone who mocks you with a grin and holds a knife to your throat? Can you like someone who has both saved your life and treated you like a plaything? Can you like someone who you will leave in the end?

"Helen," he says. "You will only get hurt."

"And get *her* hurt."

He exhales. "Yeah, kid," he says. "I'm sorry."

The ground is scorched beneath me, the pillars crumbling, the blood swirling at my feet. We are always, always burning in this house. Dying over and over again. Me and Mama, Paris and I.

And never, ever my father.

I allow Tommy to coax me inside, to walk me to my rooms, to tuck a warmer blanket about my shoulders. "Your fiancé will want to see you later," he says as he approaches the door. "But for now, rest. I'll call for Erin, and she can bring up a tray of food."

But when he leaves, I do not rest. I pace my rooms, the balcony, the hall, and I feel the soft carpet beneath my bare feet, feel the places on my skin where Paris touched me with hands that are no longer whole.

I pace and I pace and I pace, and when I close my eyes on the balcony and feel sea spray on my cheeks, I see something for myself beyond the life I have been given.

For the first time in years, I do not even dream of the sharp white cliff and the escape below.

I dream instead of taking my place on his throne.

Tommy would have words with me if he knew what I was about to do, but I wait until he leaves to take Paris home that evening. I asked if I could see her—of course I did—and Tommy told me she was still groggy from anesthesia, which was likely a kinder way to say she would have told me to fuck off if I'd seen her in that condition.

My father is not in his office now, after sunset. He is taking his scotch in his private library, which juts out on the opposite side of the house, his balcony facing away from Troy.

When I enter, he is seated in an easy chair near his fireplace, the double glass doors open to the sea breeze that comes in over white cliffs.

"Helen." He does not look up.

"We need to speak of the alliance," I tell him. Around Paris I fumble; around everyone else, I command. Even, at my best moments, my father himself.

He does look up now, swirling the scotch idly in his glass. "Is that so?"

"I want to make a deal with you, Father," I say. "I want more power, and more responsibility. I know you worry about—the impulsiveness. The bombs in the past. But I have grown, I am no longer a girl, and I want in."

I have never been sure if it was my impulsivity with explosives earlier in life that he did not trust, or my withdrawal from bomb-making entirely after Mama's death.

My father sets down the scotch. "Paris mentioned you wanted her to report her findings to you," he says, steepling his fingers together and watching me with a thoughtful expression. It strikes me: my father rarely learns the names of his employees, but Paris must have left her mark on him, if in a subtler way than he left his on her. "I have no issue with you wanting an update, but do not try to go around me, little girl."

Mama taught me bearing, that when you are afraid, your face remains the same, your spine remains straight. So I fold my hands and nod. "Then I need you to let me in, too," I tell him. "I want more of a role in the family business."

"Do you?" he asks. "Is it truly the business you want to be involved in, or do you just want to have this affair before you settle down?"

This rankles more than Tommy's question did, that my father, too, believes me to have no interest in anything but Paris.

"I am your daughter," I say. "The only heir to your empire. Milos and Marcus are new blood, and—"

"Have your affair," my father interrupts. "So long as we dispose of her afterward. That should not be a problem, should it? If you are as ready to return to this work as you say you are, the death of one woman should be nothing."

"Of course." I smile at him as serenely as I can manage. "The fixer is nothing to me. I want some idle amusement before I marry someone as dull as Milos."

At this, my father tips back his head and laughs, the sound warmer with understanding than I would have expected. "Should I have given you his younger brother, then?" he asks me. "I thought you would have preferred the boring one over the violent one."

"Why choose, when both are mine for the taking?" I say.

At this, my father laughs once again, shaking his head at me.

The truth is far more dangerous: that the only person I wish to choose is *myself.*

Not Paris, kiss or no kiss.

"I am pleased to see you are taking an interest in the business," he says. "But see to it that this affair does not consume you. It is no interest of mine who you see beyond that. You could be fucking the pope for all I—"

"Father."

"Well? You can have whomever you please. But they must be playthings, Helen. Too many people would use you if your emotions were involved, and you know how much our Family has already lost because of that."

"If Paris is my lover, it will be easy to get her close to the queens," I say. "We need to know which of them moved on us, and she could travel with me when I pay them a visit."

He smiles at me now and nods his head to the other chair.

Mama used to sit here, before the bombs. She and Father planned and worked while I played at their feet. How many nights has my father sat opposite the empty chair, the hollows and dips in the leather reminding him of all he'd lost, letting his grief warp him further and further from anything resembling a man?

I settle into the chair, folding my hands gently. "I am sorry it has taken me so long to choose this, Father," I say. "The scare the other night—I think it shook me awake. And I am ready to do this, if you are willing to guide me."

There is a light in his eyes, a warmth to him that I have not seen in years.

"I am pleased to hear it," he says. "So settle in. Let us discuss the queens, and their old alliances. And." He offers me—of all things—a wink, a gesture I am sure is intended to be fatherly, or at least familial. "Tell me about this fixer you've decided is worth your time."

The fire dies down to embers before my father returns to his suite, our night spent discussing trade routes and politicians, wars and alliances, money and power.

When he leaves, long after dark, I linger there, in this one place where I can almost feel my mother's long-missing presence. And I call Hana, one of the few people remaining who once called my mother friend.

She answers my call on the first ring.

"Darling," she says. "I'm so pleased to hear from you. Are you well, after the unfortunate business at your party?"

"Very," I tell her. I play my role, my voice soft as silk, polite and measured. "I called to see if you were well, and to see if I might pay you a visit and make my apologies in person."

A pause.

"Is he allowing this?" Hana asks me gently. "Even after the unsettling business at your party? We had assumed you were the target, poor dear, unless?"

Her voice ends in a lift, a question waiting for me to answer.

"I make my own decisions about my movements on this island," I tell her smoothly, but her words rankle—both the insinuation about my powerlessness here, true as it may be, and the thought that my mother's friend could be playing a game like this. "Our fixers will leave no stones unturned, of course."

"Of course," Hana says. "I'll see you—would Thursday do, then?"

She blows a kiss through the phone, and hangs up before I do, a subtle gesture, but a gesture nonetheless.

I watch the dying flames reflected in my mother's bracelet, illuminating the words inscribed there while I think of Paris.

Of kisses and storms and stepping off the edge into the unknown.

Méchri thanátou.

Unto death.

CHAPTER 15

Paris

It is harder to dress the next day with an aching, swollen hand. I could call Perce or Thea, and they would help, but Thea's words—*leave my husband out of this*—echo in my head all the same.

Thea's warning to leave this island, too, sits heavy on me.

You can have a better world than this, if you want it, Kore had told me once, when we were young and fresh-faced and flying across the harbor away from Troy on a stolen boat. There had been six of us from the group home that night—Kore and Cass and I, twins named Milena and Yara, and a girl named Eris with night-black hair who was good with a gun and an explosive, so good she was snatched up by one family or another around the time Thea left.

It has been years since I dreamed of a better world. In the world I have, we burn and no one comes to save us.

In this one, my hand aches and rescue does not come for me in any form.

I spend the first half day after my injury changing the bandages, cursing the gods, and drinking. I spend the rest of it on the phone with Helen—who thinks it is "unwise" for us to be seen together daily, whatever that means.

In the days that follow, I dig through my own connections, such as they are: I ask a woman I knew from Troy—someone who left long before the bombs fell—about an old warehouse, which was once used by bomb-makers and may be worth exploring.

On Thursday evening a black SUV pulls up in front of my apartment building, later than Helen had promised when we spoke.

Helen steps out of the car, taking Tommy's offered hand, and my heart stutters in my chest. This woman is never what I expect: the other day, dressed in silk, today in a simple dress that hugs every curve and pulls my eyes down her body before I can help myself.

"May I come in?" Helen asks, though not as if she expects an answer.

I jerk my head to the door and walk ahead of her without a word. If she compels me this much, I can at the very least not let her see it.

Tommy checks me—and the apartment—at length, for weapons, though despite his skills he misses the knives at the back of the cupboard.

"Really, Tommy," Helen says, settling onto my love seat as if she owns it. "That is unnecessary. Can you give us a moment?"

Tommy nods, pausing before he goes, his gaze falling on my arm cradled against my chest. "You all right, kid?"

"Sublime," I tell him flatly. "No thanks to you."

"That sounds about right." Humor flickers in his look, though it is threaded heavily with grief and guilt. "I brought you some fresh bandages, and a wound cream I used when I first got this." He gestures to a long scar that runs the length of his arm, from his elbow almost to his wrist—and he does not apologize for what happened to me, but this is as close as we come. "You two behave yourselves."

Helen flushes a little.

When the door closes, I meet her gaze. "He told you what your father did." When Tommy had half carried me to the car after, I told him I did not want to see her—but the truth was that I *only* wanted to see her, and that was somehow worse.

"I—I am sorry," she says, a hint of tremble in her voice. "You must know. I had no idea he would . . . well, I suppose it doesn't matter that I didn't know. But I think I have bought your safety now."

I arch an eyebrow at her. "And how is that, exactly?"

Her flush deepens, her eyes flicking downward. She clears her throat once and then again, studiously avoiding my gaze. "We should talk about how to approach today's meeting with Hana," she says, evading my question with much less grace and tact than she usually commands. "I have a basket of specialty imported fruits and cheese and—"

"Helen."

Her body reacts to the sternness in my tone, whether she wants it to or not.

The blush has crept to the tips of her ears now. "I told him we were having an affair."

The laugh that rips out of me is so sudden my wounded hand aches at the sudden jar. "Well done, Princess," I tell her. "And are we?"

"I—are we—*what*? It's a good cover," she says rapidly. "And we will need to plan away from prying eyes and ears."

"Show me, then."

Helen twists her hands together, still flustered, but there is that look in her eye I first saw the night of the party. Stubborn, all the way through. "Are you asking if I am committed to our cover?" she asks primly.

"I'm asking if you mean it, yeah."

Mine, the hunger in my chest says. *All mine.*

"So . . ." Her eyes dart to the bed, and she clears her throat, but that determined look remains in her eyes. "I have never consummated a business partnership in quite this way," she says finally, but there is steel in her eyes—and something playful beneath it, something hungry and excited. "But I am happy to prove my commitment to this partnership."

I grin at her, wolfish and just as hungry. "Get on the bed."

Helen, who had looked so at ease and in control earlier, stagger-stands before she realizes she has done it. "Very well," she says, shrugging off her dress and looking back at me defiantly, as if expecting I will call this before she does.

"I have never been afraid to own what I want, Helen," I tell her calmly, letting my eyes sweep her head to toe. She is everything. Perfect round breasts and full nipples, smooth curves that narrow at her waist just a little and then widen at her hips, forming a perfect V—

"And—what is that?" she asks. "What is it you want, Paris?"

"You, Helen," I tell her. "At my mercy."

The negotiation about what she wants is a longer conversation—with a lot of fumbling on Helen's part. But she obeys me, Helen who is used to being obeyed.

I guide her onto my bed.

"Are you—are you sure—" Helen looks so embarrassed to be asking that I almost reconsider my plan.

"Very. You will tell me 'red' if this gets to be too much," I tell her as she settles back on my bed. "'Green' means good, continue. And I'll tell you the same."

Helen's eyes flicker to my bedside drawer, cracked open. "At least make it interesting," she says, before blushing at her own boldness.

"Oooh." I stretch the word out longer, looking down at her without bothering to mask my hunger. "I should have guessed you liked it rough, Princess. Fine, then. Wrists, too."

Helen gapes at my words, face furiously red.

"What is it?" I know my grin is mocking, but it is unsurprising that the princess is both inexperienced and intrigued. "Are you telling me you *don't* want this?"

"I—no," Helen says, and then I forget everything else because she unclasps her bra and lies back on my bed, holding her wrists out for me to restrain. "So long as you know how to tie a good knot."

She is delicate and dangerous and cruel. She is afraid of me and drawn to me. She is letting the power slip into my hands, and it is a heady, endless thing.

Almost enough to make me forget whose daughter she is.

Almost enough to make me want to stay.

I take one smooth wrist and bind it to my bedpost, and then the other.

Helen is trembling, perfect legs spread.

I splay my hand out over one ample leg, slide my fingers up her thigh until I am just a breath away from her clit.

She moans, catching her breath with a sharp little sound that nearly derails me. She is slick with moisture already, waiting for me.

"Helen."

"Paris?"

"I'll see you when I get back."

"What?" Helen's face shifts from eager and embarrassed to confused to furious. "You're—oh, no the fuck you are *not*."

It is the first curse that I have heard slip past her lips, but I grin, shrugging on my jacket. "Happy to stay and play another time," I tell her, tugging open my window.

"I will have you killed," she snarls, tugging at the restraints. "Paris. Paris, listen to me. I will—"

"You didn't say 'red,'" I tell her, and then I vault through the open window, leaving the little goddess herself writhing in my bed, frustrated as much with the absence of my fingers inside her as she is with my trickery.

The car I hired is waiting in the alley, out of sight of Tommy, who presumably is still outside my apartment door.

The walls are thin; it will not take him too long to realize the thumping and screaming coming from my bed are not as pleasant as Helen had anticipated. If he does not—well.

Then she can lie there, wishing I was on top of her, doing as I pleased, and learn to *wait* for once. If I have read her correctly, it will make her come harder later, waiting at the edge of pleasure and pain for so long only increasing her enjoyment.

We pull up outside of Hana's mansion about twenty minutes later.

Hana's largest mansion is on her own private island due west of this one, but she spends most of her time here since the escalation between Zarek and Troy. It cannot be a carefree existence here, away from the home she built herself, near the man she cannot fully trust.

She walks a knife's edge in her position in Zarek's world, and if she has in fact positioned herself in my way, I intend to topple her off it.

Two of Hana's guards join me at the gate where my hired car has parked, flanking me as if I am being led to an execution.

Hana's manor is sugar-white, modernist simplicity contrasting dramatically with the pen of peacocks north of the house. It is her signature—the peacocks, the white cliffside manor, the cascading turquoise pools on the west side. Peacocks and pools and bloodied fragments of bodies mailed to family members.

I press my own injured hand to my chest. It aches. It aches. It aches.

We walk through an entryway guarded by two more men. Hana waits for us, a woman on each side of her. She is known for this, too— the two women who remain by her side, guards, confidantes, lovers.

"Fixer," she greets me coolly. "Helen told me *she* would be visiting, not sending her investigator to interrogate me."

"Hana," I say. "Helen sends her regards."

Of course Hana is suspicious. I was not a fixer until the engagement-party bomb, and it was only Thea's word and Helen's choice that made me one at all. But there is another story I can sell: one that begins and ends with Helen.

Hana arches one perfectly threaded eyebrow. "What do you want?"

"To hire you," I say.

When Hana smiles, it is a deadly thing.

"Do you, then?" she asks. "Come in, Paris of the island."

I follow her and her attendants down a long hallway to the back terrace, which overlooks the three cascading pools.

"Let us discuss, then," Hana says gently. She gestures to the lounge chairs beside the pool and sits before I do. She is wearing some loose silk thing that opens to smooth calves and bare feet. She lounges back as if she is used to being this: magnetic, powerful, wanted.

But she is nothing like Helen, anxious, furious, damaged Helen with glass in her beautiful hair and distant, ravaged eyes.

Helen of the island, Helen of the gods.

Helen, tied up in my bed.

Helen, whom I intend to destroy.

"I look forward to our partnership," I say. I sit down beside her before her companions have the chance to, which draws a raised eyebrow from Hana.

"You have confidence, child," she says, glancing at my bandaged hand. "Zarek doesn't like that, I'm assuming?"

"He and I . . . have different approaches," I tell Hana. "By the way, Helen wishes very dearly that she could be here. But she is a bit . . . tied up currently." Her eyebrow lifts higher.

"Oh," she says. "*Oh*. The princess has finally taken a lover, and decided to do so *now*, right before a marriage? And what is it about you that has so compelled her, when she has been locked up in her little tower these many years?"

I shrug one shoulder, the weight of Hana's suspicion landing heavy on me.

"I am not here on her behalf," I tell Hana. "Or on Zarek's. I am here for *me*."

This is a better story than a brand-new fixer: a story of wanting Helen. Of crossing whomever I need to in order to have her. Of course, it's not entirely false, even if it is not true in the way that Hana might think.

Hana smiles, ever so slightly. "I wondered if you would be honest with me," she says. "Or if you would try to play the game."

From the queen.

And is there anyone else in the world of the Families as regal as Hana?

Helen. But Helen is back in my apartment, writhing in the ropes I left her in. *My Helen.*

"You don't strike me as the type to start a war," I tell Hana, my throat suddenly dry at the image of Helen spread on my bed. "You seem more like the type to finish one."

Hana smiles again, full red lips pressed together. "Flattery will get you nowhere, my dear," she says. "But come. Tell me what it is you wish to know." She steeples her fingers, hands resting on her chest as she reclines against her lounge chair. "I am being interrogated, am I not?"

"No," I say. "I want the kind of help you're known for."

Her round blue eyes narrow. "My help?" Her words drip with honey and violence, and the look she gives me is skeptical. "*Zarek* wants my help? Or Helen?"

A shiver snakes down my spine.

"Helen and . . . Helen and I would like your help. With a sensitive matter," I say. "Regarding an upcoming alliance."

"Ah," she says. The wind whispers against us, gentle and warmer than this morning, just lifting her dark-brown hair. "Yes, of course. The marriage."

"The marriage is an alliance, of course," I tell her. "But we—I need to know if all parties can be trusted."

"Are you asking me to learn something useful about Milos?" Hana asks, her voice gentle. "Something Zarek does not know?"

"Of course not." I tilt my head, my gaze raking down her face. "I know you already have *that*. I'm asking about his brother Marcus."

Something in her expression settles, and I can see it: the slight loosening of her shoulders, the way her steepled fingers relax against her chest. I have pacified her, passed the first part of her test, at least.

"What would you like?" she asks. "Do you have a preference if it is real or falsified?"

Marcus is the kind of man with blood on his hands going back years and years. Connections or not, he will be easy to find dirt on. And Hana is a master of her craft.

111

"I want whatever you can find," I tell her.

"Well, you are in luck, child," she says. "I do so like to be helpful when it comes to marriages. Come," she says as she shrugs off her silk wrap. She is wearing nothing but some lace briefs beneath it, and she descends topless into the pool.

"Swim with me."

It is an order, but nothing like the orders that Zarek gives.

I shrug off my jacket, and after a moment's thought, I kick off my boots and black jeans. When I descend into the pool wearing only my tank top and briefs, her lips quirk into a smile.

Did she swim like this with Lena, when they were young, living on Troy? They were friends, once, from the sound of it. Are they still?

"Just a week ago you were no one, Paris of Troy," she says. "Not a fixer, not a guard. Not a damn thing, no record to be found. And now Helen herself calls your name. What changed?"

I am being interrogated, too, and I am at least smart enough to know it.

"I was just a girl at a bar the other night," I say. "She sat beside me."

"I was there." Hana moves deeper into the pool, to the edge where the water cascades down to another pool a few feet below. "I saw the two of you together. You must know Helen's reputation. She gets close to no one."

"*I* get close to no one." I smile slightly at her, let the silence hang there between us until she fills it herself.

"See that you keep it that way," Hana says. "If you want to survive on this island."

Oh, but I know more about survival than a queen born in a gilded castle. I know about hungry nights, and just how cold pavement is beneath my back. I know about loss, and I know what it is like to be the life that no one values. I know about fighting just to survive, and about fighting for a place at the table, in a way that Hana, born to power, never will.

I think of earlier, swollen lips and fire in Helen's eyes.

"When he took your finger," Hana says, "did he promise to take your hand next, if you did not deliver?"

I smile at her. "Who are we talking about, Hana?"

The turquoise water ripples gently, warm against my skin. I am taller than Hana, if only slightly—the water just over waist high for me, though closer to her breasts. The wind gusts over us, and her nipples tighten, the small hairs on her arm standing up.

"The man who took your finger," she says. "Who else?"

"It is a beautiful view," I say. "On clear days, can you see Troy? Can you see the home he stole from you?"

Her expression darkens, and then she moves between me and the edge of the pool with the cascading water. A second later, she pushes me up against that wall, her body pressed against mine, her thigh edging between my legs. Her skin is smooth, flawless.

This kind of threat is much more enjoyable than Zarek's.

I smile at her, all teeth.

"What are you saying?" she snarls, but the madness in Zarek's eyes is absent in hers.

"Do you miss home?" I ask. It is a dance, a game, and I am pressed against every inch of Hana's body. "Do you miss *her*?"

It is a dance Helen wanted from me, too, because the gods are nothing if not hungry for those of us they see as playthings.

More, the thing inside me growls. *More.*

We are talking about Lena, even if we do not say her name. We are talking about Lena, something too dangerous to do anywhere on this island—because Zarek kills anyone who speaks of his great loss, and because presumably Lena would kill anyone who speaks of her survival.

Has she been rebuilding, all this time? Has Hana been helping her?

"Do *you*?" Hana asks. "I know she funded your home. I know she would have been devastated to hear what happened to all those girls."

I flinch.

It is the one blow I have never learned to brace for.

If Kore or any of them could see me now, in this lavish pool beside the god who owns it, what would they think of me?

"She had her favorites," I say. "Were *you* one of them?"

It is true, that Lena's Family funded our group home, a supposed act of generosity. It was full of girls who later joined her Family on Troy, before Zarek killed them off in one bloody weekend.

Hana's eyes flick to my leather jacket, discarded on a poolside chair, and she does not answer my question. "*That* looks like a Lena gift to me."

I freeze, just for a second.

I have had the jacket, a flame-retardant leather jacket, since I was seventeen, since Lena—on one of her many charitable visits—stopped to greet me.

Me.

Shame curdles like sour milk in my belly at the memory of my excitement that Lena, Lena of all people, the god of the Trojan Family, had wanted to talk to me.

But starry-eyed adoration turns to ash when gods—Zarek's bombs, but her match that lit this war—unmake your family.

"I was never one of Lena's favorites," I tell Hana. "Were you?"

Hana sighs. "We were friends, long ago," she says, eyes distant with grief as she runs a finger over the locket resting against her throat.

Does she know that the person she speaks of with such veneration is still alive, her new empire rebuilt above the bones of my sisters? Or did Lena keep it from her all this time, no longer trusting a woman who had fled to Zarek's side before the flames in Troy had even stopped burning?

I will not get that from Hana tonight, no.

But the only question that really matters, when it comes to Hana, is this: Will she stand in my way, or can she be used?

"So what do you want from this game, Hana of the gods? Because Zarek is on that hill just waiting for an opportunity to start a war with you."

Hana's eyes flash, heat and danger dancing there. "I like you," she says. "You are strong. And you don't take shit. But this was never a game. And if you forget that, you are going to die before you ever get to make your mark here."

As if making my mark here would have ever been enough for me.

I tilt my head back and stare up at the stars. The night is cloudy, but the brightest stars are still visible in the night sky. "Hana," I say gently. "May I be honest with you?"

She leans forward, close to me again, close enough to kiss me, close enough to cut my exposed throat. "Of course, darling." Her dark hair brushes my bare shoulders, and she leans in, presses a kiss, featherlight, against my collarbone. "I was hoping you would."

"I want Marcus to die," I tell her. "Milos is weak—if he is my only barrier, I can have Helen whenever I want her. The only thing between me and Helen now is Milos's guard dog."

Hana's eyes spark. "I see," she says. "You want more than just a fling, then. You want her for your own, long after she is married. And is that all you want, Paris?"

"I want a world where I have enough power that this"—I extend my injured hand toward her—"never happens to me again."

I want Zarek to die. I want Helen at my mercy. I want them all turned to dust.

The magnitude of what I will do weakens my knees.

A true smile uncurls across Hana's face, a light in her eyes as if she has just won.

Hana trusts me now, or at least trusts what she thinks she knows about me. She believes I have told her the truth, and I have, in a way. I have told her enough.

Hana leans close, her locket brushing my skin. "Oh, Paris," she says. "You are going to be so much *fun*."

She kisses me then, tongue pushing between my lips, her hand splayed across my chest, sliding upward until her fingers are wrapped around my throat.

I kiss her back, just as slow and smooth and firm, though the only thing I can think about is that she does not taste and feel like Helen. *No one can feel like Helen.*

As Hana kisses me, I slide my hand up her arm, touch her throat, her jaw, until my fingers trail the back of her neck. The clasp on her locket slips easily, the small bit of metal falling into my hand.

And then I break the kiss, and climb back out of the pool, leaving her behind as I go. I stand dripping on her terrace, the wind ruffling my hair.

In the lounge chairs, Hana's women look on carefully, their expressions guarded. Neither of them is rushing to stop me, to peel apart my loosely closed hand, so they must not have seen me slip the locket from her. She touched the locket as we spoke of Lena and Troy, of the gifts Lena gave us. If there is some record of where Hana's loyalties lie, it may not be in money trails or whispered secrets or any of the things I asked her to find on Marcus.

I hesitate, and then lift Hana's silk wrap from the poolside and slide into it. I glance over my shoulder at her.

A small smile plays on her lips as she watches me. "Think of it as a gift." She extends a hand toward her robe, now soft and warm against my skin.

I brush my hair over my shoulder with my good hand, my injured one still pressed against my chest. "Good night, Hana," I tell her, as if we play on equal ground now. As if we ever did.

As if I were not here to topple them all.

CHAPTER 16

HELEN

I had been so lost in pleasure, Paris's ringed fingers slipping just inside me, teasing at my entrance, that I had not seen the tide turn, or felt it until it was far too late.

And I am humiliated now, bound and spread in a bed that smells of the woman who left me here: cedar and eucalyptus and worn leather, with the faintest hint of TNT.

It is hard to imagine a woman in motion like she is at rest, but there is a dent in her pillow proving me otherwise, and it is so unbearably Paris: the sheets are a soft gray; the bedspread a worn, woven thing; the pillow compressed as if she has tossed and turned upon it every night.

She will die, now, of course.

Not because my father will dispose of her when this supposed affair is done—though can it be called an affair if I have not even been allowed to *come*?

But no, Paris will die because I will kill her myself, the second she unties these fucking ropes.

I strain at them now, pleasantly firm against my wrists.

Damn Paris and her expertly crafted knots.

I maneuver myself toward the side of the bed. Perhaps I can get some purchase on the edge, use the bedstead post to break the loop over my wrists.

Tommy is still outside the door, and he will come if I call. But the thought of Tommy seeing me like this is unthinkable.

I twist, pushing myself up to reach the bedstead, only to lose my balance, bound as I am, and fall, face down now, into Paris's pillow.

I struggle again, biting my lip to keep from making noise, and then slump over in defeat, embarrassment only heightening my arousal. I will kill her—whenever she finally returns.

It feels like ages before I hear Paris again—an hour, maybe more. Finally, footsteps sound in the hallway just as I am trying to push myself back up off the pillow. I only succeed in getting my knees under me when Paris's footsteps are outside the door, her old black boots sharp against the thin carpet of the apartment hallway.

And then Tommy's voice—

"Where the *fuck* is she, Paris?"

He shoves through the door so hard it slams against the wall.

"Oh, for fuck's sake."

It is a small mercy that I cannot see Tommy's face.

"Goddamn it, kid," Tommy continues.

"Get out!" I yell at Tommy. "Get *out*."

Paris, damn her, laughs. I am turned so that I cannot see her face, but I can feel her gaze singe me all the same.

The door shuts, almost as loudly as it was opened, Tommy safely retreating from the horror he witnessed.

"I'm going to kill you," I snarl at Paris.

I am without the grace and dignity and mask I have worn my whole life. I am snarling and desperate and still slick between my legs.

"Oh, Princess." Paris is beside me suddenly, her footsteps silent when she wants them to be. Then her fingernails trail down my spine, my ass, one finger reigniting the sensitive place between my thighs.

"Have you been good for me while I was away?" she asks, her wandering fingers stilling at my entrance.

The words make me twist against her, shoving myself backward to grind against the firm pressure of her hand.

"Fuck you," I gasp, but my writhing belies my words. "I'll kill you, Paris."

Her fingers disappear, leaving me aching at the sudden absence.

Then she slaps my ass, hard.

I gasp. *"Paris."*

"Shall I update you on what I've learned?" Paris asks, a laugh in her voice.

She is vicious. Cruel.

And I want her to be *worse.*

Disappointment overshadows relief, and all of it mixed with embarrassment, when the ropes around my wrists loosen.

"Get up, then," Paris says. She settles into a chair at the end of the bed, leaning back, both arms lazily resting on the armrests on either side. She sits with her knees spread, head tipped back slightly as she watches me with cool disinterest, as if none of this meant anything to her. As if she felt nothing while she was taking me apart.

I stagger to my feet, knees wobbling so hard I have to steady myself with the bedpost. "Paris."

"Stop your whimpering, Princess," she says. "Do you want to hear what I learned?"

"That was *my* meeting," I snap at her. "What about the gift I was going to bring to her? How will I get an invite back *now*?"

"Oh, I told her you were otherwise occupied." Paris smirks. She nudges the gift basket toward her with her foot. It is a beautiful assortment I brought—imported cheeses from France, expensive chocolate from Switzerland and Germany, among other things. "Here," she says with a slight sneer. "Aftercare."

She unwraps one of the chocolates and tosses it to me, taking another for herself.

I sit on her bed, for lack of a better place to sit, and eat the chocolate despite myself.

"I hired her," Paris tells me.

"You—*what*?"

"Well, I asked her for help with a delicate matter," Paris says. "Which, in Hana terms, is the same fucking thing. I asked her to find dirt on Marcus."

Oh, no.

No, no, *no*.

This game requires a subtler hand than this, but Paris is burning her way through with all the tact of a grenade. Which, I suppose, should not surprise me for a woman who insulted my father enough to lose a finger only days into working for the Family.

"Why Marcus?" I manage. "And why would you not consult my father to see what he already knows about Marcus?"

Paris waggles her injured hand at me, one sharp brown eyebrow arched in my direction. "What do you think, Princess?"

"I could at least have gotten you the dossier my father compiled," I tell her wearily.

"But Hana needed to trust me," Paris says. "Or at least trust that she knows what I want. And we already know Marcus is obsessed with you."

My head snaps up.

Obsessed with me?

Only Tommy knew that Marcus had visited my room. That I had *sent* for him.

"What is it you think you know?" I ask her.

She shrugs one shoulder. "Everyone looks at you like you're this untouchable god," she answers. "I saw it at the party. Milos looks at you like you're a pretty toy he's excited to have. But Marcus is the unstable one. The dangerous one. And he looks at you like—"

She stops abruptly, shaking her head.

"Marcus doesn't trust me," I tell Paris, debating for a moment if I should tell her about the visit I had with him. "He loves his brother. That's all."

"He *wants* you," Paris repeats with unarguable assurance. "And besides all that, he's a good target. Milos wouldn't be reckless with your alliance—but Marcus? He'd be reckless if it meant protecting his brother."

She sounds so confident, almost as if she can relate to that particular kind of recklessness. That particular kind of violence.

"So you're trying to frame him?"

"I'm trying to learn about him," Paris corrects. She pulls a small golden locket from her pocket, holds it out for me to look at. "How well do you know Hana?"

Not well, if I am truthful.

She was my mother's friend, once, and then she was my father's.

But she has never been mine. I am held at a polite but immense distance, a smile and a kiss on my cheek when she sees me, but questions directed to my father, to others in the room, and never to me.

"She has been in this world since before the fall of Troy," I tell Paris carefully.

If Paris really knows this world she is trying to belong to, she will understand what I am seeing: the loyalty of new blood, like Marcus and Milos, is easy to determine. There is only one power, now, to ally oneself with.

But old blood, like Hana? Anyone who worked in the smaller satellite organizations like Hana's has loyalty that is muddy at best, mostly allied to Troy before its fall, now exclusively allied to my father. If you believe them, that is.

Paris holds the locket out to me. "I took this from her," she says. "I did my research on her—on all of them. She's always wearing it; it means something to her."

"You . . . you *took* it?"

"While she was kissing me," Paris says, so casually I am not sure, at first, if I have heard her correctly.

And why does *that* make me want to kill her more than tying me up and leaving me did?

I snatch the locket from her hand. "It doesn't say anything."

Heat has climbed my face, giving me away.

Paris grins and jumps to her feet, crossing the apartment in a few strides. She grabs a hammer from a drawer, then stalks back over, snatches the locket, and sets it on the floor. She hits it once with the hammer, warping the metal, and then peels the locket open.

"That mean anything to you?"

She slides the warped metal toward me.

Inside it is—not a picture, like I would have assumed.

No, engraved on the inside is a symbol I recognize.

It's not Hana's symbol—her house has a peacock on a white backdrop, Altea's an *A* in red ink, Frona's a pomegranate, my father's an intertwined symbol of *Z & L*, still representing his love for my mother.

But no, Hana's locket has something else entirely, an old symbol that no longer represents any house in the Families.

It is simple, an *L* with a snake curling itself around the letter.

When I look back at Paris, there is a darkness to her eyes that I cannot read, but recognition that tells me she knows, too:

This was my mother's symbol.

CHAPTER 17

Paris

Helen stares at her mother's symbol with awe. "Do you know what this is?"

Oh, better than Helen does. I grew up with the symbol emblazoned on the wall at the head of the table in our home. We were never allowed to forget who owned us.

"Lena's," I answer Helen, throat dry.

How could any of us have grown up anything but loyal to Troy, when it was drilled into us from our first moment there? Maybe that was why Zarek melted our doors shut with his bombs.

The memory of Lena in my *home*, where my sisters died is not enough, this time, to quench the guilt that stirs when Helen looks at me, bereft.

"Mama's," she confirms.

"Was Hana in love with Lena?" I ask, looking away from Helen's grief and back to the locket, turning it over in my hand. "Did your mother have an affair?"

To my shock—and horror—tears spark in Helen's eyes.

"If they did, I never knew of it," she says. "I know they were friends, long ago. But Hana has always been so distant with me. I always thought

. . . I thought she could hardly bear to look at me, but maybe that was because I reminded her of who she lost."

Lena is only lost because she chose to be lost, something Helen will learn eventually. Still, the tears on her face make my chest squeeze painfully.

I reach out, brush them roughly away with the pad of my thumb. "There now," I say roughly, because if I do not, and the words come out soft—I do not know what I will do. "Come on, Princess. We'll be all right."

She nods, catching her breath. "I'll keep this," she says.

Not a question. A statement of fact, whether I like it or not.

"Oh, were you trying out a bit of bossiness?" I ask her, grinning at her as if she could not have me killed with a flick of her hand.

To my endless delight, she blushes again as she places the locket gently in the pocket of her dress.

"We should let Tommy know we're done," I tell her. "And then— you'll take me to Frona's on Saturday night."

Frona's is not a house, not like Hana's. Frona once lived on Troy but now lives full-time on her floating pleasure city, a massive gathering of yachts with a small, repurposed cruise ship at the center and bridges connecting all of them; they are usually docked far enough from the islands to be in international waters, rendering any activities that take place there harder for governments to regulate.

"Does Frona know this?" Helen cocks her head. "I can get us an invite, of course. But people will talk about the two of us visiting *there*. Maybe even to Milos. And nothing says an affair like visiting Frona's pleasure city."

Frona trades in sex and secrets; world leaders and celebrities vacation on her floating city, experiencing the beauty and discretion that Frona provides. And in return, Frona takes a secret from each of them.

"Call her." I wave a hand at Helen, who bristles.

"Do you give me orders now?" she asks.

"Yes, Princess, that has always been the arrangement."

"And do we have a lead to track down?" she asks. "Do we have a *reason* for this?"

I lean across the space between us, set one hand on her thigh. Squeeze tightly.

"The reason," I tell her. "Is that I told you we were."

I do have a lead, of course. A bomb-maker's warehouse on an island past Frona's floating city.

Red creeps up the fair skin of her neck until the blush has engulfed her.

"I—"

"Will have me killed, yes," I repeat. I lean closer, my lips near her jaw as if I am about to kiss her. She stares at me, waiting, but makes no move—and if she will not make a move or even *tell* me what she fucking wants, then she can keep waiting for it, too.

Either way, watching Helen breathlessly stare at my lips is better than seeing the grief on her face when we talk about Lena. I could tell her. Show her, even. Let the truth slip past my lips—but that would change everything. She could tell Zarek, ruin the horrific surprise I have planned for him. She could even run to her mother's side, disrupting everything I've worked for.

I jump to my feet, snatching my jacket—something I will think twice about grabbing every time now, after what Hana said—and nod at her. "And to answer your question, bomb-makers used to use her space, and some of the islands adjacent, to gather materials and test them."

Thea dabbled, back in the day.

And Cass was learning, under some unnamed benefactor, when she was still a teenager. Unnamed, but we all knew who.

Cass would return to us with ash on her hands and a wild light in her green eyes, until the day she didn't. Until the day it all ended and the last I saw of her was her eyes, wide and staring as the ceiling collapsed in on top of her.

Helen nods, pulls her phone from her pocket. "Frona's it is, then," she says.

Tommy takes us Saturday night, in a large, stable catamaran that knifes through the cold water of the bay until we reach open waters, the turbulent waves comforting.

It takes two hours to reach Frona's, though Tommy goes fast.

When we dock the boat, the floating city is alive, music spilling from cantinas, people dancing in the corridors of the small city. There is sex and dancing and drinking, and any other day, any other lifetime, I would take the hand of the first beautiful person I saw and fall into all this pleasure.

But tonight the atmosphere feels discordant and harsh, in sharp contrast to the violence I am trying to survive and the violence I am trying to perpetrate.

Frona is waiting for us in the dark. The first vessel in her city of boats is smaller, quieter than the rest, and it is empty except for her. The lights are not on, so we have only the dim glow from the lanterns outside, and there is no sound for a long minute besides the cry of seabirds and the slap of waves.

Frona is tall, willowy where Helen is curved, and if she were not standing beside Helen I would think of her as beautiful.

From the queen.

Was it this woman before us, pacing at the edge of the boat, her golden hair swept up to reveal smooth white shoulders? Does she fancy herself queen enough to vie for power against Zarek?

She is goddess of secrets and sex, and both are obvious in the tilt of her chin and set of her lips. She is beautiful, but never in a way that could have rivaled Helen's.

"Helen, darling," she says coldly, and then leans in to kiss Helen on both cheeks. "How can I help you?"

"Thank you for having us," Helen says. "This is my . . . well, you know Paris is investigating a matter for me."

I nod to Frona, who nods in return.

"Tonight, of course, we're not here on official business," Helen continues. The blush that follows her words helps with the cover story: we are here for the same reason every other guest is.

Here at this oasis just for our own pleasure, paying in secrets.

"Oh?" Frona tilts her head. "You know the game, darling. *You* have a standing invite, of course." She nods her deference at Helen. "But this one—" Her gaze falls on me. "Owes me a secret."

Helen raises her hand, opens her mouth to speak.

But I step forward, lean close to Frona's ear and whisper—

"I had Helen tied to my bed just two days ago."

Her eyes widen, a glimmer there that was not present before.

"And?" she asks.

"And I'll tell you the rest when I visit next," I tell her, meeting her eyes as I shift back a little. "Perhaps I will even tell you what I am willing to do to keep her at my side."

She smiles slightly. "Many have said the same, Paris," she says, but she dips her head. "Enjoy your stay."

She leaves us, and Helen turns to me.

"You're laying it on thickly enough," she tells me tartly. "This affair is becoming an absurd cover."

Behind us, Tommy clears his throat.

"Tommy's right," I say, delighted when Tommy has to cough to cover his laugh behind me. "You wouldn't sound that embarrassed if you thought what you were saying was true. And it wasn't much of a cover when you were tied up in my bed."

Helen gasps with indignation. "I—that's not—"

"Let's go," I tell her.

Helen follows me, too shocked in this moment to do anything but follow my lead.

I know where we are going, but only because of my sisters. I lost Cass so long ago I cannot always remember the way her laugh sounded, but I could still recount the stories she and Milena and Eris told about working with their "benefactor." Eris left before the bombs. Thea too, of course.

But when Cass and Milena and Eris were young, and still training with benefactors, first they were always taken to the city of boats, and then to a small raft that carried them to a nearby island.

They spoke of it as some grand, glittering adventure, and perhaps it was. Perhaps it always would have been, if Lena had cared to return for them. Cared to pull them from the wreckage instead of waiting for their bodies to burn before building her safe house.

The words emblazoned in my group home echo differently in my memory now: *en morte libertas.*

In death, liberty.

Our death.

Her liberty.

Tommy only protests a few times when I lead us from yacht to yacht, holding Helen's hand in mine in front of patrons who are drinking and dancing and—in some cases—fucking, where anyone can see them.

Helen should not still be innocent, at this age, but her eyes dart away, her bearing breaking when confronted with the pleasures unfolding in front of her.

And because I have never missed an opportunity to add to her discomfort, I offer her a grin. "Would you like me to get you an audience next time?"

She gasps, trips over her own pristine little flats, clinging to my arm for support.

Tommy shakes his head at me. "Never ask a question like that in front of me again," he says. "That's not in my job description."

Helen slaps my hand away, blushing furiously as we make our way over the last yacht toward a collection of small rafts and dinghies.

We take a raft, the way my sisters once did, Tommy accompanying us.

"You are sure about this?" Helen asks me.

I am as sure as I am of the memories: Cass climbing into my bed instead of hers, curling up beside me, dark hair spilling across me as she spun stories of all she had learned and all she had seen.

And, oh, Helen can never imagine the side of this world I have lived, or how well I know the mother she still speaks of with so much love.

Lena used my sisters, and when it was convenient: she let them burn.

When we reach the island Cass spoke of, it is nothing but a dark slab of land rising from the nearby choppy sea, a few long, low buildings sprinkled across it.

The first is empty, a storage facility with abandoned lockers hanging open.

The second looks more like a warehouse, but as I approach the door, Tommy's hand stops me, drags me backward.

"If these housed a bomb-maker," he says sharply. "They will have this door rigged."

"They don't," I tell him.

I would know if they did.

I would smell it; I would be able to *taste* it, ash coating my tongue again. Perhaps it is part of what helped me survive the flames of Troy. Perhaps it is why I ran for the window when everyone was running for the doors, clambering over each other when it was already too late.

"How the fuck do you know that?" Tommy demands, guiding Helen behind him.

If it all burns, he will stand in the way of those flames. He would die, if it meant she would live.

It cuts me somewhere deeper, some soft bit of me that I did not know I still had, to think of having someone like that. Something we never once had on Troy.

"Trust me," I tell him, and then I kick through the door, just above the handle, before reaching through the gap in the splintered wood and turning the handle from within.

The door swings open with a creak, and I step through, flicking a switch. The building lights up, dim light bulbs swinging gently from their chains in a row all down the room.

I comb the warehouse from front to back and then over again, Helen joining me at the far end of the room where barrels line the wall. At the bottom of one—the one tipped on its side—is a handful of dark-gray grounds, the scent of them overwhelming.

"Solidox," Helen says, the most confident she has ever sounded.

I turn on her with a snarl. "How do you know?"

She looks taken aback at my ferocity. "We all learned what we needed to, Paris," she answers finally. "I was not as good as my mother or her assistants. But I know what I am looking at."

"Did you—" I cannot quite get the sentence out. Her *assistants*. Was it Cass, assisting Lena here? Or was it one of the queens—Hana with her long-held love of a woman whose supposed death she seems to grieve? Frona with her empire of secrets, seeking more power than the secrets can provide? Or is it Altea, branching from trading guns into something more incendiary, beginning with a move against Zarek himself? "Did you help her?"

"I did what I had to," Helen says, drawing back a little.

I might throttle her right here, right in this warehouse, the rest of my plan be damned. No grand ending to the Families, just Helen dead in a bomb-maker's warehouse.

"Did you ever make explosives for your father's Family?"

Helen takes a step back from me, her eyes darkening. "No," she says. "No, I never did."

It does not ring true. Not that much she says does.

"Would you?" I close the space between us, my hand drifting toward her throat but landing on her collarbone instead. I slide my thumb along her collarbone slowly. Let it drift to the hollow of her throat, where her pulse is beating wildly. "Would you if he asked you to?"

She does not break eye contact. She does not back away. Instead, she leans in, deepening the pressure against her throat willingly. "No," she murmurs, her breath warm against my jaw. "No, Paris, I would not make bombs for him."

I let my hand fall to my side. "You are lucky I believe you."

It snarls in me all the same. She *could* have. She is a bomb-maker like her mother, a player in the wars I am supposed to die in.

Who *was* his bomb-maker when he cleared Troy off the map? Was it Lena's explosives, left behind when she faked her death that were used against her own people?

Helen huffs. "There is nothing here," she says. "Just a bit of solidox and sugar, and what can you really do with all that?"

Kill a houseful of girls.

Bomb a party.

Any number of things.

"Would your father?" I ask, "Blow up his own party?"

"Careful." Tommy's voice cuts through the silence.

When I look at him, he shakes his head.

"Kid, don't go saying things that will get you killed," he says.

"He wouldn't, anyway," Helen says. "It's not that he's above staging something he wants staged. But he's embarrassed that this happened, and angry that it happened under his nose. This wasn't him."

In the silence of the warehouse, we are left staring at each other, both of us holding back. Zarek's rage tells me there is truth in what Helen says, but my gut tells me there is more to this recent bombing than we yet understand.

The warehouse shows nothing—there are footprints outside leading to the door, telling me that there have been visitors since it last rained a few days ago, but it has been cleaned—or at least visited—fairly recently.

"Tommy," I say. "You'll need to get the boat moving as soon as we're done here."

"Whatever it is you're planning," he begins. "Is it going to get you both hurt?"

"I'm going to blow this place up," I tell him. "And leave a message for the queen."

Helen's eyes light. "I can help," she says.

"I know you can, Princess." I grin at her, enjoying the blush that answers my use of the word *princess*.

Helen runs a hand down her face as if she can wipe away the heat there, and turns to Tommy abruptly, hiding her face from me.

"Tommy," she says. "This is the fun part."

He pinches the bridge of his nose, shaking his head. "You two," he says. "Are going to be the death of me."

CHAPTER 18

Helen

I have not laid charges in years now.

Not since Mama and I played on abandoned islands. Not since my father decided he could not control my impulsiveness any more than he could control my ability to blow up a building. A marina, once, because I was angry. An outbuilding on our own property, because my father screamed at my mother and me and it incensed me. A cliff behind Altea's very own house once, just because I was fifteen and I could.

But as I place explosives, as I use the solidox and sugar to make something that will bring a building down, I *feel.*

I am in my body.

I am here, feet firmly planted on this island Paris brought us to, the cool of the night chasing goose bumps up my arms, Paris beside me.

I feel.

I am here.

I am alive, for the first time in ten years.

I gather some of the discarded materials, pack them into an old, heavy workman's bag. I have not had a bomb-making kit in so many years, and I—I am sure my father has supplies that I could use, but I find I would rather have materials all my own to rely on.

I lay the last charge and walk outside beside Paris.

She holds her lighter out to me, a hard metal shell with a *P* engraved on it, for all the world looking like her own symbol, the kind that would be emblazoned above a door if she was one of the Families.

"Paris," I breathe, closing my fingers around the lighter.

She is looking at me strangely. "Oh, Princess," she says softly. "I've never seen you quite like this."

This—this is how I am meant to be. My fingers are dusty from the work, my jacket discarded beside me, sleeves rolled up.

"Mama would love to be here for this," I blurt, because I cannot help it, because I am so alive it is all spilling out of me. "She would have helped us with this, Paris. She would have helped us with all of this."

Something almost like guilt flickers in Paris's eyes for a moment, her hand falling away from mine.

"If your father didn't keep you locked in that mansion all your life," Paris says. "Who would you become, Princess?"

If he didn't stop me—if he was no longer in my way—I could be anything.

I could even, perhaps, be queen.

"I think there would be more of this, certainly." I grin at her. I know I must look a sight, hair falling loose from the style Erin had chosen for me earlier, clothes askew. I must look much like I did after leaving Paris's apartment.

I expect a smile in return, but Paris's expression remains hard, her jaw set but her eyes holding an emotion—or many—that I cannot quite untangle.

She nods to me, and I light the charge.

And when the building flames and tilts and finally falls, nothing left but ash and dust, my pulse is thundering like the waves.

We are coated in its remnants, Paris and I, and when we step into the boat, she reaches for my hand. For a moment she opens her mouth as if to say something, and then shakes her head and shuts it again.

"Helen," she says finally, after Tommy has started the boat and we are leaving the bomb-maker's island behind us. "I think you're right. If Lena could see you—she would be proud."

CHAPTER 19

PARIS

That night, as I toss and turn and lie awake, thinking of the building collapsing, of Zarek's knife flashing and leaving me bloody, of Helen tied to this bed, of Thea's warning, of all of it folding in on me so tight it chokes me—

A package slides beneath my door.

Footsteps retreat immediately and are gone by the time I open the door, knife in my hand.

It is a thick file, a note on the front, written in immaculate handwriting:

He wants what belongs to you.
—H

Hana has delivered what I asked of her, then.

I lock my door again and open the file.

It is thick with surveillance pictures; she has held on to this information a long time.

Pictures of Marcus, outside Helen's window. Pictures of Marcus, eyes fixed on Helen at a dinner with her father. Pictures of Marcus, standing on a yacht, holding a drink, eyes never leaving Helen even while his brother holds her hand.

He wants what belongs to you.

And he will die for it, if I have any say in the matter.

Tonight I will tell Zarek the story I want him to hear. And he will believe me, if only because I do not belong to these Families. I belong to Troy and to the group home and to the sea.

I belong to myself.

I wait to make my call until I have crossed the island. And before I do, I place solidox and sugar in the car that transported Marcus to the engagement party.

Zarek, god of all the Families, answers when I call.

"Name," he says curtly.

I can picture him in his office, eyes hard and merciless. He is as they all are: broad-shouldered and tall and beautiful and perfectly tailored, but a man nonetheless, and one that can be killed.

Marcus wants what belongs to me.

And I don't need him to be the bomber to want him out of my way.

So I open my mouth and tell Zarek:

"The name I have for you is Marcus."

CHAPTER 20

HELEN

I wake to the house aflame with light and bustle and noise, heavy footsteps running and Erin's hand, shaking me urgently awake.

They are both dressed, Erin in the gray trousers and blouse that most house staff wear, a poppy embroidered on one sleeve to signify her as my attendant, and Tommy in tactical.

"Get up, kid," Tommy says roughly.

"What's this?" I ask groggily. I am here and then not. I am in my body and then away, everything muted. "What happened? Is it Paris?"

What does it say about me that Paris has become the first name upon my lips when I wake?

"Your father received some information about Marcus," Tommy tells me. "We're getting you down into the bunker. *Now.*"

They don't wait for me to dress—though Erin does toss a few things for me into a bag—before they pull me to the trapdoor in my closet.

My father had this escape route built during the reconstruction after my mother died, when he first gave me the suite of rooms that once belonged to my mother. Beneath my room, a long, narrow staircase winds down, the walls on either side still unfinished, solid rock. It is lit only by a few hanging lights along the way, which flicker wearily as we descend.

At the bottom is—a bunker, it could be called, or a cave. It is a room hewn out of rough rock, complete with supplies and weapons and a hidden bay, big enough for not more than two boats, which rock idly in the night-dark water.

From the outside, it looks like unbroken rock—but the wall of the cliff opens inward with the push of a button. The only way to trigger it is my bracelet, an escape built just for me.

"What did Marcus do?" I ask again when we have settled in our little bunker, Tommy rummaging for more weapons from the case on the wall.

"Tommy? Tell me. Please tell me."

I grabbed my phone, at least, the one thing I managed to remember.

I text Paris: **They have me in a bunker. I don't know what's going on. Stay safe.**

Stay safe?

What a meaningless thing to say when my father is on the rampage—it does not matter who was responsible, because once my father has decided someone will die, they will die.

The idea I had when Paris and I blew that bomb-maker's warehouse to hell crystallizes further. My father should not be allowed to continue reigning like this, unquestionable and all-powerful and utterly bloodthirsty.

If Mama were here—if I was not trapped in my father's house all this time—

I could be queen.

"Marcus had some materials," Tommy tells me tersely, once he had strapped yet another handgun to his thigh. "In the car that brought him to your party."

The text sends for what seems like ages.

And then *delivered*, and immediately Paris's three dots, indicating her typing.

Congratulations to you, Princess. Got another secret admirer leaving you bombs?

Ah, at least Paris is safe enough to be ridiculing me. Strangely, it returns me to my body, the stone beneath me becoming real again. It is not ten years ago. It is now, here, as real as the smirk on Paris's face when she typed that message to me.

Tommy snatches the phone from my hand. "Are you telling someone where you are?" he demands. "You don't know what Marcus is doing, or what he is capable of. Kid, you cannot be serious."

"Paris doesn't work with him."

"Jesus." Tommy shakes his head.

"They're investigating now," Erin tells me, squeezing my hands. "They haven't found him yet, which is why we need you down here."

It takes the better part of the day to receive the all clear, by which time I am restless and tired but not otherwise the worse for wear. My father refuses my request to meet with him, too busy to answer my questions about Marcus—or perhaps because he does not believe I can handle the answers. Does he think, after all this time, that I will lash out the way I used to? Lay explosives on his doorstep and take my revenge?

The first thing I do, of course, is call Paris.

She does not answer the way I answer her calls, at the first ring. She makes me wait, even in this.

"What's up, Princess?"

"What did you hear about Marcus?" I ask.

Paris laughs. "Meet me at Altea's tomorrow night," she tells me. "And I'll tell you what I've got."

I may not know much, but I know my father has a standing meeting with the three queens on their joint interest in expanding the weapons trade. It is always held at Altea's, usually on her weapon range and sometimes in her office. I only once had an invite, as a teenager accompanying my mother, but my own impulsivity on the gun range—asking a young guard if she wanted to have a shooting competition with me—put an end to that.

"How the hell did you get an invite to that?" I ask Paris.

"Charm," she tells me, and hangs up.

The next night brings a sharp chill and news that my father has found Milos and Marcus and will be occupied longer as he . . . does what he always does.

While I am no longer being kept in the bunker, I have been offered little freedom, the security in the mansion still rigid—so when it is time to leave for Altea's, I am eager to go.

We take a boat, Tommy and Paris and I, and dock in Altea's private cove under the watchful gaze of the armed guards above it. One of Altea's attendants waits for us as we make our way up the stairs from the cover toward the cliff top where Altea's house sits, a guard beside her.

At Tommy's request, they show us upstairs to the rooftop garden.

Altea's rooftop garden is not so lush as mine—more wind-battered, less tended, but I love the peace of it. Green vines sprawling across the whole of it, winding around the legs of the white outdoor chairs. Tommy wraps me in one of the throw blankets and leads me to the couch.

"Okay," he says. "We should be safe here. No microphones."

"Is this why you wanted the garden?" I ask Paris.

She nods once. "We can speak more plainly up here."

Tommy ducks his head at me. "I'll give you two some room to breathe."

He will be just inside the doors, listening for threats, waiting for summons.

"Tell me, please," I say to Paris as soon as the elevator doors close behind him. "No one will tell me anything, least of all my father. But I know he has Marcus and Milos now."

She cocks her head at me, a smile unfurling I have never seen before—glee, almost, or joy. "Oh, does he?"

Paris drops into a chair near the elevator doors and puts her feet—still in their scuffed combat boots—up on the table.

"Paris." I join her, drop into the chair next to her and glare at her.

"It worked, then."

"What worked?" Realization settles coldly over me.

"I think it's time we have a conversation about what we both want here, Helen," she says. Her voice holds a dangerous chill.

No one has ever thought me anything more than a pawn. No one has ever looked at me and thought I might be something more than a pretty face.

But Paris of Troy is looking at me as if she sees me for all that I am.

It is a different type of cliff I stand on now. A different steep drop, a different danger.

A different freedom waiting for me here, too.

I take the plunge.

"My father is cruel," I tell her. "And dangerous, and often unstable. The Family needs a new head."

She tips her head back and looks at the sky, eyes sparking as she laughs, full-throated and bright. "And you want it to be you."

I bristle. "And who else would it be?"

"Does it have to be anyone?" Paris is looking at me intently now.

I startle.

The end of the Families? The end of this industry that has funded half of this country's politicians and much of those in Europe and beyond?

Who would smuggle drugs, or weapons, or steal secrets, or move behind the scenes of elections when necessary? Who would step into that kind of power vacuum, if not me?

"Oh, is ending their rule not something you even considered?" Paris gets to her feet, brow furrowed. "I should not be surprised that you think you could be a lesser evil—that the problem is your father, and not the power itself. So that's it, Princess? Instead of helping you escape, I'm here to help put you on that throne?"

I stand, too, facing Paris. Confusion stirs in my chest, replacing the excitement that had risen when we blew up the warehouse together. "And why not?" I ask her. "You have no love for my father. No loyalty, either. You have not hidden that once." My eyes flick down to her hand. "I would be a ruler that ruled differently. I would not have—"

"You would have to grow a pair to be able to do that," Paris says, dismissing me. "But very well. And what do you propose we do? Test Altea's loyalty and see if she, too, misses Troy?"

My heart thunders against my ribs.

It is treason. The kind of thing that would get us killed. That may yet get us killed.

"Yes," I breathe.

Find the queen, but not for my father.

Find the queen, so that we may see if, though her loyalty is no longer to my father, it may yet be to me. I am not just of this island. I am not just of Zarek.

I am Lena's daughter, after all.

And that makes me a daughter of Troy.

CHAPTER 21

Paris

So the princess wants to rule now.

That was not entirely unexpected, though the disappointment I felt when she told me certainly was. Helen trying to dethrone Zarek will only help me in destroying him, her connections and money and power and access to weapons unmatched.

If only I can forget the light in her eyes when she told me she wanted to live, to rule, and she wanted me at her side as she did.

If only I could forget the way she looks when she grieves her mother.

Helen stares breathlessly up at me now. "What—where do we start?" she asks as the attendant dips her head and retreats, giving us space to talk in private as she waits by the elevator. She stands again, wobbling a little before taking my hand. "Do we try to gauge Altea's loyalty? Because I can tell you Altea likes to interrogate people on her shooting range."

I tilt my head, looking at her until she explains.

"Not with us downrange," she laughs. "That's more my father's vibe. She just likes to outshoot you and prove who she is."

"So can you outshoot her?" I ask. "Because while you do that, I'll have a look around."

"You can't," Helen says. "She'll catch you."

I shrug. "And you'll get us out of here. Make that name good for something, Princess." I reach over and smack, my hand colliding with that ample ass.

I am rewarded with a little shriek. "I'll go down first, while you ask to have your hair styled for the dinner party. The wind has taken it down, anyway, so it's not a bad cover," I tell her. "I'll put Altea at ease, shoot with her for a little while. When you join us, I'll take my leave."

I bite back the last of what I wanted to say: that I like Helen's hair, wild like this. That I like when she looks at me like I am an explosive she cannot wait to light.

When I tell the guard Helen will join us below when she is finished with her hair, he nods without a word—and if it is strange to him that a fixer gets a solo audience with a queen, he does not remark on it.

We walk in silence, down long, spacious hallways and empty, opulent corridors. Altea may not have Zarek's power, but she is old money, old gods. Lena was like that in the heyday of Trojan power—her old money combined with Zarek's growing power, and they were a new kind of god while they lasted.

Altea joins me on the north side of her home, almost at the cliff's edge, and dismisses her guards with a nod. "Paris." She greets me with a smile, something hungrier than the other gods have shown me. "Thea has always spoken so highly of you. And now look at you. A grenade, a few weeks, and you have the most powerful woman in Greece at your side."

The memory flashes in front of me: Helen spread out on my bed, wrists bound to the headboard, mouth rounded into an O. Eagerness transforming into fury as I stepped away and left her behind.

"Is she?" I laugh at Altea's words, the sound a cold, sharp burst. "The most powerful woman?"

She links her arm through mine.

"She's certainly one of them," Altea answers easily.

She is not like Hana, or Helen, women whose bodies are soft and supple even if their minds are sharp. No, Altea's arm is lean, hard muscle, her grip tight. There is a reason she can wave away her guards without worry for her personal safety.

"I was delighted that you wanted to speak further," Altea says. "Shall we step into my office? Or are you like me—I prefer to have my most important conversations on my shooting range."

Perhaps this is a test, an attempt to divine if I am here as a fixer in some capacity, or perhaps just a test of what kind of woman I am. Can she see it in my eyes, that I am not here to make peace, or stop the coming war? That I am here to incite the violence they have brewed for years, if I can?

"Shooting range," I answer.

Her grin broadens. "I thought as much."

I follow her down a long, winding staircase.

At the base, set somewhere deep beneath the rock—close to the water, because I can hear the waves outside—is a long, open room with targets at one end and a wall of weapons at the other. Mostly guns, of course, mostly *rifles*, because this is Altea, but in one corner, a javelin, a machete, and various blades.

"Ah," Altea says. "That look Helen has when you touch her? You have that when you look at my weapons."

She lifts a rifle with a long scope and holds it out to me. "This is a favorite of mine. The newest Barrett. You've heard of it?"

Heard of it, yes.

Held it, no.

It costs more than six months of my rent, but she must know that.

I take it from her, run my thumb reverently down the barrel, my rings clicking faintly where they touch it. "Thank you."

She nods briskly and lifts another rifle—another Barrett, though I am not well versed enough in expensive long-range hunting rifles to know which mark. "Shall we?"

We shoot in silence, just the two of us, Altea in her gown and gold sandals, and me in my black jeans and combat boots. She shoots first, unerring, no trace of hesitancy.

When she replaces the paper target and nods to me, I place the rifle against my shoulder, its weight solid and comforting, step forward, and make a choice—a badly calculated, too-reckless, too-threatening choice. Just like every choice I have made since I tackled Helen to the ground and saved her from the grenade.

I, too, am unerring, though I learned from shooting stolen shotguns and handguns that Milena smuggled into Troy when we were too young to be that close to bullets.

The first was when I was twelve: my small fingers curled around a handgun, Milena teaching Cass and I how to hold it.

I shoot high now, adjusting my angle just slightly with every shot. Altea shoots like she knows she will not miss.

But she has never known scarcity.

I shoot like I know I *must* not miss.

When the magazine is empty, I set the rifle down and retrieve the target. I hand it to her wordlessly, flipped over so she can see the pattern that I shot into it.

It is an ⊠—for her—overlaid with a *T*, the old symbol of the Trojan cartel she was once allied with, the remnants of which Zarek obliterated on Troy. Altea survived, adapted, allied herself with new power.

But if I am right, if she is like me—

She never stopped longing for home.

For a second, the paper trembles in her hand. Something flashes in her eyes, something dark and furious and damaged—

And then she steps away from me. Sets the paper down. Lifts her rifle.

"What do you want, Paris of Troy?"

"I want a new world," I tell her. "And I want a piece of that world."

Enough truth, just as I gave Hana when I said I wanted Marcus out of my way.

Altea is still facing away from me, her shoulders tense, one finger ghosting over the trigger of her rifle. "Who will you be in that world? Who will Helen be?"

"I will have *her*." The words ring truer than I want them to.

I will have them all, and I will have them on their knees. I will have my revenge on all of them, everyone from Zarek to Hana to Altea to Frona to—yes, to Helen, too, even if that last thought has begun to turn my stomach. And when the power Zarek has collected around him is nothing but ashes, then—

Then he gets to die.

A tilt of the rifle as Altea checks the magazine. A click of the bolt sliding home. "And that is all, Paris of Troy? A piece of this, and Helen at your side?"

I need to know, too, if Altea grieves Lena and resents Zarek—or if she knows Lena is alive and is keeping that a secret. If Lena wanted to rebuild without Zarek knowing, she would need anyone loyal to her to keep that secret for her—and is Altea one of those still loyal?

"If Helen wants to take a more active role in this business," I say finally. "We will need your help. Can we count on that?"

"If I say yes," Altea murmurs. She slides the rifle to her shoulder. "That is disloyalty. That is something Zarek can kill me for. What could you and Helen possibly offer me to risk my life and everything I have built?"

I do not answer her, not with words.

Instead, I tap one finger on the paper target with her old Family symbol.

The room is so silent, so still, that the gentle brush of the paper against the table beneath it feels apocalyptic.

Altea has angled her body away from me, her face cast in shadow. "Call for your plaything, then, Paris of Troy," she says finally. "Helen and I have much to discuss."

CHAPTER 22

HELEN

I arrive to the shooting range dressed in black silk and, like most women in a dress like this, ready for war.

"Darling." Altea greets me with a kiss to my cheek and a rifle held out for me.

Paris ducks her head. "Zarek is coming later, is he not?" she asks.

Altea nods. "When he finishes with those brothers," she says carelessly. "Do you really think they did it, Helen? Do you think a man like Marcus is capable of a bomb so beautiful?"

"That is for my father to ascertain, I suppose," I answer—or give her a nonanswer, rather.

Paris withdraws gracefully, making some excuse that she would like to give us time to talk, just Altea and me.

I wait until she is gone before I take the weapon from Altea. It is heavy in my hands, smooth and cold and beautiful.

I have not fired something like this since my mother taught me almost fifteen years ago. We have a beautiful shooting range on a lower floor of my father's mansion, a wing reserved just for family—my mother and father and me, once. Now just my father and me.

"But what do *you* think, Helen?" Altea asks me thoughtfully. "About the new blood?"

"I do not think Marcus capable of that explosive, no," I tell Altea. "But he is capable of hiring someone."

"Why?" Altea asks bluntly. "Why would Marcus want to destroy what is very nearly built?"

It is an honest conversation between Family, something I have not yet experienced, daughter of Zarek though I may be. It makes my whole body feel light.

"Marcus came to my room the night of the bombing," I say. I had not believed him capable of it, then—there was a wildness in those beautiful eyes that told me he wanted to know his brother was safe, and nothing more. Still, the story I can spin for Altea can be something different, and her answer can show me something about *her*. "He seemed frenetic, unbalanced."

"Like others in the Family, then." A smile plays across Altea's lips as she lifts her rifle and begins to fire.

Beside her, a used paper target lies discarded.

When she sees me looking, she nudges it behind her with her foot, pushing it out of sight.

"Indeed."

"And will you match that instability if you marry his brother?" Altea asks.

It is a weightier question than it sounds: it is not a question about Marcus.

It is Altea asking, with the usual subtlety of these queens, if I will rule like my father—or if, instead, I will follow in the footsteps of my mother.

"My mother had a different touch," I say. "I would follow in her footsteps, if I could."

Altea nods to me, stepping back from the shooting range.

I lift the rifle she gave me to my shoulder and step forward. I fire, each bullet unerring. Each finding its target.

When I turn back to her, Altea's eyes are glinting, and I know I have found my first ally.

She ducks her head to me, the gesture nearly deferential.

"Welcome to the Family, Helen."

CHAPTER 23

PARIS

As soon as the doors have closed behind me, leaving Altea and Helen to the business dealings of the gods, I walk confidently down the hall with the key card I lifted from Altea, my hood up.

I make my way back downstairs, key card in hand. It will not be long before she notices it is missing, but until then—until then, I have unfettered access.

Altea's office is just above her weapons range, and while she showed me up a staircase at the far end, there must be direct access from her office. Which means there may be more—more hidden doors, more secrets here that could pit her firmly against Zarek, or Lena, or both. Despite the revenge plan I have spun over many years, I do not particularly care which of them dies first.

If Altea is still loyal to Lena and the house of Troy, then they both are the reasons my sisters are dead.

If she is only loyal to whomever has the most money and power at any given time—Zarek when Troy fell—then she is an opportunist who profited from the death of my sisters.

So I will toy with each one. Make them all suspect each other. And when they are weary and weakened, when they have experienced what it is to be small and afraid—

I will burn them all to the ground.

Helen included. No matter how she may sometimes surprise me. And no matter how she looks in my bed.

I swipe the key card and shove open the door to Altea's office, pushing aside the tangled thoughts of Helen.

Altea's office is wide, the walls rounded, with windows opening toward the sea on one side and north toward the island and Zarek's mansion—Helen's mansion—on the other.

The office is strangely bare.

It does not seem like much for a woman who is attempting to expand across eastern Europe with a range of automatic weapons.

I pull open each drawer. None are locked.

I run my fingers just beneath the desk—I find the handgun first, and then a second handgun, stowed where she could access them in an emergency. And then, just past that, a small lever.

I push the lever, and the ceiling above me opens. The boards move back, and, slowly, a narrow spiral staircase extends downward.

I climb the spiral stairs. When I round the corner at the top, I find myself in a tiny round room with a desk, a laptop, and a row of rifles hanging behind the desk chair.

A shiver snakes down my spine.

Was the assault on Troy planned from a room like this? Did Zarek sit in a room like this one when the bombs melted the metal doors shut so we could not escape? Was he safely hidden in a room like this when I left behind Cass, her familiar green eyes staring, unseeing, as our world ended?

And Lena—did she know when she faked her death that the price would be so steep? Did she try to stop it, try to warn anyone? How could we mean so little to her that she let us all die?

I breathe deep and exhale. From here, I can see what Altea sees. From here, I stand in her shoes. Through one window, she could see her home island on a clear day. Altea's longing is palpable in every inch of this home. I know the vastness of that kind of emotion. I have felt it myself. I have seen it in the way her eyes stray beyond the horizon.

I knew it when she stared at her old Family symbol and had to turn away to mask her feeling. She may have been only a satellite of Troy's in the heyday of its power, but Troy was always better than Zarek at one thing: building loyalty.

And it seems Altea's has never left her, something I knew when her eyes lit as I offered her a chance at going home.

The other window faces north toward Zarek's mansion, visible in all its impenetrable marble glory.

In front of the north-facing window is a large object hidden beneath a blanket. My pulse is racing as I draw the blanket back. It is thunder beneath my rib cage as I see, for the first time, a weapon made to kill a god.

It is a gun, a big one, something long range. No, not a gun.

A rocket launcher, and Zarek's mansion sits squarely in its scope. More than that: the scope rests directly on the level of the home and the side of the mansion where I know Zarek's office to be.

Has she pored over copies of the floor plan as I have, deep into the night, hoping and scheming for something impossible?

Altea, queen of weapons, queen of war, has her sights on Zarek.

Helen is a few floors below me, and I am steps away from her, imagining blowing her home off the face of this island.

Instead, I record a video on my phone—the weapons, the secret room, the sights trained on the mansion. I send it to Helen, first.

She responds immediately. **Dear god.**

Just me, I text back. **No gods here.**

We're headed to her office. Where are you?

Shit.

The sound of voices stops me, seconds too late to make my escape.

She must have entertained Zarek in the office below many times, the ceiling closed, the spiral staircase retracted. Did he stand beneath this room, never dreaming she had her weapons trained on him, just waiting to fire?

Altea's voice is first, and then a man's voice, his a lower rumble. I don't hear Helen, not yet, but she will not be far behind.

I yank the lever, and the stairs rise slowly, slowly.

They click shut, conceal me away, just as the office door below opens.

I crouch at the floor, at a small gap in the floorboards, and peer down.

They enter together—Altea arm in arm with Zarek, who must have finished whatever godawful interrogation he was doing with Marcus. Tommy follows with Helen on his arm and takes his place at the door as they all sit down.

And then I am trapped, all the gods below, and death waiting for me if I am found.

Could Helen save me from this? *Would* she?

My chest aches strangely at the thought.

"Hana is on her way," Zarek announces below me without preamble. He does not need to dally on greetings and pleasantries.

As if on cue, Hana enters the small office, flanked by her attendants.

A shiver snakes down my spine. All these brutal women missing their home and hating the man who took it from them.

And me, shit from Troy, hiding in the wings, waiting to topple them all.

"Thank you all for coming," Altea says, inclining her head to Zarek. "Frona sends her apologies. My attendants will have refreshments for all of you on the terrace afterward. I can send Saanva for drinks now if anyone would like?"

"It is our pleasure," Zarek says. There is a smile on his face but nothing in his eyes. Nothing at all.

I will take your whole fucking hand.

I clench my injured hand so tightly that pain unfurls inside me, a grunt escaping before I can stop it.

Altea stiffens, but otherwise she does not react. "Will Milos be joining us tonight?" she asks smoothly.

Of course she pretends not to know: no one is supposed to know, but of course everyone does.

Helen, however, shifts in her seat slightly.

Zarek places his hand on her back, fingers splayed open possessively.

Helen is not mine, despite the little game we are playing for the benefit of the Families. Still, the sight of anyone touching Helen as if he owns her makes the knot in my chest expand so wide I can hardly breathe.

Perhaps I would have waited them out otherwise. Perhaps I would have made the rational, safer choice. But the sight of his hand on Helen's back, the way she shrinks into her own body while still leaning into his touch—

That pushes me into action.

I have the small bag of solidox from the bomb-maker's warehouse.

There is sugar beside the teapot on Altea's desk.

My lighter is in my pocket.

So I crawl to the edge of the room, wait until the conversation below grows in volume, and then pry the vent off with a pop.

I shake the solidox and sugar together in the bag, and then crawl back over and peer between the slats of the floor.

I can see it all, the push-pull of power between them, the way they all seem to rotate on an axis around Zarek, as if they are planets in orbit and he is the goddamn sun.

En morte libertas.

In death, liberty.

The only way to escape the Families.

It was a saying the girls of Troy had, a foolish, morbid, furious thing we said to one another. Cass had screamed it into the waves. Milena had it tattooed on her knuckles. Even Eris used to say it to us before she, like Thea, left our home for whatever work awaited her. And Kore whispered it like a prayer.

I had said it to Helen, let it slip in a moment of weakness.

But once, surrounded by the girls I called my sisters, Kore had said *en morte libertas* and I had said:

In our death? I had asked her. *Or in theirs?*

Yes, Kore had said, and the girls had laughed, but I had not forgotten.

Not in my death.

Not in mine.

En morte libertas.

They are fascinating, opulent, untouchable.

I am a nobody, a forgotten girl, hidden in the ceiling.

I twist one of my rings, push my thumb hard against the flame engraved there. One for the girls I lost. One for the brutal will to survive that kept me here when I had not earned it. One for the Families—not gods, no matter what they think—whom I will destroy.

And then I drop the solidox mixture into the vent, wait for it to hit the bottom with a small thump, just next to the wall where Zarek is seated. Some of the mixture catches on an exposed wire on the way down.

Helen is below, smooth and unruffled and far from me even though we are separated by only a thin layer of floorboards.

And suddenly it is not enough. Not enough to blow apart a room. Not enough to cave a wall in, ruin a party, scare Zarek a little.

I sit down behind Altea's desk.

I lift her phone, the encrypted line she uses, and send a message to anyone in her contacts affiliated with Zarek's house.

Clear the house. Clear Zarek's wing.

I wait, watch lights flicker and turn off in Zarek's mansion. Below, his phone begins to ring, loud and shrill.

The voices below rise, too, fury and unease, but I do not hear them.

I do not hear anything but the sound of my sisters laughing as our boat cuts the waves, Cass holding tight to Milena as Kore drives. We are limitless. We are free. We are *alive*.

En morte libertas.

So I remove the safety mechanism. I pull the trigger.

I light the fucking match.

And Zarek's house begins to crumble.

CHAPTER 24

Helen

My father is shouting with rage.

That is the first thing I hear, above all the rest.

There was a *boom* above us so loud I cannot hear anything else, and Tommy is half carrying me away from it all.

They are all fleeing, Altea running with iron in the set of her jaw, and fear on Hana's face, and I want to scream for Paris, Paris, Paris—

Until I look out the window and see the damage and I know:

Paris has started a war.

She joins us as we reach Altea's marina, Tommy still running, shielding me with his body.

"I am going to kill you," he tells Paris, but she seems unbothered.

"Her targeting is *excellent*," Paris says a little breathlessly, utterly ignoring Tommy's threat.

Tommy nearly throws me into the waiting boat, Paris vaulting in after despite her injured hand, and then we are tearing out of the marina.

When I look up, Altea is standing on the cliff above us, looking down. There is a rifle in her hands, and even from here, I can see the look on her face.

Betrayal, after she thought we were building an alliance.

Fury, after I had almost come home.

I put two hands against Paris's chest and shove as hard as I fucking can. "What—the—fuck"—I punctuate each word with a shove—"was—that—"

She catches my wrists easily, jaw set. "That, Princess," she says coolly, "was doing what had to be done. If you wanted it, you could have the whole world—or at least all of your father's empire."

"I trusted you," I snarl at her above the roar of the boat. Why does it feel like I am being split in two, when I knew all *along* I could not trust her? Why, then, does it feel like I am bleeding?

To my surprise, Paris's face mirrors the pain on mine. "I am—"

Sorry does not make it past her lips, but I could see it hovering there.

"You should know," she says finally, "that your trust means something. It does."

We are inches from one another, her hands still closed over my wrists, our lips a breath away from touching.

"Tommy," I say without drawing back. "Take us somewhere quiet, where Paris and I can talk."

Fifteen minutes later, he has us docked on the far side of the island, where the coast is rugged but not entirely impassable, and the night is dark and silent.

He climbs out of the boat, stands off to the distance where he can do what he always does: watch over us, and let us have some time.

"Helen," Paris says, taking my hands in hers again. "Altea had her long-range weapon system trained on your father's house. On the wing of the mansion where his bedroom is. If she was willing to blow your house off the face of this island, she was never going to be an ally of yours."

"But—" I sputter. "But you could have *told* me. You could have given me a *chance*. Are we partners, Paris, or am I just a plaything?"

She drops my hands, looking stricken. "Do you want us to be more?" she asks cautiously.

And there it is again, the question that always seems to divide us: *What do you want, Helen?*

"Was I a fool for thinking we were?" I ask. "Paris. You started a *war*. You must care about that."

"And you think you know me, Princess?" she asks.

Paris does not spill secrets like blood. Paris's jaw is set, and she stares past me at the blackness of the sea, knuckles white as she twists her hands together, careful to avoid her injured finger.

"I *do* think I know you," I say. "I think you grieve your sisters every day. I think you are angry at my father for what he did. I think you resent me—and I think you *like* me."

Paris stares at me, shocked—and then she crosses the space between us, hooks a hand around the back of my neck, and pulls me into a bruising kiss, her tongue tangling with mine.

When she withdraws, both of us are breathless.

"Paris," I say against her lips. "Paris, I want *more*."

I want us, together, the two of us on the throne, changing the Family forever.

For half a wild moment, I think of bringing Paris to the secret entrance to my family's home, to climb the stairs together, all the way to my bedroom. To hold her hand, to feel the cold stone of those ancient steps beneath our feet, to burst into my room like invaders, with secrets no one would ever suspect.

"We need to talk about what happens next," Paris says. "You and I. This war."

Because it is that, now.

"He will kill so many," I say. "We have to stop him, we have to change something—I can talk to him, calm him down, if you can get Altea and her people to flee, maybe to Troy, maybe farther—"

"Stop," Paris cuts me off. "Helen, *stop*. Why would we stop this now? Why should we care if it burns, if it weakens your father's rule and one of your rivals, too?"

But I can see it in her eyes, I *can*, that she is haunted by what she has done tonight.

"And how are you different?" I snap. "How is this different than my father bombing your home? If this is how you are going to—"

Paris's hand closes around my throat, her rings cold against my skin, and she is shoving me backward against the side of the boat, making the boat tilt wildly.

Tommy is there before I can even think to call him, dragging her backward, yanking her hands from me. "Enough," he says sternly.

If it were anyone else, they would be bleeding at my feet.

But it is Paris, *my* Paris, and Tommy seems to know well enough that she is . . . well, mine. And not to be harmed.

"You," Paris snarls at me, lunging at me even as Tommy holds her firmly. "Do not *speak to me of Troy.*"

"Easy," Tommy says, almost as if he is comforting her. "Both of you take a minute, all right?"

Are we bleeding right here on this boat, Paris and I? Bomb after bomb, ripping through our lives? Are we always destined for this violence?

Me in my home, Paris in hers. Caught in the wars of the gods.

"Zarek killed teenagers," Paris snarls, ignoring Tommy's low, soothing tone. "Girls I *loved*. Do not compare me to him, Princess."

Tears are stinging my eyes. I swipe the back of my hand across them, vanishing them with one motion. "I didn't—I didn't mean—"

But what can I say to Paris, after this? She carries them with her every day. I see it on her, all those girls like her, trapped beneath bombs while I survived my grief in luxury.

I can scarcely breathe.

I'm sorry, I want to tell her, but it is not enough. It will never *be* enough, no matter how long I rule and how well. No one can give

Paris back her girls. Paris does not look at me, her face cast mostly in shadow.

And how did you live, Paris? How did you make a way out of the impossible? What secrets do you carry in that closed-off soul, in that singed jacket under your arm? How did you survive when others burned?

"I can make it home from here," she tells Tommy. She does not look at me as she leaves.

I watch Paris go, her body thin and wiry and appearing so fragile next to Tommy's broad shoulders. She disappears soon after, the black of her clothes fading into the darkness of the rocky shoreline.

You could have the whole world.

But, oh, Paris.

What if it isn't just the world I want?

CHAPTER 25

Paris

Helen will be the death of you. Thea told me that ages ago—or maybe only days ago.

Then Helen spoke to me of Troy tonight, as if she had any right.

And still, and *still*, I cannot let her go.

I must have paced the shoreline for almost an hour, long after Tommy took Helen home, before I call him.

"Tommy," I say. "I need to speak to Helen."

Tommy's sigh is a blend of annoyance and resignation. "You two," he mutters. "Did you not cause enough trouble together tonight?"

"We did," I say. "But will you send a car for me anyway?"

He does, of course he does, and brings me to Helen's rooftop garden without a word.

It is a different place at night: though I know it cannot be true, the plants look more tangled, the wind wilder, and—Helen.

Her hair curls, unbound, past her shoulders. "I am sorry," she says, stopping still before me.

The silence is as long and dark and empty as all those nights after I survived the bombing, after Kore and Cass and Milena were gone and it was just me, sleeping on concrete beneath the stars. And because I cannot bear a silence that lasts that long, I do, finally, speak.

"I am sorry, too." I have not said those words in years—not since before I lost my sisters. It was a part of me I cut away, because if I was sorry, I could not do what I needed to do to survive. Helen stretches out one smooth hand and takes mine.

My aching, bandaged hand.

And she is so gentle with it, so purposefully tender that tears bite at the backs of my eyes. Oh, Helen. Plaything and power. *Mine.*

"Helen," I say, and then she is kissing me there in defiance of gods and families and every power that has ever bound the both of us.

It is brief, and it is wild, and the only taste I know is her lips.

And my plans for revenge be damned, there are no gods I would not defy to get another taste of Helen.

Perhaps her vengeance and mine are the same after all. Perhaps we do not have to be one another's pawns or playthings.

Perhaps—*perhaps.*

My lips taste of Helen long after our kiss is past, and I am thinking about her concern for the innocents, about her dismay over the coming wars as I pace the worn floorboards in my apartment later that night.

Zarek will destroy Altea for this.

The weapon is in her house. Fired above his very head.

It will be over by morning, but I call her, all the same.

"What have you done, Troy?" Altea answers my call, her voice sharp as a blade.

"He knows what you long for," I tell her. "What all of you long for." *Home.*

They have all built houses here, mansions close to Zarek's. But their islands—Altea's homeland, Hana's old place on Troy, Frona's home before she lived full-time on the floating pleasure city—are far from this island, out past the bright-blue waters of the Mediterranean, far from Zarek. And perhaps they all want their homes back.

Do they know that Lena is still alive? Do they know each other well enough to know that they all seem to share the same hatred of Zarek?

"Is this what you wanted?" Altea asks, voice soft as velvet. "Is this what you planned?"

From the queen.

Which of them was taunting him, at that party that feels like lifetimes ago? Which of them considers herself queen above all?

"No one planned anything," I tell her. "I found an opportunity, and I took it."

I want to be free.

"And this talk of an alliance? The message you left me on my shooting range?"

"I was honest with you," I tell her. "I want Zarek to fall."

Silence at the other end, for a long minute.

"Was it for Troy?" she asks softly. "For what happened all those years ago?"

For Troy. For the girls and the caved-in doors and our melted skin.

She is the first of all of them to guess the truth.

I twist the rings on my fingers.

En morte libertas.

"I call you as a courtesy tonight, Altea," I say, though it is not to her that I offer it. "So you can get your innocents out before they bleed."

She will; of course she will.

The alternative is unimaginable.

"And Helen?" Altea asks coldly. "What is she to you? No more games, Troy. You owe me that truth at least."

I catch my breath.

And the memory: soft curves and full red lips and the sight of her, disheveled and joyful, crossing the wild rooftop garden toward me. My chest aches.

"Helen?" I say, and I am thinking of her lips, and her rage on the boat, and how I will lose her before all this is done. "She is nothing but a set piece to me." And then I leave Altea to it, to plan and scheme and aim her weapons at Zarek.

I have walked their halls and played their games and survived their violence. And now?

I light the match. I light the match. I light the match.

CHAPTER 26

HELEN

I leave the bunker in the early hours of the morning, and I fall into a restless sleep at last. My father came to my chambers, only briefly, to tell me that his belief in Marcus's loyalty has been restored.

He does not say Altea's name.

The rest of the house is livable; the only wing destroyed my father's.

We are safe, he tells me.

I do not tell him he is not, not anymore.

I wake early the next morning, the sun still new in the sky. Erin wakes when I do, fetches a tray for breakfast. When she returns, she is pale, quiet.

"Any word from Paris?" I ask her.

I was wrong last night—to bring up Troy. But so was Paris, to dismiss my concerns about Altea. To dismiss me the way I have always been dismissed.

"Would you like some water?" Erin holds out a glass to me, ignoring my question. Her face, her voice, her mannerism, as pleasant and distant and calm as ever, but her eyes betray her.

I take the water, my hands trembling. "Can you send for Tommy?"

Tommy.

Tommy will know.

He will know if my father has already taken his vengeance swiftly.

Erin does not meet my eyes. "Your father has responded to Altea's attack. And Tommy . . . Tommy was assigned to work with your fiancé's brother this morning. A special project for your father."

The cup slips from my hand, water spilling across my legs, the glass shattering on the floor. "What special project?" My voice is splinters and sandpaper.

Erin turns away from me. "I do not know more than that," she says. "I apologize, ma'am. I could ask your father—"

"No," I tell her.

Because we *do* know. We both know what kind of special projects my father sends men on. What kind of bloodshed Marcus has been known for ever since he was a boy.

My father's response to Altea was always going to be personal, his violence scorching—and Marcus is just the man to lead it.

And I know, I *know* Tommy has been sent along as a punishment for me.

It has always been this way: since I was very small, Tommy willingly killed to keep me safe. But the rest of the violence? He never had the heart for it.

So this, then, is what my father meant about Marcus restoring his loyalty. It is how Marcus made a name for himself, how he solidified a place for himself and his family among *the* Families.

I reach down to pick up the glass, and Erin brushes my hands away. "You'll cut yourself, ma'am," she says.

But perhaps I want to feel. Perhaps I want to bleed for my own mistakes, just this once.

"Leave it," I tell her, but she does not stop, and she does not let me help, and I sit there at the edge of a luxurious bed in a mansion I did not earn.

The only thing I have ever caused is bloodshed.

I push myself to my feet, avoiding the glass.

Erin is humming under her breath as she finishes cleaning.

"I need a motorcycle," I tell her. "And I need to go unnoticed."

And I need a handgun, though I am not sure whether or not I should tell Erin that part.

She freezes, her shoulders still hunched over the mess I made, but the song she was humming disappears into nothing against shattered glass and marble.

She stands finally, her mouth just slightly ajar as if she is about to ask what ill-advised plan I've concocted this time.

"And send a car for Paris," I say. "Someone you trust. Tell no one else."

But do I damn her with this? Working behind my father's back, asking her to do the same? When I am afforded protection and she has none?

Erin moves with more urgency than I have ever seen. She pauses at the door, something wild in her dark, ever-serene eyes. "You will do what you have to, Helen," she says, but I can hear the question in her voice. "You will try."

"To stop this?" I say. I could not stop my father's carnage on Troy, child that I was—but perhaps I have a chance at stopping this one. "Yes. I will try."

And so she goes to do as I have asked of her and—perhaps for the first time in years—I choose my own clothes, and I dress myself.

White jeans, torn at the knees, buried at the bottom of a drawer at the very back of one of my closets. A soft red top that hugs the rolls and curves of my soft, pale stomach beneath, with a bird taking flight across the front. Combat boots from the very back of my shoe closet. A black leather jacket to cover it all.

It feels like something Paris would wear to a party where cocktail gowns were expected, and the thought of her gives me strength.

I have always been dressing for war, but this time I am slipping into a different uniform.

I go to my father's study. He is pacing at the windows, staring out over the sea.

"Helen."

"Father."

"Was it your fixer?"

I steady myself on his desk chair, my hands closing over it tightly. No. *No.*

He cannot possibly know—because if he does, Paris is already dead, and *that* I cannot live with, no matter how many times I have tried to convince myself that I could. "No," I tell him, with as much certainty in my tone as I can muster. "Why didn't you send me along on the project this morning? I have asked you for a greater role. This would have been a chance to prove myself, and you wasted it on a man like Marcus."

There was a time when I would have chosen the violence. Laid explosives myself. But pretending to care about my father's business seems to be one of the only things currently keeping Paris alive—so I will do what I must.

He turns at last, raising an eyebrow when he sees what I am wearing. "You are dressing like her now?"

"I am dressing comfortably. And you didn't answer my question," I say, but what I mean is *Am I already too late?* and what does it say about me that I am more worried it is Paris he killed this morning, and not Altea's entire household?

"I sent Tommy," he says. He watches me carefully, searching for some reaction. "Helen, this kind of upheaval is a threat to *our* power. Not theirs. When you rule, any war is a reason for the people who follow you to leave, or betray you, or question *why* you rule. You have always been impulsive—you have been kept out of the Family business for years because you couldn't stop yourself from blowing up marinas when the whim took you, Helen. Is that what you've been doing this time? When your fixer was poking around, did she offend Altea enough for that bitch to *fire upon me?*"

I hang on to the back of his chair and let out my breath slowly. So not Paris.

Not yet.

"I'm not sure what Paris has to do with it," I say. "Altea had the weapon, not my fixer."

My father's eyes are cold when they meet mine. "Maybe so. And maybe not. Either way, you have allowed her too close to you," he says. "You have allowed her to mean too much to you, little girl, and that is *always* dangerous."

"I allow nothing," I tell him coldly. My heartbeat is thundering in my chest, nearly drowning out my ability to hear my own words. "Paris is nothing to me."

Paris is everything. Paris laughing on the open water. Paris with a blade to my throat. Paris's hands—

"If that is true," Zarek says. "Then finish this fling with her and let me take care of things."

"Let me at least have until the marriage." I try to make my words sound casual, careless, as if she is just a plaything and killing her too early would be an inconvenience, nothing more.

His eyes narrow. "That does little to convince me she means nothing to you," he says. "If she does not matter, you can have a new toy before the wedding. Let this one go."

"Then let it be Tommy," I say, and I taste ash on my tongue as I say it. "Offer me that much, Father. I have asked for so little. A quick death for Paris."

He nods, just once. "Very well."

It is acknowledgment and dismissal, and I turn to go.

I stop at our private armory and gather a handgun and a few magazines, packing them in a holster beneath my jacket.

Erin is waiting for me at the garage.

She helps me put the helmet on and tucks in the strands of my dark hair beneath it, and then we walk together, our strides matching, to the motorcycle that waits for me. There, she presses the key into my hand.

"Shall I send a guard behind you?" Erin asks.

I shake my head and swing my leg over the motorcycle. "I am going to find Tommy," I tell her. And even to Erin, I do not tell the rest: *I need to save Paris.*

And then the motorcycle roars to life beneath my gloved hands, Erin opens the garage, and I am gone, speeding across the island as if I was born for this.

I do not stop the gods today.

I do not stop the carnage or the cruelty or the despair.

I do not arrive in time to save innocent staff, and I do not arrive in time to save Tommy.

I do not arrive in time to save anyone at all.

There is blood spilled across the gate, and a guard who looks like a boy impaled there, his blood still leaking out of him in slow, steady drops. His brown eyes are fixed on the sky, waiting for a rescue that never came. His stomach is open, and parts of him are spilling out that are supposed to remain inside.

I slow my motorcycle, and every muscle in my body aches to escape. I could just let go, could leave my body, could leave all this horror behind.

But the boy at the gate, his body bent back, his mouth open in one last gasp—the boy says I must stay.

That I must witness this, even if I still struggle to look upon it.

That I must let the blood flow beneath my feet as it always has.

The iron gates are bent inward, his youthful body arched over them. As if explosive force blew them in.

As if Marcus did not once try to negotiate or ask or knock. As if he came here only to do what he does best: to make them bleed.

I drive through the gates slowly, past two more guards laid out just inside the gates. There are weapons beside them, but there are knife wounds, slashes on their faces. As if Marcus had his fun before he killed them.

And then there are twin bullet holes, one in each of their foreheads. They, too, are still bleeding.

And this I recognize as Tommy's work.

Ending their pain without the torture Marcus would have asked of him, defying Marcus. I wonder if Marcus has made him pay for it yet, if he would dare. Fury and fear thread together through me, winding around my spine and reaching up to wrap cold fists around my throat.

Marcus.

The name is a destructive promise echoing in the back of my mind.

Farther I go, past more carnage.

Was it a mistake? To come here first?

There are no right moves, it seems. There is no path I take that does not end in blood and loss and horror.

Altea's drive is long and winding and bloody, and I pass a guardhouse and a dead woman my age, gun still in her hands. I pass the inner gates, blown in like those at the road. Another guard, older, maybe Tommy's age. The kind that has survived so long as a guard he was probably like family, at least to Altea.

This man has a hole through the center of his chest.

Shotgun blast, point-blank.

Marcus.

I round the last bend and, finally, there is Altea's mansion, stark white against the bright sun, incongruously beautiful against this nightmare.

I stop the motorcycle, gasping.

I can smell blood in the air as I dismount.

And then I see it as I walk toward the house: the first sign of life. North of the house, on a smooth white stone terrace, beside a fountain that gurgles gently.

Six of Marcus's men—or my father's men—and in front of them, three women. Even from this distance, I know what I see: a young woman in a maid's uniform. And on either side of her, two of the women who have been Altea's personal attendants for years.

Run, one of the men says.

I am close enough to hear the taunt.

I know this game.

The women do not move. They do not play the game.

They stand with jaws set, shoulders back, defiant and proud even when they are past hoping for survival. Even the young one, the maid.

They are Altea's women, through and through.

The men raise their guns, and I am running toward them, running—

"*No,*" I shout, and I raise my hands, waving desperately to stop them.

The guns fire.

Three splashes of blood across white stone.

And they fall, beautiful and proud and fierce to the end, into the fountain, red blooming in the water below them.

The men with the guns turn to me, all six of them.

There are tears cutting my cheeks beneath the motorcycle helmet, and something beneath my rib cage cracks open.

"*Run,*" I shout as I shove my helmet off.

They raise their guns, confusion as clear on their faces as violence.

I draw my gun, and they hesitate, because they see me, they know who I am, they cannot fire upon me.

It is not a fair fight. It has never been a fair fight.

I am my father's daughter.

And I kill every last one.

CHAPTER 27

Paris

A car waits for me outside of my apartment, but I slip out a back entrance and make my own way to Altea's. Whether that car was sent by Helen or Zarek, I have no way of knowing—and this morning, I'm not sure I want to risk it. I get her text when I am already on my way to Altea's: destruction at Altea's. My father's men. And Marcus.

When I arrive at Altea's, that is exactly what I find.

She had time, she had *time*, I gave her time. And she let them all die for her anyway.

I walk past fallen guards and gates blown in. I marvel at the courage, and it makes me furious, too.

That the gods let us bleed for them, let us be fodder in their endless, endless struggles for power.

That I have become a *part* of it, that I chose this and walked into it with my eyes wide open.

Still, I warned her so they would *live*. So that innocent maids and doormen would not be slaughtered.

Perhaps that has always been the difference between me and these gods: if someone had given me warning on Troy, I would have spent my last breath getting every single one of us out of there.

I walk toward the house, empty now.

The hit team is long gone—Helen's text said Zarek sent Marcus with two dozen men. I know enough of Marcus to know he would *want* to be a part of something like this.

He wants what belongs to you.

I circle the house, stopping when I reach the terrace on the north side of the house. There are dead servant girls, bloodstained uniforms visible in the swirling red of the fountain. I stagger, my legs scarcely willing to hold me up in the face of such loss.

"I told you she was dangerous."

I spin around. Thea stands at the north entrance to Altea's ravaged house, her eyes narrow and furious and full of a wild grief that I feel like a blade between my ribs.

"She didn't—" My voice catches strangely.

Because it wasn't Helen who did this.

It was me.

"All because you wanted to fuck power." Thea's mouth twists. "You know, for all your talk about the Family not owning you, you ended up with them all the same."

"Like *you* didn't," I snap.

"Do you think I had a *choice?*" She throws the words at me across the bloodied ground between us. "Do you think any of the girls at Troy had a choice when the Families told us to *come?*"

I stare at her. "You wanted—"

"I *wanted* nothing," she snarls. "None of us did. It was no honor, like they told us it was to be chosen. They took the strong, they took the girls with an affinity for weapons and explosives." She hesitates. "They took the beautiful."

It was true.

"And now. *These* girls," she says softly, extending her hand toward the fountain. "Altea and I stood side by side and those girls—they shot them, right there. We watched them die from the safety of her hidden office." Thea's eyes are haunted as she says it. "They were Troy girls."

Girls who grew up with bars on the windows.

Girls who died in someone else's war.

"They were *mine*," Thea says fiercely.

Tears are hot on my cheeks before I realize they are there. "They were *ours*," I say.

There are tears cutting lines down the sharp angles of her face, too, and she takes a step closer to me. "And do you know what else I saw from that office window?" she continues. "A girl on a motorcycle, trying to stop it. A woman in a black leather jacket, facing down a hit team. And I thought it was you at first, trying to save them. But it wasn't, was it?"

My body stills.

Helen.

And then it is too much for me to bear. Too much. Wars and gods and a woman who will change everything.

"Why did you warn Altea?" Thea asks. "And why did you warn her too *late*?"

Helen on that boat, accusing me of being just like her father.

My hand around her throat, because the only thing unforgivable was *that*.

But she had been right, after all, and innocent people have died in a war I began.

"She could have saved them," I say, but I am trying to convince myself of that, and it shows in the tremble of my voice. "She could have sent them away."

But I wish I had, I wish I had stilled my trigger finger, I wish I had killed Altea and Zarek and Frona and Hana and Lena myself so that all the innocents would still be alive, but I did not. Instead, I played games and told lies and spun stories and considered mercy too late, just like every other member of these Families.

Instead, I prepared myself for escape. Because where does my loyalty lie if not my own survival, first and last and always?

"You hate them," Thea says, her voice cracking. "We all hate them. But we choose how complicit we are, Troy. *You* chose." She jabs a finger against my chest.

I let her.

"You played the game of the Families," Thea continues, voice barely a rasp. "And look at the mess you fucking made."

There is nothing else to do. There is nothing left.

So I go to Thea's, at the end of it all.

You played the game. Thea's words echo in my head no matter how much of her bourbon I drink. No matter how roughly she and I touch each other, or how gently Perce touches us. No matter what we do to one another in Thea's spacious king bed, the words echo and echo and echo.

Hours later, when we are all three of us spent with exhaustion, Perce pushes himself to his feet.

"I'll make some tea," he says, fingers trailing gently over Thea's shoulder.

She catches his hand in hers, presses a kiss to his knuckles. "Beloved," she says.

When the door shuts behind him, she sits up and pulls one of the blankets around her shoulders.

"Troy," Thea says. "I have something to say to you."

"Why were you there?" I blurt, pushing myself up, too, and I pull on my tank top, as if a layer of clothing can shield me from Thea's sharp gaze.

Thea hesitates. "I would have saved them," she says. "If I could. I was always trying to save them, Paris."

"But why were you *there*?" I glare across the bed at her. *Are you part of them?* I want to ask. *And what else—who else—do you answer to?*

"Because I have a husband I want kept safe," Thea snaps. "Paris, how is this so impossible to understand? I worked in this Family to keep us both alive. I stood beside her today because when I follow their orders, my husband stays safe."

"But why did she want *you* there?" I persist. "Why did she want you with her today?"

Thea shrugs one shoulder. "Why do they do anything? Maybe she wanted me with her because she wanted to know I was loyal enough to stay at her side until she could make her escape. Maybe she wanted something to hold over my head. I don't fucking know, Troy. All I know is that I keep their secrets to keep us alive. *All* of their secrets, Troy."

I freeze. "All of them," I repeat.

Years ago, when I first learned Lena was alive—and using our old group home as a hideout—it felt like a secret I had to carry alone. Because how could I have my revenge if Zarek found out first, and took his?

"I think you know," Thea says. "I think you have known about Lena for a very long time."

Even here, even in her bed, we have not always been honest with one another. We have not always spoken freely, because homes can be bugged and guards can talk. But on this bloody day at the beginning of a war, Thea gives me truth. A gift, after years of secrecy and planning.

I breathe in. Out again. And then I nod. "And you?" I ask. "Why didn't you say?"

She shakes her head again. "Zarek would have tried to kill Perce if I left his Family," she says. "And Lena would have tried to kill Perce if I told anyone *her* secret."

"Thea," I whisper. "I—I am sorry. That I did not trust you. That we could not be more honest with each other."

She stares me down, the look on her face hard and unchanging. "And I told *you*," Thea says. "That you would die if you did this. And

I thought you would, Paris. Long before you would cause this much wreckage."

I open my mouth and then shut it again, shaking my head. "Thea."

"No," she says. "No, listen to me. You were reckless and stupid, and you wanted revenge above everything else."

"No," I stop her. "No. Not just that."

The silence between us is heavy and final. Helen is in all the spaces between us, dark eyes and deadly power. Her pinkie brushing mine and changing everything.

"You cannot be serious," Thea says. "Paris? After all this time?"

I have wanted revenge.

I have carried my rage like a banner. I have kept anyone from loving me. Kept myself from loving in return. Until—

"Helen," Thea breathes. "Does she—do you—"

"I wanted revenge," I tell her finally. "I always have. You know that. I wanted them all to die. I wanted them all to lose everything. And then—then I met her, and then I *still* wanted them to die, all of them but . . . her."

"So you kept going," Thea says. "Because—"

"Because I didn't care if it was the most reckless plan," I whisper finally. "If it kept me at her side."

"That's not the only option you have. There's the option where you run," Thea tells me firmly. She opens a drawer at her bedside table. Inside are two passports and a small box. "I know you have a fail-safe. I've been working on one for Perce and me for years. So take Helen and run. Let her burn a thousand ships in your wake if they come for you. But get out of here, Troy, and have a shot at living. To do that you have to let go of that group home."

I stiffen. "They died," I snap at her. "Every last one."

"Not every last one," Thea says. "Not yet. But they will. And you and Helen will be used and used, and the Families will keep solidifying their power, and nothing you do will change that. So run while you can."

"But how?" I lean forward, resting my elbows on my knees as I look at her. "Thea, I—I don't know if I can."

But I know, now, that I *should.*

"Do you think you can convince her?" Thea asks, her expression shifting, the hard look in her face fading as she looks at me. "To go, and leave power behind?"

I am balancing on a knife's edge. Revenge on one side. Life on the other. And Thea, the only real family I have left, is telling me go, go, go. *Live.*

"But Lena," I say, meeting Thea's dark eyes with mine. "She is building her empire there on our *grave.*"

Thea's gaze flickers, and then she sighs deeply, as if she knows she has lost. "Not just Lena," she says.

Again, my body is rooted in place. "You mean—"

Thea hesitates, and then nods. "Yes," she says. "All of them. All three queens. They have been loyal to her all this time. Paris, I—"

But I am already pulling on jeans and my socks, I am already halfway gone, because if the queens are all using my home together—if they are *all* involved in building a war room on Kore's grave—

Thea calls my name, and Perce, too, as he passes me, carrying tea in his gentle hands.

The knife tilts. I fall, again, toward vengeance.

The dead girls at Altea's should have been protected—but I made choices, and they died.

And I know, even now, even with guilt clinging to me like a fine layer of ash, that I will make more choices like it before the end.

From the queen.

The girls of Troy are burning and burning and burning.

And this time it's me who lit the match.

CHAPTER 28

HELEN

I find Tommy hours later, pacing the cliffs at the edge of my father's property. His clothes are still bloodstained, and there is a look on his face that makes me want to drag him away from the edge of that cliff.

He looks up at the sound of my steps, soft as they are.

I have changed back into a dress, a wicked, scarlet thing.

I have not been able to wear it before. It had reminded me too much of blood.

But now?

Now I wrap myself in blood and pace the cliffs.

I have had enough of grief and waiting and hiding. I have had enough of doing as I am told.

"Tommy," I say fiercely, and he breaks.

He hugs me to his chest, and then his own shoulders are shaking with a violence I have never seen.

"Kid," he says, and then just as suddenly he steps back, his hulking form still trembling. "*Jesus.* You shouldn't—you shouldn't be comforting me. Not after what I've done."

"Marcus's men," I tell him, ignoring his words and taking his hand in mine, squeezing it. "The six that did not make it back."

He stares at me, and then recognition dawns, brutal and beautiful, across his face.

"They killed those women," I tell him. "And then I killed them." I pause. "I am sorry I was not there in time to stop it. To do more."

He shakes his head. "Kid," he says. "I made a choice. I always have. I always will."

"But what kind of choice was it?" I ask the question rhetorically, because I know my father, and I know he gives orders no one disobeys. At least, no one disobeys and lives. But Tommy answers me, quiet and heart-shattering.

"He said," he tells me softly, "'Who will it be tonight—Altea or Paris?'"

I inhale sharply. "No," I say. Because I can save them both. I *can*.

"Because he knows," Tommy says, and then that is all he says. "He knows Paris is not and has never been his, and the only reason he has not yet moved on her is because she is *yours*. Your plaything. But his patience will not last forever, Helen. And how will I do it?"

His eyes are haunted.

I sit down on the white stone, my palms flat against them. "Sit with me," I say.

He obeys.

"That was no choice at all," I tell him.

But he does not look at me.

He does not believe me.

"Tommy," I say, because I cannot bear to tell him what my father is about to ask of him. "It will be okay."

He stares out at the wild sea, crashing below us, echoing the thing inside me that came untethered today. Finally, he opens his mouth. "Promise?" he whispers.

There is blood caked beneath his fingernails.

"Promise."

CHAPTER 29

Paris

I do not know if I will see them again, but we leave it there, Thea and I, between the blood-soaked fountain at Altea's fallen mansion and the tangle of our limbs in her bed.

And I go to Helen.

After all this time? Thea asked me, and I had trembled and thought of Helen, lips parting, eyes sparking with joy.

My bag is packed—the fail-safe Thea talked about, the poppy Helen gave me at the party, a passport with a new name and enough cash to get me to freedom—when the knock comes. And with it, relief.

Because I was never going to leave. Not with the knowledge that the queens have been using Troy. Not with the knowledge that Altea knew her household would die for her and she *let* them. And not before I could tell Helen about Lena. Lena, who she still adores, despite it all.

Tommy is at the door, looking older than he had just days ago. "Helen," he says, and that is all. Helen summons me.

"Did you?" I ask.

He does not have to ask what I mean. Perhaps the carnage is all he can see, too. His eyes are dark and lifeless, and he stares somewhere past my shoulder, as if, like me, he is seeing gates blown in and boys with holes in their chests and bloodstained fountains. "Yes," he answers.

I hesitate, and then I step forward and wrap my arms around him.

He pauses, body stiffening, and then returns the hug, cupping my head against his broad chest for just a moment. "I don't deserve that, kid," he says.

I draw back. "None of us do." I shrug on my jacket, shooting another glance at him. "What does Zarek want?"

Has he decided it is time to be rid of me?

Tommy's eyes find mine, finally. *"Helen,"* he repeats. "Helen wants you."

Helen wants you.

The words ache somewhere nameless beneath my ribs.

Would she let me die for her, the way those who loved Altea died in the carnage? Would she hold her head high afterward, because I am just another commoner and she was born to a throne? She accused me of being just like her father—but she is the one who wants to rule.

She is the one longing for a throne.

After all this time?

"What does she want?" I ask him. My heart is pounding—not from the danger closing in around me, but from the weight of what I have kept from Helen. The weight of what I am about to reveal, come what may.

Wherever Helen goes, whatever she chooses—I owe her this, at least.

Tommy has already turned to go. "Come on, kid," he says. "Let's go."

I follow him, my footfalls heavy and slow and inevitable.

We are just two playthings of the gods, Tommy and I.

And we do as we are told.

He stops me before we reach Helen. His hand is on my shoulder, gentler than it has any right to be.

"I need to know, kid," he says.

My own gaze snaps to his. "You need to know what?"

"Is it real?" he asks. "For you. Is it real for you?"

I am frozen beneath his hand. "Tommy."

"I know what you are after," he says wearily. "Ten years ago, even, I would have believed it my duty to stop you. I would have believed my loyalty to this family. But there have been so many monstrous things. So very many. And now my loyalty is to the little girl I raised, and her only. So I need you to tell me, Paris."

After all this time?

I flick my lighter open.

The flame trembles there.

"Yes," I tell him. The word is raw in my throat.

Tommy leans back, satisfied. "Good," he says. "Because I think it is for her."

The silence hangs between us, and then he looks at my injured hand, still bandaged, and he shakes his head. "I am sorry," he says. "That I did not protect you that day. That I lacked the courage to do what I should have done years ago."

"Forgive yourself," I tell him, even as the hand still aches. "I do."

"Will you get her out of here?" he asks. "After all this?"

There's an option where you run, Thea told me.

If Kore was here, would she be saying the same? Would she be telling me to *live*?

Tommy looks far away, as if imagining the world that exists beyond these warring islands and their restless gods. As if imagining that beyond this boundless sea we could reach a place where Helen could be free, where I could be with her, where we could leave the violence behind.

He rests his hand on my shoulder a moment longer. The gesture is gentle. Familial.

Strange for a woman who has no one left.

"You take care of her, kid," he says as he pushes the door open. "Promise?"

I nod. "Promise."

185

There was a day a lifetime ago, where I was brought to the rooftop garden where the sun shone down and the wind ravaged our skin and hair, and Helen climbed across a stone table to reach me. To kiss me.

But today is not that day.

Today is gray and still and lifeless, cold in a way that reaches down to the bone. Today there is only carnage between us.

Helen sits upon the couch like a throne.

"Paris."

The sound of my name in her mouth wraps around me, pulls me forward. Undoes me.

After all this time?

"Helen."

I stagger on my feet, the ground itself unsteady after the monstrous things I have done.

Glass blown in.

Helen beneath me, soft skin and warm breath.

A grenade for a god.

"Paris, I told Tommy not to tell anyone I was bringing you here," she says. "My father is gone today, meeting with Milos and Marcus, but we only have a little bit of time. He's decided—well, he's decided I care too much."

I stare at her now, unsullied and perfect, her dark hair swept up into a loose knot, curls spilling over the curve of her neck. Soft scarlet gown, sweeping down to her feet. A flash of bare ankle beneath. The words barely register. "He's decided it is time for me to die."

Ironic, then, that I have decided this about him. A whisper of wind touches her, ruffling her hair, the folds of her skirt.

The hairs on the back of my neck stand up.

She stands, scarlet spilling down over her curves.

I want to bunch my fists into the soft folds of her dress. I want us to be simple and unhurt, just us. Just Helen, just Paris.

But we were never just Helen, just Paris. God and commoner, and nothing to bridge the gap, no matter how desperate I am now.

"Walk with me," she says.

Helen reaches out her hand and takes my arm, and I am trembling at the weight of this.

Helen and I.

Helen and I.

"Did you see—the men I killed?" she asks me finally. "At Altea's?"

"I did."

Next to the girls in the fountain.

And for a moment, Helen had been just another girl from Troy, taking her revenge.

Girls from Troy.

It comes back to this, always.

We pace together at the edge of the rooftop, Helen and I.

"I could not save them," she says.

"I know."

"I wanted to save them," she continues. "For *you*. Because I am not going to rule like my father or the queens. And I want—I want to save the rest, if we can."

I pause, wavering at the edge, staring down at the water that crashes against the cliffs below. "How?"

"I mean what I said," she says firmly. "My father cannot be allowed to do this. Not again."

No one, *no one* who came for Zarek has ever had a chance. But what chance does *he* have when the weapon in my hands is his own daughter—and the power she is now choosing for herself?

She is just a set piece to me, I told Altea. I had tried to mean it, even. She is a weapon I can use to unmake Zarek himself. Thea said I would be used and then killed. Thea said I had no chance against them. But with Helen beside me—

"What are you saying, Helen?" I step away from her, still my shaking hands when I clench them into fists. "What are you willing to do, and are you willing to do it with me?"

"I know you love them," Helen says. "Your girls. I know you love them and grieve them and I know you're not as hard as you let on, and I know that's *why*."

"Helen—"

"Let me finish," she continues firmly. "I was wrong about you. And I think you were wrong about me, too. I think I can be better. I think I can *rule* better than they have, and I think we can do it—I think we can do it together."

She sounds desperate, hungry, as if this is more than ambition. As if she needs this to *live*.

But I do not, do not want to rule.

"Helen," I attempt. "Helen, I don't think you *can*. In these Families, this world . . . people always, always get hurt, even when you don't mean for them to."

Helen snatches my hand. "I need you to do this," she says. "Paris, don't you understand? If we don't do this, he'll kill you."

I have survived him once, and Helen should not underestimate me now. "We have more options than just overthrowing him, Helen," I tell her sharply. "There is no way to rule that saves the girls of Troy."

"You're wrong about that," she argues. "About me. My mother was a better ruler than my father—her people loved her, were loyal to her."

I *was* her people.

And she let us all die.

"Aren't you listening to me? My father wants to *kill* you," Helen continues. "Tommy is loyal to me. He could lead some guards, if I asked him, hold my father hostage in my study, and meet with the queens. We could make a bid for power, you and I—"

"Helen." Her name comes out in a rasp. "I—I have something I need to tell you, too."

Lena is alive, and she may have bombed your party.

Lena is alive, and she may be moving on the throne you want for your own.

Lena is alive, and will you still want me at your side when you learn what I once planned to do to you and your family?

But before I can find the words for any of it, the elevator doors open behind us.

I turn my head, and—it is too late.

Too late for us all.

Because there at the door is Zarek, flanked by all his guards, Milos and Marcus at his side, their guns trained on us.

CHAPTER 30

Helen

They are not supposed to be here, not yet—not until this afternoon. We were supposed to have time to *plan*, Paris and I, to make something out of this horror. To change things, just this once.

Milos is wearing his usual pressed shirt, but without the suit coat. He is deathly pale, the weapon in his hand trembling violently.

I can feel myself slipping away—away from the person I only ever am with Paris or Tommy. The mask slides back into place.

"Father," I say, willing my voice not to tremble. "Milos, darling? What is the meaning of all this?"

"Helen, move," my father says, waving his gun at me. "Paris. Tommy. Kneel."

Tommy's face is unreadable, but Paris's expression is all rage.

Tommy moves past me, setting a hand warmly on my shoulder as he goes.

"Tommy," I say. "Tommy, Tommy, *no*. This isn't—Father, you can't—"

"It'll be okay, kid," Tommy says. "It's all right. It is."

The smile he gives me is warm, after everything, and then he kneels on the windswept rooftop, hands behind his head, fingers interlaced. Welcoming the inevitable.

Paris stands still, stance wide, scowl on her face. "Come and make me, then," she says.

"Kid," Tommy says gently.

This time he is not talking to me.

It is this—and not the guns—that makes Paris step forward, passing me without casting a look at me and kneeling beside Tommy. They face straight forward, their expressions calm in the face of all this.

Milos's expression is unreadable as he takes my hand. It is cold and limp in his, and I do not feel it.

The sensation is gone from my body, hidden away. I am somewhere above it all, pieces of me in the high marble ceilings and the ladder we could use to escape and the railing that juts out over the sea. Part of me everywhere, in grains of sand and whispers of wind and the poppies, scarlet against the night sky.

And none of me is his.

Not when he takes my hand, not when he pulls me in for a kiss.

Milos, I would tell him if I were there. *It's time for you to leave. I don't want you here.*

"Are you ready?" Marcus asks me.

"Can you—can you tell me what is happening?" My voice carries so much weakness that I do not want Paris and Tommy to hear it, not when they kneel there with such unwavering courage.

Milos draws me closer to his side, still holding my hand.

We were meant to walk together, hand in hand, through marble hallways and through the years. We are every inch the king and queen.

I had thought I could rule. I had thought, even, that I could rule and do *better.*

But perhaps this is all that ever waited for me. Perhaps this is what it meant to rule.

My father draws closer. There is the fury of war in his eyes. I have seen it before, before he avenged my mother's death, before he destroyed the whole island of Troy in his rage.

"Helen."

"Father."

"Milos, give us a moment."

Milos drops my hand, and I return to my body, if only briefly.

My bracelet burns my skin, this homage to my mother. I rub my thumb along the thin band of metal, over and over and over again.

Méchri thanátou.

Unto death.

"What is the meaning of this?" I manage the words, manage to drag myself back into my body. Paris and Tommy, kneeling just there.

No.

No.

"Do not play coy with me, little girl. You have been knee-deep in this game with Paris," he snarls. "Did you really think you could do as you pleased in my house?"

"Do not pretend you cared for my life," I tell him coldly. "Do not pretend you care about *any* life when you treat them all as if they are at your disposal."

He looks as if he wants to raise a hand to me now—but something stops him. Is it something he sees in my face? Is it the fact that after all this, I am still a bomb-maker, still my mother's daughter?

"Am I a daughter?" I ask him again. "Or a bargaining chip? Which were you afraid to lose to Paris?"

"You are both," he says. "Helen, you *know* that. You have always known that. I can love my daughter and value my business. I can care for you and value your contributions to our *Family*. Do not play, little girl. Not after all this."

"How long will you keep me small? How long will you deny that I have the power to rule at your side?"

"At my side?" he asks. "Or in my stead?"

Paris and Tommy are kneeling there, guns trained on them, and I will do what I must.

I do not hesitate. "Together," I say. "Family."

My father pauses, considering me, considering my silence. "Very well. I will make you a deal, then, *daughter*," he says. He leans forward, violence in his eyes. "But you must prove your loyalty if you want your place here, if you want your guard and your paramour to survive this. You must earn it as your mother did."

When my mother was young and newly married to him—nineteen, or perhaps twenty—he sent her off alone. On what sort of mission, she never told anyone. But Tommy told me she came back empty-eyed and haunted, with blood beneath her nails and ashes on her boots. She spent long hours walking with Tommy along the cliffs, and if anyone left alive knows what she had to do to prove her loyalty, it is him, and his silence is unbroken.

"What would you have me do?" I ask him.

Who would you have me kill?

Because for Paris, I would. I would.

"You will marry Milos. Tonight. You will seal this alliance. You will prove your loyalty to me."

My father must see the hesitation in my eyes, must see the fear and fury there, because he smiles.

"If you are thinking of killing me," he says quietly. "Know what it would do. Have you seen a power vacuum before, little girl? Have you seen the wars that will be fought? Do you know who would die, how *many* would die?" His hand closes over my bicep, fingers digging so hard I know they will leave a bruise. "But in case the body count does not matter to you." His breath is hot on my face. "I will keep your insurance until this ceremony is done."

He gestures toward Tommy and Paris.

Tommy.

Tommy, on his knees, hands woven together on the back of his head.

Tommy, with a handgun pressed to his temple.

Paris beside him, the fury of the last ten years flickering dangerously in her eyes.

"No." I rip my arm from my father's grip. *"No."*

"It's okay," Tommy says quietly. "Kid—Helen, look at me. It's okay."

"Promise?" I whisper.

They hit him hard across his face with a pistol. The blood is immediate, pouring from a cut in his lip, and he does not answer me.

Milos is behind the circle of guards, face pale. "Helen?" he asks uncertainly.

After all of this, he remains the fool, shattered all over again at the knowledge that he and I will never be anything more than an alliance.

"We are getting married," I say dully, but my eyes are on the barrel of the gun, at the smudge it has left on Tommy's forehead. "Milos, we are getting married tonight."

"Like this?" He gestures to the guns, to Tommy, to Paris, and he looks bereft, though the emotion evaporates a second later, and then he looks—

Then he looks furious.

"Like this," I answer.

I turn to my father. "I will remember my place," I tell him quietly. "I will play the game. I will rule at your side. But if anything happens— to either of them—"

I let the threat hang there, bolder than I have ever been with my father. The memory of laying explosives with Paris surges through me. The joy, the way it felt like my chest was expanding, the feel of her hand in mine.

I am more than Zarek's timid daughter.

My father nods, just once. "And you," he says. "Remember that there are things you love. That there are things you could lose."

I dip my head in response, a gesture between equals, between rivals, between gods.

"Helen," Milos says hesitantly. "Helen, I thought—"

I walk past my father toward Tommy, move the barrel of the gun from Tommy's head. Take Tommy's hand and pull him to his feet.

He stares down at me sadly. "Kid," he says.

"No," I say. "No, not anymore."

"Paris stays there," my father says.

I meet her eyes.

I am standing, and she is kneeling, but I feel smaller than I have in my entire life.

You are the power, she told me.

And I can feel it, pounding against my rib cage, begging to be released.

I kneel in front of Paris and cup her face in my hands.

"Whatever I must," I murmur, and press a kiss to her lips.

And then I walk, hand in hand with Milos, to become his wife.

A man I do not know arrives to perform the ceremony, and Milos is quiet and Tommy is quiet and Paris is furious and the room is a tomb and Mama and everyone who died at Altea's are here bleeding and all of it circles back around me, but still I stand, still I stand unshaking, and I do what I must.

Tommy takes his post beside me. He brushes hair from my face and looks down at me with an ocean of sorrow in his eyes, but he says nothing.

They keep Paris between two armed guards, flanking her but not touching her—if they touch her, *if they touch her* I will draw the knife from beneath my dress and cut their throats.

After our vows, Milos turns to me. His face is almost blank, almost empty. But not quite. "Helen," he says. "Helen, I didn't want to marry you like this. I thought we could be *something.*"

I cup his face with one hand. "I am sorry," I tell him. "I am sorry."

How can he have been so naive, to think this marriage could become something it was never meant to be?

"This is an alliance," I tell him. "Our families are now one."

"But—could we come to care for each other, do you think?" he asks me. "Does it always have to be this way?"

I pull enough of me back into my body to answer. To answer, but not to feel. Because after Paris's hands, how could I ever want anyone else's hands on me? How could I ever go back? "How could it have been any other way, darling?"

It is easier to look past him and pretend I am talking to Paris. She is watching me, her body still but her eyes blazing. I can use words like *darling*, and I can imagine it is her hands cupping my neck. Her hands, long, lean fingers with those rings that drive me mad, dancing across my skin.

And if after all this, I cannot save her—cannot save Tommy—

I turn to my father.

"Father, may we go?"

"Not yet." His voice is sharp, dangerous. "Milos, in my family, loyalty must be proved."

Tommy moves toward me, the gesture automatic. He can hear a threat in the change of tone, and he moves to protect me now, his body between mine and my father's.

And I want to rewind it all, return to a time when I was a little girl and Tommy could just hold me close and call me *kid* and tell me to be better, but it is too late, too late for both of us, because—

They force him to his knees beside Paris again.

There is a gun in my father's hand. He hesitates.

Not one of us moves.

Then he holds it, hilt out, toward Milos. "Your brother's loyalty was brought into question," my father says. "I do not tolerate disloyalty in any form. He has done his part. So pay your debt, Milos Vasieleiou. And buy your brother's safety."

The words hit Paris before they register in my own mind, because she begins to struggle against the guards that are holding her until they shove her to her knees beside Tommy.

"No," I say numbly.

Milos does not look at me. Does not meet my eyes. Not even once.

I do not plead with him. I do not plead with my father. I know better than to ask for mercy, so instead it is Tommy I turn to, and for the first time in my life, I do not look away.

"It will be okay," I say to him. "Promise."

Even now, even here, the word comes out a question.

Promise?

Tommy is calm and still, his breathing even. Unafraid as he has always been. He meets my gaze and opens his mouth to answer as he always does, to say *promise*—

And Milos pulls the trigger.

CHAPTER 31

Paris

Tommy is so calm as he dies.

He is looking at Helen. He is promising things will be okay.

His blood is splattering against my jaw and hair and ear.

And then Helen's knife is in her hand and the guards nearest her have crumpled to the ground, blood spilling. She is running for us, and Milos and Zarek are running for the exit, because they know—they know she will come for them next.

Blood soaks the scarlet tulle of her dress. Blood drips down her jaw.

And then Tommy is cradled in Helen's arms, and his eyes are open, unseeing.

Only then do I falter. Only then do I slip to one side, bracing myself on the bloody ground with one hand.

And then Helen is screaming, cradling Tommy's body against her, and screaming *promise, promise, promise* over and over again.

"She—what the fuck?" Milos is at the elevator doors, gun still trembling in his hand. He has not seen this Helen. He has not seen her unmasked, as brutal as her father and far more dangerous. "She *killed* those guards."

Helen is dangerous.

Oh, and only a fool would have taken so long to see it.

Helen is wailing, a high keening sound worse than anything I ever heard on Troy, but when he speaks, she looks up at him. "You," she says. *"You."*

They have gathered themselves now, Zarek and Milos, after the initial shock of Helen killing the guards.

Zarek holds up a hand, stopping Milos before he can call for the elevator. "Helen," he says. "Look at me."

Helen does not move.

I want to shake her by the shoulders, tell her to use her knife and finish this, but instead I am frozen at her side, Tommy's eyes still staring, unseeing, at the spectacle unfolding on the rooftop.

"You asked me not to kill her," Zarek says. "And I have decided, this time, to spare her. But remember there are things you love, Helen. And things you can lose."

Helen lifts the knife, the movement sudden, her hands trembling. Then she meets my eyes at last, hers wide and haunted, and the knife clatters to the floor.

Zarek tilts his head. Smiles. "Ah," he says. "So you *can* control your impulses."

"Helen," I say softly. I place my hand on her arm and look at her, because I cannot bear to look at Tommy. Tommy, who was gentle when neither Helen nor I deserved it. Tommy, who cared for me patiently when no one else ever really has.

"Let us do the decent thing," I say to Zarek. "And give him a burial. He kept her safe for many years. You owe him that."

Zarek's eyes flicker.

Milos is still staring at Helen as if he has never seen her before. "You—Helen, what *are* you?"

She looks at me desperately. "Your wife," she says, but she is looking at me and not at him, as if I did not kneel here during all of it. As if I cannot taste blood in my mouth from the force of the shot. "Your *wife*. But you were supposed to save Tommy." She looks up at Zarek. "You promised."

The last part comes out a whimper.

"Take care of him," Zarek tells me, waving his hand at Tommy, as carelessly as if Tommy has not spent almost three decades caring for Helen, as if Tommy has not been loyal in a world where no one ever is.

I reach forward and close Tommy's eyes. Gently, gently, I brush the blood away from the entry wound. It is not enough, not nearly enough, and he deserved so much more than this, but it is all I can give him. It is more than I gave my sisters on Troy.

I take Helen's hand. "Come," I say. "Come, Helen."

They leave us there, and I let Helen cradle him against her for far longer than I should.

Finally, I coax her to her feet, and then we carry him as best as we can. He is heavy, so painfully heavy, especially in his tactical vest and gear, but it seems so much a part of him I cannot bear to take it off. We could call someone to help, but neither of us can find our voices, and we both seem to have decided that this we have to do ourselves.

It takes us so long, so very long, to find our way to Helen's room. I pause there, grab a fistful of poppies from her bedside table, and then Helen guides us to a trapdoor in the back of her closet. There is a staircase hidden there, leading down to a private cove where a small speedboat and a few canoes are moored.

We set Tommy down at the edge of the water, and I fold his hands over his chest. His hands, so gentle with us, so brutal with the rest of the world, are still.

And then the first sob rips through me, rips apart my chest where all the bombs of the gods could not.

"You were not supposed to love us this much." I bury my face against his chest, so still and quiet.

I want to feel the steady *thump*, want him to call me kid and sigh when I do something utterly stupid, I want him to call me *kid* even when I insist that I am not.

Helen lets out a noise that is more snarl than wail this time. "No," she says. *"No."*

We Are the Match

"I'm sorry," I whisper, and we lean on each other, our strength gone. There is so very little left of us, just as Tommy had warned us. Just as so many had warned us.

Helen sighs, a soft release of breath.

"I want to send him off," she says. "Will you help me?"

In the end, we pull a boat in, one of the smaller canoes docked here, and help him into it.

I hold out poppies from Helen's bedroom.

She places one in his hands, folded now over his heart, and I do the same.

She says *I love you* and *I'm sorry* and *promise*, so many times I think my heart will break.

Tommy, who loved Helen so much it killed him.

I fold his hands over the poppies and smooth his dark-brown hair, speckled with gray. I straighten his coat, button the buttons over his heart.

We send him to sea, our Tommy, to rest at last, to rest away from this gods-cursed place.

"Helen," I say at last.

She is so, so far from me now.

"Paris," she says finally. "You should take this speedboat and go."

I reach for her without thinking, and she steps farther into the water, holding out her hand between us.

"No," she says. "No. I am—I am sorry. You should be far away from me. Everyone I love—everything I love. He will take it from me." Her face is streaked with tears, eyes red and puffy and desperate.

"Helen, wait. Listen to me. We should go upstairs, get you a shower, a change of clothes."

"Everything I touch—" Helen's chest heaves. "I—I can't stop it. Paris. I can't make it—I can't make it stop."

Helen is trembling in the water beside me.

"Helen of the gods," I say softly. "I am not afraid of you."

She is shaking violently now, her makeup running in rivers down her face, sweat beaded along the crease of her forehead. "Please, Paris."

"I always thought you would be begging me under very different circumstances," I tell her, but there is no mockery in my tone.

"Go."

"You *are* dangerous, Helen." I reach out and close my hand over her arm. Loving her is dangerous, yes, that much was always true, but it cannot dissuade me. So I hold on to her. "But so am I."

Helen stops mid-sob, the shock of my hand touching her enough, apparently, to jar her back into her body. "Paris," she whispers. *"Paris."*

We are both trembling.

"Are you done?" I ask her.

Helen laughs, only half mirth, and more sob. "I am sorry," she says. "I am—oh, Paris. Will it always be like this?"

Helen's shoulders sag, the last of the fight going out of her before I am able to answer, and then I wade forward into the water and catch her as she falls.

CHAPTER 32

HELEN

I lean my head against Paris's chest, and she wraps her arms around me tightly.

"Stay with me," she says tenderly. "It was like this, after Troy. For so long. But it won't always be, Helen."

Promise?

Promise. "I miss him," I whisper against Paris's hair.

"I know," she whispers back. "He deserved better."

He did.

My Tommy. Too gentle, despite it all.

Finally, Paris and I climb back up the long, winding stairs to my room, and it is wrong, wrong, *wrong* to be doing this without Tommy.

Promise? I keep asking and asking and asking. But he is cold and silent in the sea.

When we reach my room, I show Paris to the bathroom, where she strips and steps into the shower, Tommy's blood running down off her into the drain below.

I leave her there and call for Erin, who brushes my hair and offers me a cloth for my face. After Erin leaves to retrieve some food, Paris emerges from the shower and dresses in some of my clothes—the only jeans I had, and a tank top, both of which are too big for her, and then her worn leather jacket. Then she steps forward without a word and pushes me against the wall, *hard*, and kisses me breathless.

"I am sorry," she says between kisses. "I am sorry."

"No," I tell her. "You and I? We have nothing to be sorry for."

It is not true, and never has been, but who is left to forgive or condemn us now? We are all we have.

I let my head tip back, thudding gently against the wall as Paris leaves a line of kisses down my jaw, my throat, my collarbone.

A knock interrupts us, sharp and persistent.

"Helen." Milos's voice sounds broken, fragile.

Rage floods me, so swift and immediate that I fling an arm out, sending the glass flying from my bedside table, shattering it against the wall. I look at Paris.

"I need," I tell her. "To do this."

"If he touches you," she says. "I will kill him myself." And then she withdraws into the next room, and I let Milos enter.

He has blood on his hands. *Tommy's* blood. My Tommy.

"Helen," he says brokenly. "I'm sorry."

"Milos," I tell him woodenly. "I have upheld my father's alliance, and he will need you for whatever he is planning next. But you have killed the only family I had left."

He is pale, eyes haunted. "All these years," he says. "I have never killed. Not once. I know—I know my brother has, when it was necessary. But what would you have done? If it was your brother? What would you have done to save him?"

"I don't care," I tell him. I don't care that he loves his brother. I don't care that he thought he had no other way. I don't care about my father's Family and his games.

"What would you have me say?" Milos whispers. "That Tommy was killed for an alliance as much as he was killed for my brother? That it was worth it to me, if it means I have *you*?" He reaches for me again.

I slap his hand away.

"You *do not*," I say. "Have me."

You never will.

Something changes in his face. The softness, the longing, the hope there twists around, around. Around. And then rage is the only thing left.

"Do you think you can make me care for you?" I taunt him. My fingers inch toward the knife beneath my dress. "Do you think you could have *ever* made me care for you?"

"And what of this alliance?" he snarls. "What of the demands your father made?"

He reaches for me—though to what end I could not say—and then—

He is jerked backward, nearly off his feet, and Paris is behind him, holding his head back by his black hair, her knife pressed to his throat with her other hand.

A drop of blood has already appeared beneath her blade, and her eyes are as unforgiving as the storm outside.

"Lay a hand on her," she hisses. "And I will bleed you dry."

Something broke inside of me when Milos pulled that trigger—and whatever was left of me shattered just now when he demanded, after all he had done, that I would be his one day. "Paris," I say. "Paris, help tie him up, please."

For once, she does not argue about who gives the orders. Instead, she brings the hilt of her knife down on his head and he staggers. She shoves him through the balcony doors, binds him to the rail using his own belt to secure his wrists.

And then I crouch in front of him.

Because I have decided something, something that has been inevitable since we announced my engagement, since the golden apple that said *from the queen*, since Paris threw me to the ground to save me from a bomb. Powers and pawns. Kings and gods and girls.

And me, destroying the balance of power in the Family with a single choice—as if all it takes to start a war is a woman saying no.

I reach toward Paris, steady myself with one hand on her hip, and pull the knife from the sheath at her waistband.

She lets me, eyes raking up and down my face with curiosity and concern and hunger all rolled into one.

"Helen," she says. "We could leave him and run."

I shake my head.

Milos is staring at me, terror in his wide eyes.

"Your father will kill her," he says. "You know that, Helen. I'm— I'm sorry. I *am*. I didn't want to kill your guard. I didn't—"

Paris rips cloth from his shirt unceremoniously and shoves it into his mouth. "If he doesn't even know Tommy's name," she says. "We don't need to hear from him." She looks at me. "Helen," she says, her voice coaxing now. "We can make it."

"Paris," I attempt, but I can't get the words out. I am not sure, now, what is even left to say. My plans were shaky at best—Tommy helping us lead an insurrection, reaching out to Hana or Frona to forge a new alliance. And now they are shattered on the ground around me.

But without any hope at all, without any chance of survival, Paris reaches for me anyway and says:

"Run away with me."

I start to weep again, fragile as I am after all I have lost today.

Milos writhes against his bonds, anger and fear fighting for dominance in his face.

"Helen." There is urgency in Paris's voice. *"Please."*

But I am not a child, and I will not be coaxed any more than I will be coerced.

"We could make it." Paris sounds more desperate, but when I look at her, it is just weariness on her face. "All this . . . Helen, all this bloodshed. We can get you away. You could be *free*."

We can get *you* away.

Does she not intend to remain at my side, then? Does she not intend to outlive this war?

The thought tastes bitter.

"Paris," I murmur. "I will follow you where you go—to Troy, to the mainland. To freedom. But wait for me at the boat below? My attendant will meet you there after she gathers my things."

Paris's shoulders sag with relief, as if she had expected me to put up more of a fight about leaving, and then she leaves with one last nod at me.

I pull the gag from Milos's mouth, alone with him at last.

"No one can hear you," I say. "No one will come for you."

"Helen, *please.*" Milos's eyes are desperate, but how dare he be desperate, when Tommy was so calm?

"Yes, husband?" I tilt my head, watch him carefully.

"We were made to rule, Helen," Milos attempts. "You and I. We were born for this. We are *royalty.*"

"Yes," I murmur. "We are royalty."

"You could embrace it." Desperation colors his tone now. "You are as guilty as the rest of us. So lean closer to this world, wife. Rule with me. I will—I will do whatever you wish."

I sigh, the release of breath a release of so much more.

"You were mine," Milos whispers now. He raises his eyes to me, beautiful man, horrible man, ruler and god. "You were *mine.*"

I replace the gag, my hands gentle and sure, and his eyes go wide again. "I was always going to rule," I tell him. "But not because of you, Milos. I have never once needed you."

He had Tommy in front of him, and he pulled the trigger. *He pulled the trigger.*

I crouch beside him. My dress is as red as the sunset sky.

"Milos," I say gently. "It will be all right."

He stares up at me, wide-eyed.

I cup his neck with one hand, so gently he relaxes beneath my touch. "I promise," I say.

And then I draw my knife across his throat, and I do what Paris threatened to do. I spill his blood across the marble, let it flood him and surround him, and I watch his eyes until the last bit of fury and fear disappears.

This was not a fight. This was not an honorable kill, not the kind Paris or Tommy would have carried out. No, Tommy was a soldier, his kills clean, painless. Paris is a survivor, her kills in self-defense— or for Troy.

But I am not a soldier or a survivor.

No.

I am a god, and this was an execution.

And I am not sorry.

I hesitate, blood trickling across my golden sandals and bare feet. I crouch there a second longer, watch blood drip over the side of the balcony, slide down the marble toward the sea.

My husband is dead.

I reach out a finger, dip it in the blood, and then I write.

A message for my father, who used me to ensure his own power over and over again.

A message for Marcus, who threatened me on this very balcony.

Now it is my turn to tell a story, to break an alliance, to burn it all down. If I was never meant to take my father's place, then at least he will know he has made himself a new enemy.

So I leave him a threat, my message in Milos's blood. My bedroom a battlefield.

FROM THE QUEEN.

ACT THREE:
TORCH SONG

CHAPTER 33

PARIS

When Helen arrives at the boat launch, she is not the woman I knew. She is someone else entirely.

She walks slowly, regally. My knife is bloodstained in her hands. Her dress—the new, soft one she had slipped into—is matted with gore. Her feet are bare and wet, as if recently washed.

She sees me staring and looks at me with dark, unworried eyes. "I made sure they knew," Helen says, "who Zarek has made an enemy today."

As if this answers my questions at all.

As if I want to understand anything but why Helen returns to me dressed in blood.

"Helen." My voice cracks. "What did you *do?*"

"He killed my family," Helen says. "He deserved it, Paris. As they all do."

This, then, is the kind of queen she would be.

"He did," I say. "He took Tommy from you."

But it sits heavy on my chest all the same: the knowledge that any chance we had of leaving quietly has evaporated before me—even without this, Zarek would have come for her. And now? What hope do we have of ever leaving this behind?

And still—I will take what slim chance we have.

"Are you ready, Helen?" I ask her. "To leave all this behind?"

"As soon as Erin joins us." Helen turns her head.

Behind her, a woman wearing a maid's uniform descends, and I startle again. Because behind a blood-drenched Helen is—

Eris.

My Eris.

Her honey-brown hair was almost black when I knew her, her voice loud instead of measured, but I—I *knew* her.

"Paris," she says softly.

"Er . . . Erin?" I ask.

And how was it she ended up at Helen's side, when every girl from Troy ended up in Lena's employ, not Zarek's?

"I should pay Marcus a visit," Helen says, interrupting my confusion at Eris's introduction. "Like his brother, he is guilty."

She is fearsome now, eerily similar to her father in her mannerisms. Would this Helen burn down a home full of sisters just to be free? Is it a different thing, to kill for freedom and not power?

I do not know, I do not *know*, but I stretch out my hand toward her, offering help to board the boat.

Helen takes neither of our offered hands. Instead, she reaches down and dips her hands in the cold water of the cave, scrubbing at the blood. It unspools under the water, red leaching from her fingertips.

"Erin," she says, her tone betraying no hint of whatever emotions must be raging inside her like the storm that raged the night we met. "Did you retrieve my kit?"

Eris—no, Erin now—holds up a small bag in response.

Helen continues scrubbing, the silence long, unbroken except for by the sound of the water. When she is finally satisfied, her hands are shaking. She stares at the knife she carried, and when she looks up at me there are tears in her eyes.

"I would do it again," she says fiercely. "I will be free, or I will be nothing."

I take her shaking hands and help her into the boat.

And then there is nothing more to say.

Helen of the gods.

Helen of the island.

Helen, who started a war, who bled a king dry for touching her.

Helen, who killed her husband to run away with me.

My Helen.

Zarek will shut down the harbors as soon as Milos's body is found and it is clear that we have fled—the airport on this island, too, so Troy is our only chance at securing a bigger boat or plane, something that can carry us to mainland Greece and beyond.

It strikes me that I do not know what Lena would do if she learns Helen has run away—if she no longer cares for the daughter she left, or if she had plans for Helen's future like Zarek always has.

"Helen," I say, reaching for her hand as Erin charts a course to the marina on Troy.

Helen jumps at the touch. "Stop," she says, just as suddenly, her voice hard and commanding—the queen, again. "We need to make a stop."

Erin's eyes flick to me and then back to Helen. "Where to?" she asks.

Helen lifts the bag—the one Erin had held up when Helen asked earlier. "My father's marina."

"That's madness," I tell her sharply. "It will be crawling with guards."

"It's dark," Erin offers. "And we may have some time yet before they find Milos."

Helen offers no explanation and no apology, a far cry from the woman I met at the engagement party.

"And what's the goal?" I snap. "If we delay our escape by an hour to go to the marina?"

"To blow it all to hell."

Our black ship is as silent and swift as Zarek intended when he built this wing into their home.

When we reach the marina, Helen climbs out without a word to me. And that is when I see what is in the dusty kit she brought with her—solidox and sugar, taken from the warehouse we explored together. Other tools, too, the kind Zarek must have in his personal stores.

In this moment, she is more Lena's daughter than Zarek's. All queen, all bomb-maker.

The question eats at me as Helen works, laying charges in boat after boat after boat, carefully covering them with rope or crates so they will not be immediately visible if Zarek commandeers these boats to follow us. *Who will you be when you learn Lena is alive?*

Erin watches Helen, and she watches me.

When Helen returns, blood still stained beneath her fingernails, the detonator slipping into her silky pocket, she says nothing at all.

She stares straight ahead as we pull away, the boat cutting through the waves, the weight of what she has begun as heavy as that weighty golden apple, blown open at the beginning of all this.

"Erin," she says finally. "When we reach Troy, where do you intend to go? Or will you make your escape with us?"

Erin turns.

In the gathering dark, her gaze meets mine.

"I have the same question myself," I tell Erin.

Erin's face remains impassable as Helen's eyes flick back and forth between the two of us. "I will remain on Troy," she answers finally. "Helen, there is someone—there is someone there who wants to see you."

Her words land like a blow, even though they are addressed to Helen.

Eris left our group home. Eris was skilled with both weapons and explosives. Eris was loyal to—

Lena.

Rage licks at me like a flame, white-hot and unbearable. Even from afar, Lena has made sure there was someone to watch her daughter's every move—or even control her.

"Tell her," I say to Erin. "Tell her who you are. Where you are from."

Helen's eyes seek mine. "You know Erin? Who is she to you?"

When Erin is silent, I take Helen's gaze in my own.

"I knew her as Eris back then." My voice is soft. A skill I have finally learned: the dagger wrapped in silk.

Erin's shoulders jerk at the mention of her old name.

"I didn't recognize the name when you mentioned her, didn't realize who she was until I met her today. But she was one of us, once. Bright and bold. She was a girl who loved flowers and makeup and dresses, was damn good at them. She was also a girl who loved rifles and bomb-making. And so they took her away to serve."

Erin shifts and stirs, and then turns away from us, staring out over the sea. "I am a girl from Troy," she says. "Taken from the group home, long before the bombs fell. Taken to be your attendant. Do you know why the island of Troy sings to you, Helen? Do you know what awaits you there?"

Helen's wild eyes seek the horizon. "What has always awaited me?" she says. "War, and war again."

"But this time," Erin says, "you move the pieces."

Erin's words settle in my stomach with a weight I had not anticipated. Is this what is meant for Helen, to take her place as a god and a catalyst and a power too far removed from the violence to bleed like the rest of us? This is not what I meant by an escape to Troy.

It was meant to be a stepping stone, not a homegoing.

Will they rule, mother and daughter, on the bones of those I once loved?

Because I am not sure I love Helen enough to let that happen.

"Helen," I say, turning all of it over in my mind. Can I trust her with this knowledge now? Or is it better to wait until we are safely away from all of this before I tell her, let her make her choice when the ground is solid beneath her feet and she is far out of both Lena's and Zarek's reach?

She lost Tommy today. Killed a husband. Ran away with me.

She will not meet my eyes.

"Come," I decide. "Rest."

She hesitates at the bow of the ship, her hands braced against the sides. And then she ducks her head and comes to me and stretches out beside me, her head resting against my thigh, her dark hair spilling across my lap.

"Paris," she whispers as she closes her eyes.

I brush hair from her cheek, tuck it behind her ear, and wait.

"I just want to be free," she whispers. "I just want to be free."

And when she is asleep, and I move her so that she is pillowed on my jacket, I stand.

"When we reach Troy," I tell Erin, "we flee. That is our plan. Do you understand?"

"You need to finish this," she tells me. Her eyes fall to my jacket, the gift from Lena that kept me alive all those years ago. "You serve a purpose, too. Just like Helen does."

My hand slides to my knife. "I have never been meant to fight for these Families," I snarl at her, but the weight of it hits me.

Is that what Lena meant by the gift? And if she did, does that mean she knew something long before Zarek's bombs ever fell?

But I have no time to ask any of it, because Erin poses an immediate problem. An immediate threat. "What is it *you* want?" I ask her.

Erin slows the boat until we are idling in the water. "I want to save Helen," she says. "I want to save the Family I work for."

She is looking out at the sea, hands resting on the wheel. She is not threatened by me. She is not afraid.

"Did you?" I ask. "Care about saving us?"

"I did," she says softly.

We Are the Match

"And did you know?" I push, though even asking these questions coats my mouth with ash. "Did you know what would be done to us?"

Did Erin make the kind of call I made to Altea, hoping someone would act? Or did she turn away from our destruction as if we never meant anything?

"Sometimes," Erin answers me finally, her gaze flicking to Helen and then in the direction of Troy again. "Sometimes sacrifices must be made."

And it is true. It is *true*.

Altea's girls are bleeding in the fountain.

I am crawling over the remains of my burning sisters.

I am flicking open my switchblade and pressing it against Erin's throat.

CHAPTER 34

HELEN

I wake to find Paris with a blade at Erin's throat, red appearing. A droplet. Then two.

I scramble to my feet, heart thudding.

Paris's eyes are locked on Erin's. "Was it you?" she asks. "Do not play games with me. *Was it you?*"

"Paris," I say. "Paris, what are you talking about?"

There was shock in Erin's eyes before she managed to erase it. Who is she, to put fear so firmly in its place even when death reaches out its hand and touches her?

"The queen," Erin answers. "The queen asked, and I answered."

"You could have been free," Paris says. "When you left. And you could have *warned* us. We could all have been free. You didn't have to be a piece in their games. *We just wanted to live.*"

This is a different rage, sister to sister.

"Paris," I attempt again. "Paris, please. Tell me what's going on."

Erin's lip curls. "We are not just playthings," she snarls, wilder than I have ever seen her.

Paris brings that out in many of us, it seems.

"*I* chose the role I played," Erin says finally. "And I would do it again."

Something flashes in Paris's eyes. "We are not little girls anymore, taken in by pretty gifts and hopeful lies," she says. "How could your loyalty be to them, and not to *us*?"

I want to take them each by the shoulders and shake them, demand they tell me what the *hell* they are talking about.

"I was not a little girl," Erin says. "And every choice I made, I made gladly."

"You were the bomber," Paris says breathlessly. "At the party."

Erin smiles. "From the queen," she says. "She wanted him to know that no new alliance, no new blood, would ever matter. She wanted him to know she was coming for him, because she could never be replaced. I made the bomb, and the girl—the girl he killed. She helped me set it."

"Who?" I ask again. "Erin, who are you talking about?"

But no one answers me.

Instead, Paris leans closer, blade pressing in. "But I don't care about that bomb." Paris's voice is deadly, sharper than the blade at Erin's throat. "I care about the ones before. The ones at *home*. Were they *yours*?"

I open my mouth to ask, again, *how*. Why a bomb-maker is my attendant. Why Erin would have laid explosives that killed Paris's sisters. How Paris knows all of this just from meeting Erin.

"She needed a place," Erin tells Paris. "To rebuild."

"The bombs," Paris repeats. She surges closer, a trickle of blood appearing on Erin's throat. *"Were they yours?"*

Erin's eyes flash, and she nods.

Paris's eyes are as empty as the night sky.

"En morte libertas," she murmurs.

And then she draws the blade across Erin's throat.

Time slows down, and then does not exist, and Erin falls.

Backward.

Slowly.

Erin, gentle Erin. Erin, who has cared for me for years. My Erin.

The sound her body makes as it strikes the sea reverberates through me, and I lurch backward, my body slamming into the wood rail of the boat. We tilt in the water for one wild, unsalvageable moment—

And then the boat capsizes and we are all in the sea, Paris and I and the knife and the body that used to be my friend.

Erin and Mama and Tommy are all around me, beautiful, broken, bleeding.

The sea is blood, thick and choking, and ten years ago is today and everyone I love is dying around me and it will never never never stop.

Never.

Not until I join them.

CHAPTER 35

Paris

I killed her.

Erin killed my sisters—Erin and *Lena* killed my sisters.

The shock of it is colder than the sea I have been tossed into. Colder than the first night on the street, concrete hard beneath my shoulder blades before I learned to sleep on my side, to let the least amount of my body encounter the cold ground.

I fight my way upward, choking on icy salt water.

And then, at last, a stillness as I breach the surface.

En morte libertas.

Helen is floating, the tide pulling her away from me.

Tommy is not here to swim toward her, to keep her safe while the rest of us bleed. He is not here to call her back to herself, so I must do it.

I am a poor substitute, my voice rough where his would be gentle, but I call her name.

"Helen," I say. "My Helen."

Helen's body goes slack, her eyes toward the sky as if she can see nothing and no one.

The boat is capsized, our plan blown apart, everything I thought I knew flipped on its head. Because Erin, *Eris*, was a bomb-maker. My sister, and a bomb-maker.

My sister, and she helped to kill so many of us.

At least Helen is alive, and Erin can use us as pawns no more.

I pull Helen onto the capsized speedboat—little bigger than a fishing boat, really—and then I strike out for land I can just barely see.

Troy.

We will arrive in splinters, leaving blood behind us.

The husband Helen killed.

The sister—the bomber—I did.

Helen and Paris, running away to Troy and leaving destruction in our wake.

And what was it all for, if it was never Zarek to blame for the murder of my sisters?

And what does it say that despite this new knowledge, I still want to take his hand from him for what he did to me?

It takes nearly an hour to swim all the way to shore, and Helen does not move, not even when my muscles are aching and I shout her name in frustration.

Nothing.

Eyes wide, staring at the sky. Her lips move, as if in prayer, but she makes no sound.

But I didn't start the war, Helen.

I was just tired, so tired, of dying in them.

I left Erin's body behind where the boat capsized, and I wonder if it floats there still. If it sank, weighed down by the leather she wore. I wonder. I wonder until it claws at the fraying edges of me, the wondering and the *ifs*.

We reach land at last, a narrow strip of it covered in underbrush and broken glass.

I pull Helen to shore, and she shudders. She sits up, but her eyes focus far beyond us, unseeing, and then she stands, staggers back toward the sea as I clamber out, exhausted, dripping.

She does not see me.

She does not see anything.

The ground beneath her feet seems to shake, her first footsteps on Troy already destructive. But no, no, that is just the vertigo from being violently capsized when Helen slammed into the edge of the boat. Still, it feels like an omen of worse ahead of us, this feeling of the earth shaking and spinning when we arrive on Troy.

"Helen." It is my voice that stops her, splits the air like a gunshot.

She pauses, and then finally, finally, her eyes find me.

We are facing each other, two killers, and we are blazing, faces inches apart.

"Paris," she whispers. "What did you *do*?"

Helen is dangerous, Thea had warned me, just weeks ago. Centuries ago. Eons ago.

Helen is as she was then: dressed in luxury, smelling of rain.

Blood and beauty. Grace and grief.

I am the one who is different: bloody hands, sister-killer, loving the god I swore to kill.

It has always been too late for me.

CHAPTER 36

HELEN

Paris spends nearly an hour gathering our belongings from the churning sea—at least what she can salvage, including the worn leather bag that holds the supplies I brought with us.

Mama had that bag first, and then me, one of the only belongings of hers I have left.

After Paris salvages what she can, she finds us a safe house and her voice is quiet but firm, as if she knows the sound is the only thing keeping me from coming apart.

She killed Erin.

I stare at her hands, long, lean fingers, her three rings firmly in place. Fingers that could pull a blade across someone's throat with no effort at all.

And yet fingers I still imagine on—

Me.

She said she had to carry me to shore.

That I capsized the boat.

I remember so little of it.

What I remember, I remember vividly, even though I know it is not, cannot, be true: Erin and Mama and Tommy bleeding on the pure marble floor in the palace at home. Erin and Mama and Tommy with their hands on me, pulling me under the sea.

Come with us, they whispered. *For the queen.*

And I went under, again and again.

Until Paris pulled me out of the sea.

Until Paris called my name.

My hands tremble violently.

I feel far, far away from my own body.

Paris does not tell me who the safe house belongs to, or how she came to know of it, but it is a well-furnished, two-bedroom cottage. There are clothes in the closet, and a hot shower waiting for me, and I could ask Erin—

I stagger, knees hitting the ground hard.

Paris is at my side instantly.

"Paris," I say when I have my voice again. "What did you know about Erin? Who did she work for? *Why did you kill my*—"

My what? Because what was Erin to me, really? We were not friends. She worked for me, and I never really knew her, that much is clear. But still, *still,* her life meant something to me. Even if we were not friends, not family, not anything more than employer and employee.

Paris closes her eyes, her face pale. "She helped to kill my sisters," she says, and she cannot look at me. "Sit down." Paris guides me to a love seat, keeps both hands on my shoulders as she does.

I lean into the touch, catching my breath as best I can. "Tell me what you know."

She hesitates.

"Helen," she says finally. "The Trojan family funded that group home—most of the Families have funded something like it, at some point. It is one of many self-serving things they do, but that one— mine—was a training ground for girls who would one day belong to Lena. Her symbol was above our door."

She says my mother's name in the same tone as she always says my father's: with rage, unbending.

But why this much hatred for my *mother*?

"Mama did not bomb your home," I say. It is a futile fight, but I stand my ground the same. "That was my father. Not her."

And how could Mama have bombed a group home after we lost her to a Trojan bomb? None of this makes sense.

Paris's eyes are distant. "She visited us often." She runs a thumb up and down the edge of her worn leather jacket. "This was a gift, the last time I—the last time she visited."

I gasp for air, clutch the jacket with one trembling hand. "You knew my mother?"

"No," Paris says, unequivocally. "No, we were nothing but her pawns. Even Eris—your Erin."

"My mother has been dead a decade," I say. I push myself to my feet, weak-kneed or not. "I won't hear this, Paris. *I won't.*"

"All right," Paris says gently.

"Erin worked for Altea, maybe," I say. "Altea loves weapons. Maybe Erin was just another one of her weapons. Altea wants to move against my father, and she did, and—"

"And either way, Eris built the grenade used at your engagement party," Paris continues. "I should have seen it earlier. The solidox and the sugar. The warehouse on Frona's island—it was where the girls of Troy were trained. My friends spoke of it—Eris spoke of it, when I knew her. A bomb-maker from the Family, they would have access to any resource they could want. But a girl from Troy would be smarter, because she knew scarcity. A girl from Troy would buy something you can get with cash, for minimal resources. Untraceable and easy to make. I knew her, you know? We were—"

Her voice falters.

If Tommy were here, he would put a hand on her shoulder, would call her *kid*. Would tell us both to rest.

If Tommy were here, Erin and Milos would not be dead, because he would have stopped Paris, stopped *me* from doing something so monstrous.

But it's just us, and we are alone, so I take Paris's hand.

Paris sways—exhaustion and something more. "We were children together," she whispers, and then she stares down at her hands as if she can hardly believe what they have done. But when she looks up at me, it is the look I saw when I first sat beside her at the bar. Furious and unforgiving. Like there is steel in her, something unbendable, something no one can break, not even a god.

"You heard what she said—when I asked her about Troy. *Sacrifices must be made.* She sacrificed the wrong people, Helen—and then she set off a grenade beside you. So I killed her."

The words echo in the small entryway.

The space between Paris and me trembles, and though we are inches apart, there is a gulf between us, as wide as the sea between my home island and hers. Even together on Troy, we are leagues apart.

"Tell me her name again," I whisper. "Tell me. Tell me."

Paris steps back, shaking her head, the gap between us widening.

Every centimeter of space between us makes me miss her, and how can this be? We both killed today. The blood is still hardening beneath our fingernails, still slicked on our blades despite the time we spent in the sea.

She took *Erin* from me.

And yet I have never loved anyone as much as I love Paris.

"How could I forgive you for this?" I ask her. And how could I not, when Paris is the other half of my beating heart?

Her lip curls, her loathing for us both. "There are things that can never be forgiven," she says. "Do you think I will ever forgive *myself?* She killed my sisters, and she was my sister. I will never forgive her and I will never forgive myself, Helen of Troy."

"What is wrong with us?" I whisper.

And this, finally, is what breaks Paris. She barks out a laugh, something furious and guttural I have never heard before.

"What is wrong with *us?*" she snarls, and then those strong fingers I have dreamed of are wrapped around my arms and she shoves me back against the wall. "*You* started this war. Don't you see that? *You.* Over and over and over again. You played god at an engagement party that wasn't yours—your father killed two people in front of all of us and still you held up his rule. You married a man to solidify an alliance and then made his death a *message*. You blow apart everything you touch. And you *like* it."

And the laugh is a broken thing in her mouth, the jagged edge of our blades.

She is furious and grieving. She hates the Family, and she loves me.

And she is *right*. Even if it was not my hand on the trigger. Even if I killed Milos for a far more personal reason than *power*. Because it didn't matter, did it?

I have run from the complicity that is part of the role I was born to. I have run from the bomb-making I learned at my mother's knee. I have run from it all.

Until Paris.

"Oh, darling," I say, and I bare my teeth as I smile at her. "But *you* like it, too."

And then she is pushing me backward again, but this time one of her hands is between my legs, the heel of her palm spreading me.

The noise I make is not quite human, and I let her push me back through the open door, into the bedroom.

She kicks it shut behind us, and it slams so hard it shakes the house, shakes me, and then when she looks at me, she is positively feral.

I let out a breath, one ragged gasp.

She circles me, half a grin on her wild face.

We are still dripping wet, our clothes soaked with sea and blood, but she looks unbothered.

I shiver under her gaze.

"Paris," I say. I try to make it sound like a command. "Touch me."

The wicked little half grin splits into a wider, hungrier smile. "Oh, love," she says, leaning in so her warm breath tickles my ear. "You don't give the orders here."

She circles me again, and I shiver.

She trails a finger down my bare arm, brushing water droplets off. Yes.

Oh, gods, *yes.*

Yes, that is what I want.

Paris tilts her head to one side. "Helen." Her voice is a soft growl. "What do you want?"

I feel the rush of wind, and suddenly we are on the rooftop at home, a platter of scones spilled between us.

What do you want? she had asked me, *is* asking me, though I had not had the courage to say the last time.

"You," I whisper. "All of you."

And then she reaches out both hands, gathers fistfuls of my dress at the shoulders, and tears it open. Top to bottom.

And when all the bloody fragments of cloth are on the floor beneath us, she takes my hands in hers. Fiery and gentle. Rough and vulnerable.

"What do you want?" she asks me again.

"You," I tell her desperately, desperately.

"What do you *want?*" she persists. She is asking me for more, *demanding* more.

"Everything," I tell her. *"Everything."*

And then I am on the bed beneath her, as I have been longing to be since she first threw me to the ground to protect me from the blast, all those weeks ago on the marble floors of my palace.

She sheds her own clothes with as much care as she used on mine, and then her fingers push between my thighs. "What do you want?" she demands, and then she leans down and bites my lip, so hard I taste blood, so hard I *feel,* and I cannot stop feeling. So that when I answer her, our eyes are forced to meet. So that she sees every inch of me.

"You," I tell her again. "I want *you.*"

Her fingers trail down, cupping a breast, tracing a path on my stomach, featherlight. And then, harder, the heel of her palm grinding against me between my thighs, her rings cold against my skin. And then fingers, lean, strong, deft *fingers*, good with a blade, and better yet—with *me*.

"What do you want?" I gasp against her mouth.

"You," Paris answers roughly. "At my mercy."

I arch against her fingers, the cold metal of her rings teasing the edge of my clit as I do. "You have me," I tell her.

"I have seen you unmake buildings and alliances and men," Paris whispers against my throat, one hand cupping my breast, the grip bruising and beautiful. "But can you unmake a god?" Her breath is hot against my skin. "Because *I* can."

Paris strokes the edge of my clit, every bit of movement controlled, intentional, meant to make me come apart.

"More," I demand, arching my hips against her fingers.

Her other hand slides up from my chest and wraps around my throat, just lightly. "The same rules as before, Princess," Paris says, a wicked glint in her eyes. "You say 'red' if it's too much. 'Green' if you're good."

I moan, arch my neck against her hand, desperate for more pressure. "Green," I say. *"More."*

Her grip tightens just slightly, just enough for the pressure on my throat to make the rest of the world drop away.

There are no wars and no gods. There is no world waiting for me outside this bed. There is just this woman holding me. Paris. *My* Paris.

"Paris," I say.

She grunts, her whole body reacting to the sound of her name in my mouth.

"Beg," she says, leaning in and pressing a searing kiss against my lips. The hand around my throat loosens, slips down to cup one of my breasts.

"Please, Paris." Gone is every ounce of trained self-control. Gone is any inhibition. "Please, Paris, fuck me with your fingers. *Please.*"

She laughs. The sound of it is cruel and sacred.

"You want this?" she asks.

And then her hands, strong and deft, are spreading me. I am soaked with pleasure, and Paris slides two fingers inside me with ease.

At the sudden fullness, my body contracts with pleasure.

Paris moans, the sound half pleasure, half pain, and I realize I am clenching hard enough to hurt her, crush those perfect fingers a little, but the pain seems to make Paris only wilder.

A third finger, and then she is fucking me hard, so hard it hurts in every way I have always wanted it to.

"Take that hand," Paris orders, pinning one of my hips with her injured hand, keeping me spread for her on this bed as if pain is not a consideration—her pain or mine. "And touch me, Princess."

I obey eagerly, letting her guide my hand to her clit. I stroke the outside of her clit reverently. Hesitantly, I draw my hand back and lick my finger, drawing a gasp of pleasure from Paris.

"Good girl," Paris growls.

Good girl.

My vision goes white.

She pushes her hips forward, thrusting her fingers deeper inside me as she does, and my head falls back on the pillow, barely holding myself together.

"Enough," Paris says. There is a note of sternness in her voice that only adds to the slickness between my legs. "Let go, Helen of the gods. You are *mine.*"

And then I do, we both do. Paris is coming apart on top of me and inside me, I'm clenched around her fingers, and she's thrusting against mine, my body trembling on and on, uncontrollable waves of pleasure that do not stop, do not falter until we are both sated, exhausted, tangled up in one another.

Hours later, when we are lying together beneath a mess of sheets, Paris props herself up on her elbow and looks down at me. "Helen," she says.

I blush, the sound of my name in her mouth an unholy thing after—all this.

She grins, but her expression sobers a moment later. "Helen," she says. "After—after tonight."

I stare up at her, waiting. "Who will we be when all this is done?" I ask her.

"I don't know." She is here with me, my head pillowed on her lean, muscular shoulder, my hair strewn across her chest, half-covering her breasts. "I—I don't know what Eris deserved. Not really. She was no worse than the rest of us. No worse than me. Did she—did she really have any choice in the things she did?"

It aches in my chest. "Did any of you?" I ask.

Her eyes cut to mine, dark with the weight of it all. "It feels like a choice," she says finally. "When I crawled over my dying sisters to reach safety. When I saved myself first. I tried, after. To go back for them. To carry them out. The only one I carried from the flames was Kore, and even then . . . even then I was too late."

I go silent and still, waiting for Paris to tell me it all. "Thank you," I whisper against her. "For telling me."

Kore.

The name is a gift, a piece of vulnerability, a piece of Paris she has never shared before.

"Our birthdays were the same week," Paris tells me, running her fingers up and down my shoulder absentmindedly. "We snuck out together every Friday night and borrowed a boat and cruised around the harbor until we ran out of gas, and then we swam to shore."

The laugh bursts out of me. "Have you *ever* taken the subtle approach?"

Her fingers wander lower, trailing a line down my stomach to my entrance, which is still slick with pleasure and tender, too. "You wouldn't want me to be subtle," she says.

"Tell me more?" I ask after she lapses into silence.

"She died on a Thursday," Paris says. "We were going to take a speedboat the next day. We were going to bring her favorite chips, and do our nails bright red, and after we went out on the boat, we were going to one of the bars."

I have never seen Paris cry. Never imagined I would, or that she could, even.

But one tear snakes a line down her face, dripping off her jaw before I catch it.

I hold her, until she sits up, taking my hand. "Years ago," she says. Her voice is impossibly tender. "When I had lost everything to the flames, I had three rings made. I melted down a fragment of the bomb that killed us, and I made them from that."

En morte libertas. One word on each ring, a flame within each band.

"One for myself and my will to survive," she murmurs, twisting the first. "One for the sisters I could not save." She twists the second, and then looks at me. "And one for the gods I hated." Paris pulls the third ring from her finger, the one that reads *libertas.* Her dark eyes are impossibly soft.

I inhale, sharp and sweet. "Paris."

Paris hesitates until I hold out my hand to her.

"Wait." I pull the bracelet from my wrist, *Méchri thanátou* and hold it out to her. She slides her hand through, eyes shining brightly.

My father gave this to me, after our home burned. I thought, then, that he was right for fighting back, for doing what he did on Troy.

But I know another side to this now. And I know my father cannot be allowed to do what he has done.

"Paris," I tell her softly. "It has my mother's slogan on it: *Méchri thanátou.* Unto death."

"Helen, I—"

"Let me finish," I tell her. "It is also the access code. The *only* access code to the cliffside entrance beneath my quarters."

Recognition flashes in Paris's eyes as she runs her finger along the edge of the bracelet I have given her, and then she places her ring on my finger, her hands devastatingly gentle where they touch mine.

Paris of Troy has wanted to kill my father since the day he rained down fire and fury upon her sisters.

And I have just given her the key to do it.

CHAPTER 37

Paris

Helen sleeps heavily, her head tucked against my shoulder. She is flushed and sated, and I ease her down onto her pillow before I slip out from under the covers.

I slide the bracelet back onto my wrist as I look down at her. *Unto death*, it says. Mine or hers or both of ours.

I stole Helen away. Helen, husband-killer, daughter of gods, bringer of war.

And then I fucked her until she screamed.

It was a different destruction than the one I had imagined once. The gods ablaze. Helen at my mercy. The Family in chaos.

Helen. Helen. *Mine.*

And come morning, we will have to reckon with this: both the love and the war.

For now, I brush hair from her face—hair I was pulling only hours ago. My hands are gentle, but she loved them when they were rough.

We have so much to explore, Helen and I.

I want a thousand nights like this one with her. I want to touch her a thousand times, in a thousand ways. I want to call noises from her she cannot contain. I want to see my ring on her hand for years yet.

I tuck a lock of hair behind her ear, and she stirs. Sighs softly.

Helen. Oh, Helen.

There was never any chance for us.

I flick my lighter open and shut in my hand, just once, before slipping it into my pocket. I twist the rings around my fingers, just two of them now.

En morte.

In death.

I shrug on my leather jacket, pull the sleeve down past the bands.

It is a reminder, as always. I am a girl from Troy, but also a girl marked by Lena's choice—like Eris was. Like Thea was. Like Cass was, until she burned.

I bend down, press a kiss to Helen's forehead.

Whiskey and vanilla, poppies and rain.

Before I go, I pull the poppy from my pocket—it is crushed now, worse for wear from being carried in my pocket and then being capsized. It is still damp from the sea, a few petals lost on its journey—but it is ours all the same.

And then I slip out the window, shrugging my jacket up to obscure my face as I go.

Just a girl in the alley with a hood to hide her face.

I had planned to do exactly what I had told Eris: once we reached Troy, I would find a bigger boat that could carry us across open water and safely to the mainland. But neither Zarek nor Lena will give Helen up without a fight—and if I am no longer willing to use *her* as my bargaining chip, I need something more.

And I can only hope it will be enough: the bracelet that will buy Lena entrance to Zarek's fortress and—hopefully—Helen's safety and freedom.

So I turn, at last, toward the house on the hill where my sisters died.

And I go to find the queen who killed them.

We Are the Match

Helen

For the first time in all the years I can remember, I wake alone.

I do not want to wake up, because Paris is not beside me.

I do not know when she left, did not feel her sudden absence, but I feel the grief of it even before I am fully conscious.

I wake with my face wet with tears, though I cannot remember the dream. I wake and I look for her and I do not find her.

I want to walk through the doors and have Tommy waiting for me at the table, waiting to talk me out of my bad idea or tell me to take care or just hold me while I cry. But he is gone gone *gone* and so is Paris and Erin and Mama and everyone else I have loved.

And all that is left of me is grief.

En morte libertas.

The phrase on the three rings she has always worn.

I pull her ring from my finger and turn it over.

She left me *libertas.*

Freedom.

And then I see it, in handwriting neater than I would have expected from Paris—a note lying on her pillow.

I have one last thing to do. Don't follow. Stay alive.

But I know where she has gone, even if I do not know what I will find there—because I know *her.* I have seen her rage and I have seen her joy and I have seen her love, all of it leading her back to Troy, this path as inevitable and brutal and beautiful as Paris herself.

And I know what I need when I follow her there:

A gown and a bomb.

I choose the gown first, from the safe house closet, something rose gold and silk that slides over my curves and hugs them exactly where I want them to.

Then I dig through the kit Paris salvaged from the wreck, and I build—a fail-safe.

237

Solidox and sugar, the weapon of a woman who now knows scarcity.

If I find three queens, united against my father, I can help them plan their next move. If, like Erin hinted before she died, one of them has been leading and that she has a plan for me, too, I can see what help I can offer.

And if it all goes to hell, I can clear a path to freedom with my grenade.

A flash of red catches my eye as I open the door. The remains of the gown Paris ripped off me only hours ago? I look closer.

It is a poppy on the nightstand, faded and drying there, wind ruffling the remaining petals. Has she preserved this since the party? Has she kept this flower since the night we met?

When the whole world was watching, and somehow she was the only one I could see. When I stayed beside her all evening at my engagement party, when she threw me to the ground to save me from the blast, when she made me laugh for the first time in months. When I pressed the poppy into her outstretched hand and changed her fate and mine.

Now, I pin the flower Paris left for me above my heart.

And I go to war.

CHAPTER 38

PARIS

Home lies ahead of me, a burned-out husk, the bars still on the window.

Troy.

Home.

I have lived a hundred lifetimes since the group home on Troy, but never once have I escaped it. The smell of flesh burning, of small, charred, reaching hands—it has been the only thing I can smell for years now.

Until Helen, of course.

Until Helen invaded every sense and pushed a poppy into my hand and ran away with me to Troy.

But this building, these barred windows, they have always been here waiting for me. They have always been standing at the end of this path, inevitable and inescapable.

En morte libertas.

Lena is here. I have known this for years and hated her for it, too—though if I had known all along that it was her bombs, I would have taken my revenge long, long ago.

If what Thea told me is true, the three queens have been helping her all this time as she rebuilt her empire and plotted against Zarek.

The group home at Troy stands silent and dark, forsaken at the edge of the water. Below me are rocks and the dark stretch of beach and the restless, raging sea.

And beyond that sea, Helen's island and Zarek and Marcus and the army they must already be raising to find Helen—and control her again if they can, or destroy her if they cannot.

I can see it now that I stand before my home. They must have reinforced the structure slowly, quietly over the years, building a base out of the ashes of my beloveds.

They have left the building that sagged and crumpled with all of us inside, but beyond those walls there is something entirely new, a hiding place for three queens to convene without watchful eyes, to expand their empires in weapons, in secrets, in pleasure until they were ready, together, to take on Zarek.

But more than that, a hiding place for just one.

En morte libertas.

I will have to face Lena when I do this, to face what she did to my sisters, and hold fast to my plan to free Helen. *Live,* Thea had said.

And will it be enough, to have our safety and freedom if I cannot have my revenge?

I lift my fist and knock.

A girl from Troy, home at last.

It is an attendant with Hana's colors who opens the door, but all four of them are inside: Hana and Altea and Frona and, of course, Lena.

I step inside my home, still wearing that worn leather jacket, the ghosts of my sisters clinging to my skin and ash coating my mouth as I speak.

"Lena," I say her name as if we are equals. "I have come to make a deal with you. A god for a god."

We Are the Match

Helen

The path up the gravel road is a lonely one.

Troy is nothing like my home island—everything here is rugged, wild, sharp as the woman who survived it.

The sun is beginning to peer over the horizon when I arrive, the light just touching a brick structure that looks more like an asylum than it does a home. I imagine her here, my Paris, growing up inside this place, her hands smaller than they are now, wrapped around the bars on the windows. Her hip leaning against the concrete windowsill, her face gaunt, her eyes shadowed.

Blood pools around my feet, and Mama is beside me. She is dying in this house. I am dying in this house. Paris is dying in this house. All of us over and over, again and again. We cannot stop it. We cannot stop my father's war.

The door swings open before I knock, and they are all there together, Paris and Altea and Frona and Hana and there, at the center of them, not Erin or Tommy, who loved me.

No.

No, at the center of it all, eyes blazing, stands the person I have been grieving for ten years.

Bomb-maker, mother.

Queen.

CHAPTER 39

PARIS

Helen arrives just minutes after I do, and I do not have time—not to beg for her safety, nor to sacrifice my old plans for revenge for a bid for both our freedom. I am too late, too, to protect Helen from this knowledge.

And when Lena opens the door for her daughter, Helen's face is white as marble.

It is a cold realization in my stomach, dread and excitement mingling.

Helen, my Helen, what will you choose now?

Helen, my Helen, I am sorry.

Helen opens her mouth and closes it again. Just yesterday, she killed her husband and blew up a boat and fucked me in a bed that was not our own, but all the power I saw yesterday has vanished, and she is silent and still.

Be with me, I pray to her silently.

The way you would pray to a god.

When she finally speaks, it is a word that destroys all of us, a vulnerable, raw thing that bursts from her like she cannot stop it:

"Mama."

Lena does not flinch, does not move at all. Something flickers in her eyes, just once, a flame she has long ago learned to control, and then it disappears.

"My darling," she says, her voice as detached as Helen's. She holds out her hands to her daughter. She is striking, this mother of Helen, the structures of their faces similar, though the queen's eyes are harder and sharper, and a long scar slashes her face from above her right eye down her cheek. "May we speak in private?"

There is no hug, no welcome, no reunion, not even an acknowledgment that Lena has spent a decade pretending to be dead, even to the daughter she just called *darling*.

But Helen allows her hands to be taken.

Allows herself to be led away.

Helen. *Oh, Helen.*

Was it worth it, everything I have done to get this far? Everything I have done to bring us *here*? I wish my sisters were here, that I could ask them. Would they have built an entire life on revenge, like I have? Or would they have moved on long ago?

The rest of us are left staring at one another in the entryway to my old home. My *home*.

If I were to look closely, I would see the echoes of the girls who died at the windows here.

Milena, a blue sash tied around her waist, twirling in the sunlight that filtered through the bars.

Thea's first love, best friend, Jasmine, hogging the bathroom so she could look in the mirror as she twisted her braids up around her head like a crown. Cass, slamming her fist against the door and demanding that Thea and Jasmine fucking *hurry*. And Kore, sitting still as one of the older girls braided her hair into twists.

It hurts to think of Eris, here.

Were they yours? I had asked her.

She needed a place, Eris had said. As if we were worth nothing if it meant *Lena* could rebuild.

I make for the hallway, to follow Lena and Helen.

Altea blocks my path. "They need to speak first. Privately."

"Fuck you," I say. "I'm staying with Helen."

Altea arches an eyebrow at me. "I can see why Zarek took your finger from you," she says. "That isn't my style, but if it was, I would have taken your whole hand."

"I would have taken more," Frona says. She is watching me coldly, cruelty in her eyes that reminds me of Zarek. "I might still if you are not careful, little one."

Hana alone smiles at me. "I like it," she says. "I like your spirit. Always have. Even when you stole my robe."

"And your locket, too?" I grin at her. In another life, I would have liked her, too. In a life where she was not a god and a war criminal.

Hana freezes, a blush creeping up her face. "I liked you less for that."

I push by Altea then, ignore the handgun strapped to her hip and the flicker of anger in her eyes. I find Helen in the old headmaster's office, where I was often sent, Kore at my side, to be lectured or otherwise punished.

I shove open the door.

Lena stands where the headmaster always stood, hands still holding Helen's. Lena is bent forward toward Helen, who is sitting in a simple wooden chair and making it look like a throne.

"Helen," I say. "Helen, are you—"

It would be stupid to ask if she was all right, but it was on the tip of my tongue all the same.

Helen stares at me—past me, really, and I can see it in her eyes, the distance. She is far away from us, from me, from her own body.

I want to take her by the shoulders. I want to put my hands all over her until she cannot *help* but be present in her body, to feel everything she wants me to do to her.

Lena stares at me in disbelief. "You may leave now. I need to speak with my daughter." Her voice is so gentle, so deadly.

I can see why Zarek loved her.

"I think I'll stay, thanks," I tell her, and I show my teeth when I grin.

"Paris," Helen asks numbly. "Did you know?"

She stares at me as if she has never seen me before.

Lena's gaze changes, just subtly, tilts toward anger—or even fear.

"She was gone," Helen whispers. "I thought they killed her."

"I must ask for privacy, Paris," Lena says gently, squeezing Helen's hands and then releasing them. "We have guards that will keep her safe, if it is her safety that concerns you."

Helen gasps when my fingers brush her bare shoulders.

"Lena will tell you what she knows of me, I am sure," I tell her. "But I would like to tell you what I may, first."

Helen freezes. "You knew," she whispers.

It is the worst kind of betrayal, as I knew it would be. I had hoped I could tell her away from all this, in some little cottage on the coast of a different country, far from the mess of the Families, safe.

But instead I am here. *Home.*

Lena holds up her hand for me to stop, and Helen's gaze snaps to her.

"Mama," Helen says, her voice faltering. "Mama, you *died*."

Lena shakes her head, eyes softening. "No, my love," she says. "I am sorry. I am so very, very sorry. It was the only way to protect you. If your father knew I was alive—if he knew I wanted to be with you—he would have used you as a pawn in a war against me."

Like she is using Helen now.

Like I intended to use Helen when I first met her.

"Helen, please," I attempt again.

But just like when I tried to tell Helen about her mother, Helen cannot hear me.

"Why?" A tear spills down Helen's marble cheek as she stares at Lena. "Mama, why did you leave me? *Why did you leave me?*"

My hand tightens on her shoulder, fingers digging in. *Stay here with me,* I am telling her. *Do not go back. Do not lose yourself to her.*

This time, pain cuts Lena's face as surely as the scar reaching down her cheekbone does. "Baby," she whispers. "My *baby*." And then she is holding Helen tightly, pulling her away from me.

When Helen finally draws back, her body trembling, I surge forward to join her again, despite Lena's glare.

"But why?" Helen whispers again, despite their embrace. "Why did you leave me with him? Was it because I was impulsive and bad at ruling and because I did not want to touch bombs after I thought I lost you forever? I would have learned, Mama. I would have *tried*."

"Oh, my daughter," Lena says. She sinks down into her chair again. "All of this was for you. *All* of it. I hope you see that, sooner rather than later. But I could not be his wife any longer. I had to build on my own, and he would never have let me go."

I had to build.

Not survive.

Not be free.

No, she left to build an empire she would not have to share.

"No," I say.

Lena starts, and then stares at me. "No?" she says. *"No?"*

Helen stares up at me.

Come back, I want to beg her. *Come back to your body and to me.*

"And what would you know of any of this?" Lena's voice is ice.

"You faked your death," I say. "You will not lie to Helen. *Everyone* lies to Helen. She deserves the truth from you, at least. *You* faked your death, and used *ours* to house your new empire, away from Zarek's eyes."

"Pray tell." Lena's fingers close over the edge of the desk, white at the knuckles with the effort it takes not to rise and strike me. "What truth would you like me to tell Helen next?"

"I will tell you the truth," I say. I am looking at Helen, and only Helen. "But I want you to know that—I tried, Helen. Before your wedding. Before Tommy. I tried to tell you. I am sorry I did not."

Helen's hands are trembling.

"I would have to start from the beginning. You know some of it already. I do not have your way with explosives," I tell her. "But I had the will to live, and I did. I pushed my sisters out of the way, Helen. I crawled over them and shoved my way through the doors, the last person through before it melted shut. I did not save them. I saved myself."

Helen reaches for me with the hand that bears my ring, but I step back, shake my head. "You don't have to," she says. "Paris, you don't have to tell me. You don't have to relive it."

"The bombs fell," I tell her. I am staring straight into Helen's strange, magic brown eyes. I am falling into them. "Your father bombed all of Troy, and for a time I thought he took his vengeance on our bodies, too, because we were one of Troy's group homes. Because girls from Troy always served the Trojan Family. So we burned. We burned."

"But not you," Helen whispers. "You survived."

"I survived," I tell her. "And this jacket—your mother gave me this jacket. It's the reason I made it out."

Behind her, Lena smiles, her teeth unnaturally sharp. Her eyes flicker as she watches me.

"I crawled over them as they screamed. As they died. I tried to carry some out. I could not carry them all."

I twist the rings on my fingers. Three flames. No—only two now. One for those girls I lost. One for my will to survive—and the jacket that kept the wrong girl alive. One for the Families, who thought themselves gods, a ring for those I would hunt down and kill.

I brace myself against the wall, but I could not fall now if I wanted to.

I am as iron as the bars on the window, unmeltable, unbreakable, unburnable. Unbowed.

"Do you know what it is like to smell burning skin?" I ask Helen. "Do you know the smell of charred flesh?"

"Yes," she says. "I do."

We are only a meter apart.

We are a thousand kilometers away from each other.

"And that is all there is to tell," I say finally. "The fire was cruel, but it could not kill me. Nothing could kill me. I crawled out, and I decided to survive."

"Ah, ah, ah," Lena reproves gently, her fingers ghosting over the dagger I know is concealed at her hip. "Do not forget the rest of it, Paris of Troy. You had a purpose, once. I gave you that jacket, and I expected loyalty in return. But instead you never sought out a single job with the Families. You never joined us. And if I could not have the loyalty I am owed for saving your life, I will at least have the truth for my daughter."

"Oh, the rest?" My laugh is coated in ash as I twist the rings on my fingers, around, around, around. "That I grieved, and I waited, and when I realized your mother was alive, I began to plan. Did you know, Helen?" I ask. "Did you know *she* bombed us? Your father bombed Troy, and at the time I thought the group home was just a casualty of it. But Lena was the one who needed a hideout where Zarek would never look. And Lena and her bomb-maker—Erin—made sure she had one."

Helen gasps. "That's not true," she says. "Paris, you can't—that's not true."

"You heard what Erin said," I tell Helen. Because after all this, even if I do not have my revenge, even if I lose Helen because of this, I need her to know exactly who Lena is. I need her to *believe* me. "*She needed to build.* Erin wasn't talking about Altea, or Frona, or Hana. I know you wanted that to be true. I know, Helen. I *know.*"

"That's enough," Lena cuts me off. "Helen, she lies and manipulates just the way your father always did. I want the whole truth, Paris of Troy. Did you not realize I was watching you all these years? Did you really think I would give you a gift like that if I did not think you would be of use to us? No, Paris. No. Tell my daughter what you were planning to do with her."

"When I knew your father was responsible for what happened to my sisters," I finish slowly. I meet Helen's gaze again. There is an ocean of grief and loss between us. "I knew your mother had rebuilt on my sisters' grave. So I began to look for a way. A way to get to Helen of the gods, the best bargaining chip Zarek and Lena have ever had. Because one day, I would bring her here to Troy, and kill her in front of them both, and on that day I would give all the burning girls of Troy their revenge."

CHAPTER 40

HELEN

I have long known that Paris wanted revenge. I had known that she hated our Families. I know she was furious, I know she grieved.

But we were more than these games, and she *loved* me.

Maybe not at first, but now.

Doesn't she? Was I ever—

"She wanted to *kill* you," Mama tells me. "Do you understand that, my love? It doesn't matter what she has told you since. She was planning to hurt you."

Paris wavers on her feet for the first time since I have known her. "No," she says. "Helen, I tried to tell you—"

It is hard to know who is lying to me now, when so many have. It is hard to know if I can trust Paris when she told me something so gutting, so cruel, that I cannot bear it. My father, responsible for bombing young girls? That I could believe. But my mother? It is unthinkable.

But there was truth in the way Paris touched me last night, and I no longer know what to believe.

"I did come to your party to kill you," Paris tells me. "But I did not—I did not expect . . . this. Us."

She was there to kill me.

And I was there to die.

There was never any other ending for us.

I laugh, the sound a detached, strange thing I scarcely recognize.

"You have always been a threat to me," I say. My hands are trembling, but I scarcely feel it. "But Tommy couldn't do anything, I wouldn't let him, because you were a threat I—"

"Loved," Mama finishes the sentence. "Paris was a threat you loved."

Loved.

Loved.

Past tense.

Because it has to be this way, doesn't it? Because I was a piece in her games, and in my father's? Because she was a piece in mine, and in my mother's?

Because the only one who has not played with me was my mother, who faked her own death to protect me from all of this.

"Helen," Paris whispers.

"Don't," I say. A sob catches in my throat.

"This isn't *new*," Paris says, her voice harder now. She stands, too, though I cannot see her face behind my mother. "You know what I am. You know what I have wanted. But I—things changed, Helen. Things changed because of *you*."

"She came to me today," Mama interrupts. "To make me a bargain, and to bring me your access code—that bracelet—so she could have you for herself and let your father and I destroy each other."

And I gave it to her. I can hardly breathe.

Paris's intake of breath is sharp as she looks down at her wrist. "No," she says, but her voice is too shaky to be believed. "That isn't why I came this morning—it isn't, Helen." The look in her eyes is soft with regret.

So much I am drowning in it.

"Then go," I say numbly. "I knew you wanted your revenge. I did. But I did not plan to be your fool, Paris of Troy. So go and kill him, then, and spare me any more lies."

"Helen," Paris says at last. "Helen, I'll leave. If that's what you want. But will you give me five minutes? Not to explain. Not to change your mind. But to show you."

I look at Mama, who sighs, but nods her head.

"Five minutes," I tell Paris coldly.

We step outside the office together.

Paris looks so very, very tired. "Helen," she says gently. She turns my bracelet on her wrist, slow and deliberate.

She says my name the way she said it last night, when her hands were rough the way I wanted them to be, but there is an ocean of tenderness in her eyes.

"I do not want you to play with me," I say sharply. "I am through being toyed with, Paris." Paris nods. Regret and grief and violence in her face. She is everything I wanted. Everything I was never meant to have.

"Can I show you something?" she asks.

Not an order, not this time.

I follow her, and when she reaches out a hand, question in her eyes, I take it, my hand cold in hers.

She leads me up a flight of stairs, and she tells me their story. She shows me their pain.

"It does not matter if I am sorry or not," Paris says. She is looking past me at a hundred ghosts. "It does not matter if I justify it to myself or if you think it was unjustifiable. It is done. It cannot be undone. And here we are. But at least—at least, maybe, you can understand why."

A single tear tracks down her cheek.

If I were tender the way she is with me, I would reach out and wipe it away. But, instead, I pull my hand from hers, draw back.

"This room belonged to my friend Cass." Paris opens the door.

Inside, now, a man is cleaning a rifle with a long scope, its components laid out beside him.

"She and Milena slept there," Paris continues, shutting the door gently. "Cass threaded ribbons through Milena's hair. That is how I recognized Milena's body. The bright-red ribbons were charred, Helen."

I do not make a sound.

This, this is history no one else has. Paris has carried it alone, has carried it for so long.

"Paris," I attempt, but her name does not quite reach my lips.

"This one was Thea's room, when she was here." Paris's voice is hollow as she pushes this door open. "Only Jasmine slept here, after Thea left. If anyone talked about taking Thea's place, Jasmine would break noses. She was vicious, and she was beautiful, and she died like all the rest."

"And this—" She chokes. "This was *mine*. Three of us in this room, because we were the youngest ones."

And only Paris left alive.

"This was . . . this was where I was going to bring you," she says. "I was going to take you to Troy, your father's ships behind me, and drag you up these steps with my knife at your throat. I wanted your father to see that his wife had left him—that she had played him for a fool. I wanted to see his rage, and hers. And I wanted them both to see you die."

It is a plan as brutal as it is bold, and I should have expected this of her. All that she has done, and I never imagined this.

"No more games," Paris says, in that hoarse, hollow voice. "Just truth. We have all manipulated you. And I am sorry that I was ever one of them. But I need you to know—everything between us. That was real, Helen. All of it."

"Paris," I say at last. It cannot be true, after all these lies. And I will not be taken in by one more.

Her gaze meets mine. "Burn me," she says.

"What?"

"Lay your charges," Paris repeats, and now her face is blank and cold, a mask of what it was. "Burn me, Helen, if that's what you want to do. Kill me, before either of your parents have the chance."

I stare at her. We are both trembling.

"Burn me," Paris repeats when I say nothing. "If you want me gone, destroy me. Finish what your father and mother began, Helen of the gods."

Instead, I open my hand, place it over hers.

Palm to palm.

My breath releases, something deep and aching, and Paris—

Paris's hand is trembling, but the look in her eyes is steady.

I stagger on my feet.

"What can you ever know of a woman like me?" she asks, so gently it is almost tenderness between us again. "What could I ever be to you? Choose Lena, then, if you must. But you will never be free if you do."

"Paris," I whisper. "You used me."

"And you and your family used us all," she says. "We are all guilty. We are all complicit. But you must decide to be free, Helen of Troy. No one can do that for you."

"This." I hold up the ring on my hand. *Libertas.* "Paris, was this—"

Her face twists with pain. "Real," she says. "All of it real, Helen."

"I cannot believe you," I tell her, my words slow and measured. "My father used me all my life. Milos would have used me, too. But the difference is that I knew when I was being used as a pawn and you, Paris, you almost made me believe I was something more."

That is the danger of Paris of Troy, that she made me nearly believe I could be something more than that.

"Helen," my mother calls across the house to me. "Helen, your father has your location, and is sending ships for you. Come. We need to prepare."

I look back at Paris.

"Go," I tell her, and it tastes like ash on my tongue.

CHAPTER 41

Paris

The ships are coming.

The ships are coming, and I must go.

"Helen," I tell her. "Stay alive."

She nods once, index finger tapping the ring on her left hand. "Paris—do you want it back?"

I look down at my own hand, at the two rings remaining.

One for loss, I keep that.

One for the gods-cursed will to live, I keep that, too.

But the last one, the one that promised revenge, the one for the gods I hated—that is Helen's to keep.

"I would have left my revenge behind," I tell her. "If you had asked."

There are tears in her eyes. "We could never have run from this."

What do you want? I had asked Helen so many times, but I had not stopped to ask myself. Perhaps if I had, perhaps if I had listened to all the times Thea had asked me the same, I would have been able to answer that in time to save both Helen and myself.

But as it is—as it is, we are only the sum of the choices we have made. Helen the god, and I the nonbeliever.

Helen is Lena's.

And I?

I have what I have always had: myself, my will to survive, and a fury that not even the weight of a sagging building, of dozens of dying sisters, could crush.

After all of it, after everything I tried to do to change course and seek my own freedom, I come back to the only thing left. The path I almost abandoned: revenge.

"I will not come back to this beach for you, Helen," I tell her.

Everything, *everything* flashes across Helen's face. She is as raw as I have ever seen her.

"And I will not be waiting on this beach for you, Troy."

"Goodbye, Helen."

She stares at me for a long moment. "My mother will kill any threat to me," she says finally. "I have always known that to be true. So go, before she decides to put two bullets between your eyes."

Helen says the words so coldly they scarcely sound like her, but her dark eyes still flicker with emotion. It was what drew me to her at the party: that although she could manage her body language and expression with such perfect control, the look in her eyes was still so uncontainable.

"Helen—"

"No," she says. "I will keep her busy in the office. You leave through the window."

It is not a goodbye—just like with my sisters, I do not get a goodbye.

I leave through a lower-level window, as I often did when Kore and I would sneak out to the boats, and Helen returns to her mother, to the war we began and she will finish.

I go now to finish what I began when I crawled out of half-melted bars on the windows ten years ago.

I will take his whole fucking hand.

I was a woman with nothing, once. Nothing left but revenge.

And then, for a few brief moments, I had everything: Helen, and a chance at freedom.

I am something new, now, as I leave my home one last time. I have lost my sisters, yes—but I have also lost Helen.

And the only thing left for me is this path I walk to Zarek and revenge.

The walk down the narrow gravel road to the marina is a short one. It is closed, of course, if you are a law-abiding citizen, but even in my days as a girl in the Troy group home, I knew how to hot-wire a boat and take off across the water.

It was usually Kore, on Fridays. But even when Kore was not there to do it, there were girls to go with me, girls with fair skin or brown skin, girls with brown and blue and green and black eyes, girls with shaved heads or long brown hair or tight twists. Girls and girls and girls.

Girls who wanted to steal across the bay under the moonlight, taste the waves and the wind and come back wilder than before. Girls like Helen, used by people who were meant to take care of them.

Girls who burned.

Girls I crawled over to escape and survive.

Girls and girls and girls.

The marina should be empty, but two people wait for me on the long dock, two people framed against the gray-blue water and grayer sky. I brace for a threat—and then I cannot catch my breath, because after all this time, my family did not leave me behind.

It is Thea at the marina, Perce beside her.

"Troy," she says.

"You—"

I stare at her.

"Yes," Thea says. "Where are you going?"

"Are you getting out?" I ask her. "The ships are coming."

"We know," Perce says. "We're trying to evacuate the island."

"The whole *island*?" I ask them.

"It's a small island. And not many of them left. All the same, you could stay and help," Perce says.

Thea shakes her head before I can.

"She has business with the man on the hill," she says, resignation mixing with the sadness in her voice.

Helen of the gods will be the death of you.

But I had never cared much about that, had I?

Had never cared much if I made it through any of this alive. I had imagined stealing Helen from that party, dragging her to Troy and watching Zarek and Lena crumple as I killed their favorite bargaining chip. But I had not planned for an *after*.

I twist my rings on my fingers. Only two rings, now. It is a different grief, a different hollowness in my chest that spurs me on now.

Thea's face twists. "You know, don't you? That I grieve them, too?" she asks. "Our girls. I wanted to take them all with me. I wanted to save them. I wanted to save *Jasmine*. And I didn't. But I can't bring them back. I can only live, and hope I honor them by remembering them."

"And by the way you cared for the living. Like me. I know you looked out for me," I say. "I know you tried to warn me—about all of this. I wish I had seen your kindness for what it was."

There is no anger in her eyes when she looks back at me. Just sadness, a decade of it. "I always thought if anyone could make it this far," she says softly. "It would be you."

"Live, Thea," I tell her finally, stretching out my hand toward her.

She clasps it, her grip firm. "You too, Troy." She hesitates, and then pulls me in, her hug fierce.

Family, after all this time.

CHAPTER 42

HELEN

Paris is gone, and Mama is here, and everything I thought I knew has shifted under me. Paris, at that party, fiery charm and sharp edges. Waiting for the right moment to kidnap and kill me. And how much after that was real? How much after that was just a tool to get close to me until I handed her the key to enter my home and kill my father?

But why—*why*, did she save me from the bomb? Why was the shrapnel buried in her shoulders instead of mine? Why did she have glass from the windows in her hair, and not me?

Confusion swirls around me, potent and powerful and terrifying.

"Helen?" Mama jars me from my thoughts. "What can you tell me about the explosives you laid in the boats?"

"I did not want my father to follow us," I tell her. "I laid charges on most of the boats in the harbor—not all, I did not have enough for that. But most. The detonator will need to be used when they are close to shore, though."

The explosions will not be controlled, or precise. Most likely, they will be bigger blasts than I intend for them to be.

All I am truly confident of, in the end, is that I can pull apart the ships and keep us all safe.

"I know, dearest." She pats my shoulder gently, and I flinch.

I am not ready for touch. I have not been ready for touch in so long, except for Paris's hands.

Paris's hands were somehow different, even if I know how vengeful they are.

"There is so much I want to know about you, love," my mother says to me. Her hands are so tender, so violent, so unexpected on my shoulders.

I withdraw again, curling inside of myself.

"But today," she says. "We will protect each other, my child. There are snipers on the roof, and they can take out the first boats. I do not want you to move until all of Zarek's boats are within range. Would you like me to decide when to use the detonator? I can take it from you now if you like."

I am to unmake my father's boats.

It seems so simple. It *is* simple. I have done it before, made the kind of explosives that could unmake mansions and men.

But all those people on all those ships.

My body shudders, but I do not feel it.

Erin is dying at my feet.

The walls of the ballroom warp with the heat, and I am giving the poppy to Paris.

"Mama," I say, twisting Paris's ring around my finger. "I want Paris kept safe. If she is kept safe, I will burn the ships."

"Darling, we need you to destroy the ships regardless," Mama says. "I know this is difficult. But I know you can do this. And once you do, your father's empire will be weakened—weakened enough you can be free of his violence. We will all be free."

"Except for the ones who die," I tell her. "They will not be free."

"En morte libertas," Mama says. "We will all be free after today, dear one. You can do this. You were born for this. And afterward, you will rule at my side."

Because Paris will kill my father, and Mama and I will burn the ships, and then we will rule in his stead.

259

That was what I had told Paris I had wanted. It *was* what I had wanted.

Until they killed Tommy in front of me.

Until Erin died, too, all for this.

Until Paris left.

And what good is it to rule, if I end up alone?

"I do not want—" I stop the words, kill them on my tongue, bitter as ash.

I do not want to rule.

Maybe none of us should rule.

"It hurts," Mama says. There is something raw in her face suddenly, a pain older than I am. "I know it does. I loved him. Like you loved this Paris. But you will live, and you will be stronger, and you will rule. You will recover, when all this is done."

"I will not recover from any of this," I snap. Not from Paris, not from this life I have lived or the violence I have done.

"You *will*," my mother says. Lena. Lena, my mother. Lena, who wants me to destroy every living soul on the fleet that comes for me. "You will survive, and you will rule, because you are Helen, *my* Helen. You came from me, and I *know* you."

Not like this.

It beats in my chest, as sure as anything I have ever known.

As sure as I was last night when Paris asked *What do you want?*

And I answered *you. You. You.*

A sharp rap at the door interrupts us, and I rise, my legs still weak from adrenaline. I know what I must do.

Paris's ring is cold on my finger.

"The first boats are on the horizon," Altea says.

"Good," Mama says. "Helen? Are you ready?"

I can see them now—burning girls, and the mother I thought I had lost and Erin and Tommy, his face weighted with sorrow when he looks at me. They are all around me.

You are the power, Paris is telling me. She is killing my father. She is kissing me. She is leaving me behind.

I am meant to uphold Mama's rule.

I am in the ballroom, speaking gently to survivors of a queen's grenade. I am taking a husband. I am solidifying someone else's alliance.

I am meant to support Mama.

You are the power.

"I will," I promise them. I promise Paris. "I will make sure we are free."

CHAPTER 43

Paris

The gap in the cliff is narrow, scarcely visible in the half-light beneath the gathering storm clouds.

Above me, Zarek's mansion towers on the cliffside, an affront to the sky and the sea and the island itself. The wing of his house that I shot with Altea's weapon is marked off, reconstruction already begun.

I reach the place in the rock where Helen held up her bracelet. I hold it up now. *Méchri thanátou.*

Unto death.

The door slides open, and I pull the boat in.

It is as much a homecoming as it was to return to Troy. I take a half-filled can of gasoline from the bottom of the speedboat and I climb.

Past the blood spatters Helen left here.

I climb and I climb and I climb, and I realize as I do that the girls I left in the group home, the burning girls, are all climbing beside me.

I am more like Helen than I want to be right now, Helen who stayed behind to make the war her mother wants her to make.

I am carrying all my ghosts with me in my mutilated hand, on my unburned back. They are beside me, skin hanging from exposed shoulders, hands melting even as they reach for me.

I will take his whole fucking hand.

My knife is sharp, and it is ready.

I have been born for this.

Any other life—one with Helen, one far from here—was never anything but a dream. Maybe for women like Thea, who escaped before the bombs. Maybe it was not too late for her.

Live, she told me.

But how could I?

Without my sisters. Without Helen. Without anything at all.

In a group home, surrounded by other girls that no one wanted, I became a blade and war unto myself. I became the worst nightmare of the man, crime lord, god who has killed so many innocents.

I took his daughter, if not in the way I expected.

And it is almost, almost over.

What will it be, not to carry the weight of being the last survivor? The only one to remember?

They are all screaming around me, and maybe I am screaming, too, but at least I have my blade.

I push through the trapdoor beneath Helen's floor and step out into her room, blinking at the sudden light. There is a smear of blood where Milos was, where Helen killed him and set herself free.

We used one another. We did.

But for a handful of moments, on rooftop gardens and runaway boats, we were something more.

And I loved her. Enough that now, even now, I come to finish this for the girls, for me—for—for—

I stop there, in Helen's room.

Helen, my Helen.

Blood and silk. Poppies and ash.

Revenge in my hands, and it is hard to summon any thought but one of Helen.

If Kore were here, would Kore be climbing beside me with gasoline and a lighter?

En morte libertas, she is whispering to me.

And I do not imagine her burning, just this once.

Instead, I imagine her free. I imagine her on a boat, not confined to the harbor, leaving Troy behind. I imagine her in a little apartment in Spain, like she dreamed of, cooking with a roommate and weaving ribbons into her hair.

I imagine her the way I imagine us all—

Free.

Revenge is in one hand, and Helen in the other. Gas can and lighter. Flame and fury.

And if I choose to burn, again, instead of taking my shot at being with the woman I—the woman I *love*, I will be letting the girls of Troy down one last time.

Kore is beside me. Milena and Cass, too. Jasmine and Yara. So many of us, so young.

We just wanted to live.

Helen's bedroom is a battlefield—blankets still in disarray, bed never made from the last time she slept here. The person who usually made the bed—Erin—dead at my hands. Milos's blood is smeared wherever Helen walked.

There's an option where you run, Thea is telling me.

En morte libertas, we said on Troy.

But what if there was another choice?

What if, like the choice I made at the party—to save Helen from a bomb, the way I could not save my sisters—I could make a different kind of choice now?

I look at them all around me. Memories of girls I lost forever. Memories of a woman I *will* lose, if I cling so desperately to my own plan for revenge.

My vengeance is finally in the palm of my hand, and I choose, instead, to live.

We Are the Match

If Helen will have me—if after all I have done, she will have me—I will lay my lighter at her feet and tell her it is time to be free.

I leave the gas can there, leave the bloodstains and bed, leave it all.

And when I reach the bottom of the stairs, there are two boats waiting, not one.

And Helen, my Helen, looking more wary, more hesitant, more afraid than I have ever seen her, but here all the same.

"Helen," I say, my chest expanding with joy—and when I stretch out my hands toward her, she takes them.

ACT FOUR: BURN THE SHIPS

CHAPTER 44

HELEN

I left my mother the detonator, in the end. I left her with her war.

Because if she wins—if we rule—and I do not have Paris at my side, how can it be any victory at all?

I wanted Tommy to be here, telling me this is okay.

Promise?

Promise.

But I am grown, I am *Helen*, and I push my ghosts aside and let the breath expand deep inside my chest, straining against my ribs.

Paris holds her hands out to me now, in the darkness of this little bunker.

"You—you're here?" she says breathlessly.

"I'm here."

She kneels, right there at the edge of the water. She smells of gasoline and fury, but she holds the lighter up to me, a promise worth more than any ring.

"Tell me to go," Paris says. "Tell me to run, and I will leave it behind. Tell me to run, and we will abandon revenge and ruling. Tell me to run, my love, and I will take you with me."

I tug at her hand, pulling her to her feet. "I came," I tell her, my voice trembling with the weight of what we have both done. "I came for you, Paris."

"I was coming for *you*," she says, eyes bright. "We don't have to wait until all this is done. We don't have to hold so tightly to the roles we played. We can be—we can be *more*."

"I thought we couldn't," I say breathlessly. "I thought there was nowhere we could run to escape them. I thought—"

"You thought right." My father's voice rips through the darkness, and then he is there, his men surrounding him, guns trained on us. I am on the roof and Tommy is dying. I am in the water and Erin floats beside me. I am in this cave, and Paris is holding fast to me.

He steps forward, my father, rage in his eyes and a knife in his hand.

"Do you know what I do to women like you?" he asks Paris.

She never shows her fear, my Paris, but she lets go of my hand and steps in front of him. "Do you know what I do to men who treat Helen like a belonging?" she asks.

Oh, Paris, my Paris.

I have always been yours.

"Lena sends her regards," Paris says.

There it is: my father frozen, just for a flash. "From the queen," he says reverently. "Yes. Yes, of course. It could only ever have been her." He wavers on his feet as if the news is as physical as a blow to the chest.

And then there is a flash of steel in the darkness, Paris snatching his arm and pinning it to the wall for just long enough to—

His hand falls, still clinging to his knife, blood erupting from the stump of his wrist.

"You will never lay a hand on her again," she says, her eyes triumphant still when my father's guards force her to her knees.

I do not wait for them to force me. I kneel beside her. I take her hand.

There is no bullet left to fear. There is nothing left to fear.

There is nothing left but us.

CHAPTER 45

PARIS

The guards are surrounding Zarek now, protecting him, one wrapping the stump of his arm, and I think as I kneel there that maybe I survived just for this—maybe I survived the bombs so that *I* could be a grenade unto myself, breaking apart the people and systems that killed us.

A guard presses his handgun to my temple.

The barrel is cold, the hand that holds it steady.

But I am not afraid.

"Shall I, sir?" the guard asks.

"No," Zarek snarls. "No, I want her to die slowly."

Beside me, Helen is quiet, steady, the way Tommy was on the rooftop. She is holding fast to my hand.

I grin at Zarek, sharp teeth and cold, sated fury.

"Who are you loyal to, Troy?" he asks me. "Who sent you? Do you work for my wife, too?"

"*I* sent me," I tell him. "I am the girl you could not burn. And I come on behalf of my sisters."

Does it matter which of them laid the charges, in the end? Zarek bombed the rest of Troy. We were all collateral to them. We were all disposable.

"Bring down her gas can." Zarek stops, tilts his head. He looks hungry now. "Pour the gasoline over her."

Helen squeezes my hand, cold metal there.

My lighter returned.

Helen, my Helen, telling me to end him.

And this is his undoing, that he wants to see me suffer, that he thinks he has any power to *make* me suffer. That he has not felt, or suffered, or burned and burned and burned just to stay alive.

And so he does not understand the way I smile at him, does not understand that I am not here for their wars or their power. I am here for Helen, but more than anything I am here for *me*.

If he will not let us go, then I will end what he began.

One guard—just a boy, just a boy, like all of them, I realize—sloshes the gasoline. It soaks my jacket, soaks my boots and my hair and my skin, every inch of it. I let them take my knives, and I do not struggle.

So when I stand and step forward slowly, they do not think to stop me.

I am not a threat anymore; of course I am not.

I am a girl, I am shit from Troy, and it is only as I embrace Zarek, wrap my arms around him as if he is a long-lost family member and I am but coming home, that they realize what I intend to do. The gasoline I am covered in soaks his clothes, soaks him and me and everything, everything, everything.

Beside me, the burning girls are smiling, skin dripping from their exposed jaws.

My rings must feel cold on the back of his neck when I pull him close. One for the girls I lost. One for my forceful will to live. I whisper in his ear: *"En morte libertas."*

I look to Helen. She is standing, too, her eyes flickering as she looks at me.

"Helen," I say.

She nods.

"No—" Zarek says, and there it is, there it *is*, the whimper of fear in his voice and—

I flick my lighter open.

CHAPTER 46

Helen

My father's men run while he burns.

He takes a flaming step toward the water, and he is screaming, and he calls my name—and he falls.

I grab Paris's hand, the flames licking at me, and we plunge into the cold water, together.

When we finally emerge, holding fast to one another's hands, Paris leans her head against me. She pushes the lighter into my hands once more.

"Keep it," she tells me.

And I do.

She is hurt, badly enough that I half carry her up these marble stairs where Tommy once had to carry me. Where Paris and I once carried Tommy.

I lay her on my bed, peel the flame-resistant jacket from her body, clean the burned patches of skin on her legs and neck.

"I will go for the doctor," I tell her. "Now that my father is dead, his physician has nothing to fear if he treats your injuries."

"Together," she says wearily. "We go together."

And she is right. Despite it all, Paris and I?

Where we go, we go together.

There is screaming below, and gunfire, so when I help Paris down the corridor, I cut away from the sounds of it, toward the ballroom.

If Mama is here—

"Forget my injuries," Paris says firmly as we reach the top of the stairs.

The doctor is only one floor away, and he can see to Paris's injuries. We need to—

"We need to go *now*," Paris says. "Before it is too late."

But it is already too late.

Perhaps it has always been.

Because there, below me in the ballroom, the queen has returned home. Lena, flanked by Altea and Frona and Hana. Mama's face is furious, her weapon on her shoulder.

Like Paris, I can smell it before it fires—not just gunpowder. Acrid and sweet, sharp and brutal. Solidox and sugar, the weapon of a bomb-maker. The tidying of a loose end.

I am moving before I can call it out; I am moving on instinct and instinct alone; I am faster than any god who has walked these islands.

I am hurtling straight into Paris of the island, Paris of Troy, *my* Paris, my body colliding with hers, *covering* hers, as my mother's final weapon finds its mark.

CHAPTER 47

PARIS

The blast hits Helen.

That is the cruelty of it.

A weapon meant for me—Lena's weapon. But it does not matter now. It will never matter.

Because Helen is slumped over me, and she is bleeding, and burned from the flames and—

"Paris."

She smiles up at me, wearily. So wearily. "Paris," she says. "Listen to me, my love."

"No," I say, because the sound of her voice is *goodbye*, and I had only snatches of time with her, rooftop gardens and warehouses crumbling and one perfect, perfect night. "*No*, Helen."

"Move," she tells me, and then she coughs, and there is blood spilling over her lips and down her chin. "They will fire again. Unless you go and finish them."

The tears are hot on my face, and I pull her close to me, cradle her against me as she cradled Tommy. "Helen." I am begging, I am begging, but she just shakes her head.

She coughs again, weakly this time, but her eyes are bright. "Paris of the gods," she says. "Will you let me watch?"

More blood is running down her jaw now.

And something settles within me.

"After everything," Helen says, holding out her hand to me. "I want to see you finish what we began."

There is something gold in her hand. Something round and smooth and beautiful.

The weapon of a queen.

Helen

The queens do not deserve a warning. Not even my mother.

When Paris rises, pulling me with her, I see their faces. Their waiting weapons.

I descend.

There is silence, and beside the glittering, living souls who are here to rule stand the dead.

There is glass shattered across the floor, strewn in bloody fragments. Tommy is there at the center, empty-eyed and bleeding. The soft clink of ringed hands is the gentlest kind of violence.

I descend.

I am a sharp shard, the bent metal of the doors blown in, blood spilled across the killing fields of Troy beneath my mother's feet. I am the glittering shrapnel they forgot to sweep up.

I descend.

The room is a mausoleum to me, and still they do not see the threat, not until I pull the pin in my gold-plated grenade, hold it in my hand a moment too long as I have always done, so that by the time it bounds down the stairs to reach them, it is too late. Too late to run. They do not see the threat, not until the queens crumble before me, one by one by one.

I descend.

I am Helen. I am half god, half girl, half fury, half grief.

I am the one who will be free.

CHAPTER 48

PARIS

In the end, it feels as if we both are burning.

The ballroom where we met crumbles around us.

The windows shatter first, and then Lena is begging, and then she is nothing.

Then she is dust, and they all are dust, weapons and silk and sharp, merciless, beautiful dust. The Families are dust. The gods are dead.

In the end, it is just Helen and me staggering out of the husk of their empire and plunging into the cold, cold sea as it all crumbles before us.

En morte libertas, I tell her, and she smiles.

Méchri thanátou, she answers me.

In the end, it all falls, ash and dust and ash. In the end, the chains of Troy no longer bind me. In the end, Helen leaves the Families behind.

The sea is bright blue, and I cannot feel its cold. Just Helen's hands, warm where she holds me to her chest.

I tore them down. Every god, every queen.

And the only one left standing—well, she wears my ring now.

We take the boat as far as we can, until we are somewhere in frigid blue waters halfway between Helen's home and mine.

It is enough, as the world gets dark around me, that I hear the roar of a boat and Thea's voice and Perce's mingling with Helen's.

I will not leave behind another sister, Thea tells me as she hauls us to safety, and then Helen and I are at the bottom of her boat, numb and cold but alive, our bodies curled together as the islands that were once our homes and our prisons fade into memory behind us.

Thea does not say much more to us, and Perce is crying as he presses something against Helen's wound.

She is not dissociating this time, my Helen. She is here, she is mine, she is holding fast to my hands, and there is pain now on her face. We are damaged and furious and brutal, gods in our own right, though we chose not to be queens.

It is done, and she is mine, and we are free.

The waves lull us, rocking Thea's boat with a gentleness I do not recognize.

It is enough, to lie in the ashes of Troy and know that this time I was not left behind.

It is enough, that Helen is the last thing I see when I fade from consciousness, that she will be the first thing I see when I wake next.

Helen. Oh, Helen. Whiskey and poppies and rain.

A love that will always burn.

It was never too late for us.

ACKNOWLEDGMENTS

This book took the efforts of so, so many people to bring into the world. I am endlessly grateful, as always, to my badass agent Claire Friedman, who fights so hard for every book I send her. Claire, in every form this book has taken, you have been the champion it (and I) needed.

Thank you to Lauren Plude for plucking me from the sub trenches and to both Lauren and Amy Pierpont for helping make this book everything it can be.

To my early readers, Jenna Voris, Brit Wanstrath, SJ Whitby, Meg Long, Alexis Ames, and Isa: thank you for reading early, messy iterations of Helen and Paris.

To Emma Warner, who read too many drafts and even the deleted scenes that nobody else is ever allowed to read: you helped me have the strength to persist, and I am so glad to know you.

As always, a thank-you to my family, for the endless support in my publishing career (and buying copies at every event). Though it might be best if you skipped some of the scenes in this one.

A very, very special part of being a writer is meeting extraordinary booksellers at bookstores across the country: thank you, especially, to Emily at Next Chapter Booksellers, the incredibly supportive folks at Tropes & Trifles, and all the wonderful staff of Red Balloon Bookshop (Claire in particular).

I would not be here without the many beloved communities that sustain me: my hapkido family, my running community, the MN writers, my many writing Discords and group chats, the eternal little llama squad group chat, and my beloved PW '18 Slack. I am grateful for you all.

And finally, my Arynn: I write romance because of you.

ABOUT THE AUTHOR

Photo © 2022 Kat Veldt

Mary E. Roach is a former teacher who now writes thrilling romances and romantic mysteries.

When she is not writing stories for and about powerful women, Mary enjoys running, teaching martial arts, and disappearing into the wilderness. Mary lives in Saint Paul with her fiancée and their very disagreeable cat, Lulu.